THINE IS THE KINGDOM

also by the author

The Origins of Solitude (2005)

GARTH BUCKNER

THINE IS THE KINGDOM

RAVENNA PRESS

2008

THINE IS THE KINGDOM
© 2008 Garth Buckner
All rights reserved.
Original text design layout: Deron Bauman
Adapted by: Cooper Renner
Cover design: Liam Gillick
ISBN: 978-0-9791921-7-3
LCCN: 2008937214

The author gratefully acknowledges Charlie Lofthouse
whose "Bahama Lullaby" is quoted within. He also wishes to thank
the Casey Kaplan Gallery, New York.

Ravenna Press books are listed at Bowker Books in Print and are available
to the trade through our primary distributor, AtlasBooks, a division of
BookMasters:www.bookmasters.com/atlasdistribution/index.html.
For personal orders or other information, contact the editor at
www.ravennapress.com/books or write to Ravenna Press, 4917 S. Thor
St., Spokane, WA 99223.

Printed in the United States of America
FIRST EDITION

THINE IS THE KINGDOM

Now this is the Law of the Jungle—
As old and as true as the sky;
And the Wolf that shall keep it may prosper,
But the Wolf that shall break it must die.
As the creeper that girdles the tree-trunk
The Law runneth forward and back—
For the strength of the Pack is the Wolf,
And the strength of the Wolf is the Pack.

—Rudyard Kipling

And forgive us our trespasses,
As we forgive those who trespass against us.
And lead us not into temptation,
But deliver us from evil.
For thine is the kingdom. . . .

—*The Lord's Prayer*

I

The Eastern Road was wet and it smelled sweetly of a passing late summer rain as I drove to the Thesingers' home, *Bangalay*, to begin work on their yacht. The road cut a serpentine track along the island's coast east out of town, lined with seamless native stone walls and shaded by thick, old growth silk cotton trees. The view was dominated by colonial homes that dotted the ridge among the palm groves. The shore rolled down to the wide harbor, fringed by stands of tall, thin coconut trees that clung to the coast. The flat waters of Montagu Bay were a patchwork of stony green and azure, ploughed by the white wakes of small pleasure craft running home from the beach and by fat fishing smacks returning languidly from the day's haul. The purple of last light pearled across the cloudy August sky above the exposed, low lying scrub cays that defended the bay from the ocean's surge and gale.

My truck's windows were wound down and the wind, freshened by the rain, whipped at my hair. The broad sheets of The Tribune fluttered on the dash where I'd tossed it, flashing photographs of a man cut to death by machetes. I dismissed

the photos as sales-driven sensationalism and stuffed the pages
into the side pocket of my backpack.

I smiled seeing the bag. I'd traveled the world with it
and it was covered in the patches of the countries I'd trekked
through; Thailand, Peru, Greece. For years after university I'd
traveled. But now, despite the troubles I knew waited for me,
I wanted nothing more than to be back on my island.

At the curve a boat trailer straddled the road. I kicked
down hard on the brake. The tires locked but kept sliding
in the wet. I veered closer, twisted my face away from the
coming impact. My backpack cartwheeled off the front seat
and up onto the dash, blinding me momentarily, and then
tipped into my lap.

But the tires bit. I was jerked forward, my ribs bending
slightly on the hard steering wheel, the seatbelt cutting into
my collarbone. And then I was chucked back, just short of
disaster.

I thought the boat trailer must have jackknifed until I
saw that the truck it was hitched to was attempting to reverse
the boat down a ramp into the sea. I gaped at the driver, my
hands tightened white on the wheel. I couldn't believe that
this fool would just reverse bang across a blind corner like that
with no regard for others. It was my right of way!

The truck was an old Ford, dark blue, with "For Hire"
scrolled in yellow script on the door. A loose chrome wing
mirror vibrated to the pulse of reggae. The truck driver
was a white boy with a long goatee and curly sideburns. His
straight, white hair was swept back severely in a ponytail and
his eyebrows were thick. One sun-blotched arm hung out of
the open window, the hand dangling, one of the fingernails
bruised blue, holding a limp vanilla cigar. He stared back at
me, his mouth hanging slack and a deep cleft creasing his
brow.

"Boy!" he called out, "Watch it, hey! I tryin' to reverse!"

"It's my right of way!" I answered. I'd propped myself out the window so I could gesture with one hand in an encompassing swoop.

"Who?" His face pinched up. "I goin' down there I tell you." He pointed toward the ramp, which was thronged with those who had come late to get their Friday fish. The simple wood tables of the fishmongers stood about the edges built up on breeze blocks, constructed of plywood, painted brightly red and blue, the roofs thatched. The people pressed close, shouting their orders, complaining, jostling. Seagulls circled and battled over slop, crying and spreading their wings in dominance displays. Blue vanilla smoke from the driver's cigar coiled in the dusk, the scent of it mixing with the burnt rubber. "You gotta get out the way!" he said.

"It's a main road!" I protested. "This is my right of way…"

"What! Man, don't tell me what's what! This land's my birthright! So carry your ass back where you come from!"

I pushed my backpack out of sight, realized that my accent was neutral and the cut of my clothes preppy. If I really wanted to come home I'd have to remember the mannerisms and the peculiarities of speech. But at that moment I was tongue-tied. So I looked around for a way out. My truck's front was just blocking the tail end of his trailer. I stretched my neck to see if I could sneak past.

Horns blared behind. Checking the rearview mirror, I saw cars lined up, shimmering in the heat and chemical exhaust. They couldn't have been there more than a moment. I held my hands up in the cab, trying to show the drivers behind the holdup wasn't my fault.

Deciding to inch by, I yanked the wheel hard over,

eased my foot off the brake peddle and felt the front left tire drop off the road edge to the broken limestone below. The trailer lurched backward in a quick, metallic jostle that spat a fountain of dirty water out of the bilge onto my windshield. The boat rocked and almost slid off its rail.

"Move, boy!" the white-haired driver shouted.

"I can't get past now," I shot back, wondering if he had meant to reverse and block me. "You move!"

"My friend, I ain't got no place to go but down that ramp. You see up here I all out of road." As he said it I could see he was right. A wall ran tight along the other side of the road. "So you need to reverse back and clear the way so I could run she down!"

I sat idling, staring at him, my jaw clenched.

Car horns wailed. I jerked myself around to look. The cars were backed right up. They went off out of range around the bend simmering and intense. An imperfect configuration of shuddering metal unhappy in the sun.

A hostile drumming snapped my attention frontward. Three men stood at the hood of my truck. One had just slapped his open hand down on the metal. He kept it there possessively, the fingers splayed, gripping and glared in through the windshield glass at me.

"You lost, hey? Ain't no hotel down this way. Ain't no tourist ride. You need directions?" the man said. He was a tall, skinny mulatto, what we call "red" on the island, and his hair was big curls highlighted with gold. His breath smelt of rum.

"I know where I'm goin'," I blustered.

"Well you ain't goin' nowhere so long as you in the way like so."

I looked at the trio. The second man was white and shirtless. His arms and face were tanned but his gut was pasty and hung out over his army surplus shorts. The third was a fat black guy with shoulder length dreads, a gold rimmed tooth, gold rings on his fat fingers and a gold chain around his neck. He took a final swig of a Vita Malt bottle and pitched it high over the wall that hugged the road.

"Move, man!" Red ordered, patting the hood of my truck again. He shooed me ever so delicately with long fingers. I shivered, cold and jagged. The black guy came over and leaned in my cab.

"What happen for you? You ain't hear the man? Reverse!"

The white man was just looking, his arms folded, chuckling.

"Man, Caleb," he called out to the trailer driver, as horns still blared, "you want me to deal with this boy? Hey?" Then he laughed big and rolled his head. My shoulders bunched.

"Hey, boss!" Caleb called to me from the trailer, "Why you don't just reverse back and everythin' cool? Why you want to cause all this trouble?"

The black guy tapped a fat finger on the top of my door. I shifted into reverse and rolled back up over the edge onto the tar, my rear bumper front ending the car behind.

"Boy, what you doin'?" the driver yelled, surging out of his Mercedes. His face was set, ready to go and his hands were violent blurs in front of his vexed face.

"Sorry," I pleaded, my voice drowned out by the loud reggae. He had that jowled bull dog expression. I had to shout. "Sorry! I'm just tryin' to sort this out." I rubbed my tense skin, looked back up, saw that I'd moved a couple of feet. The trailer driver, Caleb, he had his room now. He could reverse. I breathed in, closed my eyes, shut out the horns and imagined boats on the water in the sun.

When I looked the blond man was reversing down the ramp. His wooden boat was beat up but painted a bright yellow, with an old diesel inboard engine and a prop rusted to a deep, flaky maroon. Her line curved well and smoothly, the bow fattening into a deep "V" that I knew from experience would ride the big weather.

Caleb's steering was deft and the trailer slowly rolled down the ramp. When the stern was submerged he got out of the cab. He wore an untucked plaid shirt, open at the chest and speedos. Leaning into the winch, he unlocked it, wound the handle, and the boat slithered into the sea. Red and the white boy helped steer the stern while the black man with the fat fingers waved his arms, directing with great importance.

When she was afloat, Caleb's boat calmly mouthed the waves detailed with lavender light. He wadded out. The clouds above him were high up pink gauze and the seagulls swarmed over the vendor's catch. He jumped up topside and stood in the stern coiling a thick anchor rope while the last warm light of day touched his skin.

Red pulled Caleb's truck off the road and my way was clear. The horns stopped. The Mercedes revved and overtook down the wet road, eating it up. I put the gear stick into drive while Red gloated and jeered. The black guy slapped the back of my truck as though he were sending a donkey on its way.

Then the insult came back to me, an insult from my island childhood that might reestablish my birthright.

"Man," I called back. "You'll bitches ain't nothin' but hog!"

II

I was late for my meeting with Thesinger so I nervously topped the legal limit and tried to make time. But my parting shot did not satisfy me. Those boys at the market were ignorant bastards. They don't own a thing so they have to own the road. And I'd remembered too late, called back when I was already too far away, the traffic too loud. They did not hear.

I didn't own a thing, either. I felt that starkly as the breezy, pastel grace of the colonial homes blurred passed. I was reminded why "The" is always capitalized when you speak of The Eastern Road. No other road has these homes, this view, its history and genealogy and so no other road is dignified with such a loaded distinction. It is the capitalization that sums up all the differences.

The Thesingers were a "name" family, one of the old traditional clans that lived out this way. The National Archives note a Nathaniel Thesinger who came over with the Puritans in 1648. Their surname meant something about the island and everyone knew who their people were. Old Jessie Theodore Thesinger had been a big time bootlegger, which passes for respectable money hereabouts. And his son Charlie had been a political fixer. Old J. T. had built the Thesinger homestead with his rum-running money and Charlie threw political shin-digs that had been a must during what they called "the season", if you were lucky enough to come by an invitation. The Thesingers were a cut above my people and I'd never met them.

The address was simply *Bangalay* as they didn't use house numbers out on The Eastern Road. It's their custom to name their homes. I almost overshot the house until I saw the name burnt into a length of varnished driftwood mounted on a limestone wall. I drove to an elegant electric gate of curving aluminum that secured the front drive, and pressed the buzzer with "J. T. Thesinger" embossed in red metal tape.

A surveillance camera watched me. I sat up straight and kept my eyes inside the cab. My gaze landed on the bloody photograph on the front page of the Tribune, peeking out of my backpack.

The gate swung in. I drove up an old, broken concrete drive toward the ridge crest that overlooked the sea. I passed through lush landscaping planted in riotous plan; tall, thin palms, bamboo and fat ficus and fig trees covered in broad leaf vines with the late shadows running long to the east. Undergrowth of purple bromeliads and orchids thronged the darkened bases of the large trees. The rhythmic pulse of sprinklers and the cool of the shade that sheltered the drive created a welcome mood of relaxed civility.

The drive topped out under a giant silk-cotton tree that stood before the house. Everything about the size of the tree spoke of age and permanence, hinted at some knowledge of the harsh climate and what could survive and flourish as assuredly as it spoke to an understanding of what should be avoided and what would die. There was wealth behind that knowledge, not merely money, but a wealth of time and experience.

Bangalay was of faded colonial grandeur, built off the ground on piers with wrap around, wide, louvered piazzas and slatted Bahama shutters. I could see, by their peeling green paint and the odd missing slat that those shutters must have weathered a few hurricanes in their time. The walls were a dusty peach accented with white quoins and keystones that whispered ancestry. It looked like it must be a battle to keep up. I admired the commitment required to constantly produce such timelessness. Whoever had a property like this had to have a nice yacht.

Two purebred Rottweilers came at my truck, all muscle and mouth with their black coats shimmering in the slanted light. They barked savagely at the tires and raced alongside as I parked in front of the twin Doric columns framing the large, paneled front door.

The dogs' tongues dangled from the sides of their jaws. These were no tournament dogs. A cloud of insects droned about them. My throat stuck. They circled and barked and I offered them my hand held out limply for them to smell, to lick and bond as I swung the truck door wide and got out.

Other cars were pulled up every which way in front of *Bangalay*, parked without regard to Thesinger's property. I assumed there were guests and I cursed myself for not being on time for my interview and now having to intrude.

Keeping the Rottweilers in sight, I went up to the front door and stood a moment to collect myself. I hoped I didn't smell of fish from the market. I cleared my throat, smoothed my windblown hair, and put on my red baseball cap. It was a favorite hat, old and frayed. But it had a badge from Sweeting's Boat Basin, where I'd once worked summers, sewn onto it and I thought the emblem meant business. Any guy who opened the door and knew a thing or two about boats would understand that I wasn't playing.

I rapped the tarnished knocker against the mahogany, paneled front door and waited with my hands to my sides, not wanting to push my luck with the dogs. A young woman opened it. I felt a rush at the sight of her. Her face was tanned and healthy and her lovely figure was clad in a sleek and elegant little black cocktail dress that showed her slender arms. She wore no makeup. Her hair, loose and rich, turned in the breeze that came through the house from the sea and which carried with it a hint of seaweed and salt. Of course a rich man would have a trophy wife like this. But then I looked into her eyes and I thought I might be wrong and that she could be the real thing.

Seeing me, she hesitated slightly. Then she relaxed, leaned against the doorframe and looked me over, apparently amused.

"Aren't you a little underdressed for the party, sweetness?" she asked in a native accent particular to The Eastern Road, a long mix of Elizabethan English and the politest Southern twang. Her eyes ran from my face to my polo shirt, from my khakis to my topsiders.

"Oh? No! I'm just here for the boat job." I could hear laughter and music from where the party must be across the house.

She smiled. "Mr. Blake?" She asked.

"Yes. For Mr. Thesinger. Is he in?" I whipped my cap off courteously.

"He is." She gazed at the whimpering dogs still circling behind me. "Quiet, poonkies. Hush now." The two dogs whined, their snouts down, submissive. She looked me over again, smiled.

"Sorry I'm late. I got held up."

"Held up?" She looked most concerned.

"Traffic."

"Oh!"

"At the fish market. A trailer tryin' to back across the road."

"Well, whatever you do, don't mention it to my husband. He loathes that market. Why don't you join the party? It's a little do to raise money for the Junkanoo festival. We're out on the piazza, on the sea side. Jacob, my husband, will be pleased to see you."

The cool inside *Bangalay* calmed me. We crossed a hall with a cut coral floor and a flight of stairs that curved up to the private rooms. The walls were an eggshell hue offset by the green of two potted bamboo palms standing sentinel in oriental urns flancking either side of the entrance to the living room. The paint on the walls was cracked and flaking in places, but to my mind this failure only added character.

The living room floors were dark-stained, hard native pine, laid perhaps by shipwrights. The sofas and armchairs were chintz-covered. The coffee table was piled high with books studded with bookmarks. The top volume carried the title of a naturalist's journeys, another discussed extinction.

Between the French doors that led out to the oceanfront piazza stood a mahogany bar on curved legs, the top of which was cluttered with hurricane lamps and cut crystal decanters of varying heights, some emptied and others full of gold whiskeys or tawny red wines.

The wall above it was covered in a geometry of framed old black-and-white photos. One showed a ketch at sea, painted black from the mast tops to the waterline, and running without lights. A blockade-runner or a bootlegger perhaps. There was another of a man in a linen sack suit and palmetto hat smoking a cheroot and standing atop a pile of whiskey casks while the coopers posed about below.

I wanted ancestors. I wanted my name to mean something, for the past to be invested in me. Then I could be off hand about it.

At the place of pride a square, underwater colour print of a young woman skin diving caught my eye. She was in a bikini, swimming underwater along a reef, with a large queen conch shell in her hand and a knife sheathed at her waist. A mask hid her face but I was sure it was my hostess.

"Comin'?" she asked. Her slight frown punished me for my uninvited examinings and pulled me on.

She walked ahead of me, her mannerisms infinitely rare and delicate. Her small bare feet pitter-pattered across the floor. Her simple grace and the naturalness of her movements had to be learned. But I thought too that I noticed a slight, almost wooden limp.

I could hear the sounds of the party and smelled the lush scent of the sea. I followed, somewhat nervously out onto the oceanfront piazza.

And there it was before me, the inevitable view. *Bangalay* faced northeast into the prevailing winds, in the path of the eye of the thunderstorms. Out there the sky was a composition of burnt red and purple streaked with movement up in the swelling expanse. Sunset painted the west and the east was touched with a fantastic high up oyster sky of mottled summer rain clouds. Famous Paradise Island glittered across Montagu Bay to the northwest. The tall hotels were fantastic, luminous things against the coming black. Beyond was the ever-changing expanse of the ocean. We were beyond the safety of the barrier islands. The coarse Bermuda grass-covered grounds fell away down to the sea that, kicked up by the storms, rode in hard and smashed against the eroding bulkheads. Over and over the spray erupted out and then fell back.

In the bay a wooden fishing dinghy stood out, anchored on a shallow sand bar. It was yellow and white, much like the boat at the fish market. For a moment the anger of my drive over flared up, but I wrestled it down. I could just make out the boat's name, *Cuda*, painted across the transom. It was picturesque, a dab of rustic colour and charm. A postcard image.

The evening's company sat out on the piazza in wicker chairs or stood out on the lawn clustered about a bar. Their faces were all the same. I do not mean they had identical features. Rather their faces had the same "set". That peculiar cut of experience. That glint in the eye. The confidence, the large laugh, the display of teeth, of verve, and then, disquietingly and suddenly, the coolness. The coolness was complete.

Their conversation died and they regarded me.

"Jacob, honey?" my hostess called out. "Your Yachty's here."

"Hey!" a youngish man greeted me, striding up the coral steps to the piazza from the lawn and extending an open hand. "Welcome to *Bangalay*! Did the dogs give you trouble? I'm afraid we have to leave 'em out, even with guests. It's not safe to put 'em away."

"No, sir. No trouble," I said, assuming this man to be yacht owner Mr. Jacob Thesinger and my new boss. He had an angular face, with a solid, dimpled chin, arched eyebrows that met in a permanent cleft mid-brow and sandy hair cut extremely short. I imagined him at Rotary Club meetings, overly involved in small town affairs and almost giggled. But I knew it was nerves.

He was younger than I expected. I'd imagined the kind of crusty aged job that would have a yacht. I was surprised to see that we were about the same age. Perhaps I was his junior by a few years, but not enough to make a difference. He was my contemporary and his success was striking. I brushed my hair out of my sunburned face, curled my toes in my topsiders and tried to stand up straight.

"Well, I expect the dogs know you're one of us," he declared. We stood for a beat, he maybe wondering if I was indeed "one of us", and me feeling anything but. He seemed to let the sentence and its implications hang.

The young women sitting close together on a swing chair watched me. They wore little black numbers and held sweet vermouths and Campari cocktails in manicured hands. These girls wore very little jewelry and their hair hung naturally or was done up in thick plaits and weaves. My throat tightened at the musk of their sexuality.

"I'm Jacob, Jacob Thesinger. You've met my wife, Arial," he gestured toward the girl who had opened the door for me and she smiled and gave a small, graceful nod.

"I'm Gavin Blake," I said stupidly, immediately knowing he knew, feeling his big grip crushing my knuckles. Under what I see as my hard-bitten traveler exterior there is about me a permanent undergraduate quality. I find this embarrassing. Only a ridged determination keeps it hidden. No matter how many traveling experiences I've had, something nervous wriggles inside, snickers, says that a boy like me with nothing to lose doesn't know the true difficulties of manhood. These insecurities fanned out in peacock display under Thesinger's studying look. Did I imagine it, or was there a native contempt behind his impersonal gaze for the boy blown in on the wind? "I'm certainly lookin' forward to crewin' on your yacht."

"Sure. You come highly recommended, Mr. Blake. Highly recommended. I'm lookin' forward to seein' what you can do with my boat. I hope all these travels of yours haven't made you forget the island ways," he winked the warning. "Now then. Let me introduce you," and he turned to his guests, enlarging the sphere of his personality to encompass all. "People, this is Gavin Blake. He's goin' to be takin' care of *Orion* while the skipper's away."

His guests were all skin colors and very well dressed. The men wore tuxedo jackets and bow ties. In contrast to their formal costume some wore Bermuda shorts and, fabulously, they wore no socks. I'd never seen such a get up before, yet it all looked oddly correct. There was one in a red velvet smoking jacket and another disheveled, deliberately bucking the code in seersucker. Even with the burst economic bubble I could just smell the money. Standing there in my topsiders I felt grotty.

Turning back to me, Thesinger said. "You'll get to see my boat later. She's down at The Creek. Now, you better join the party. These people are my friends. But don't trust 'em. They talk fool and tell lies." The company laughed at this outrage, perhaps used to such slander. "Now," he said, owning the moment to be delivered, putting the eye on me, he laid out the all-important islander question, "who your people?"

III

I suppose I'm a Cracker, if you really want to know. That's what I'm always told. Not that I was born in Florida. It's just something I've inherited from my father's line. His people settled by Tallahassee after the Seminole War and he was brought up in the Panhandle. That I have stemmed from such a place and tradition is something I've always had trouble admitting to. Not that I'm ashamed of my father's roots. It's no stigma. But I was delivered right here in Nassau and this is the only home I knew as a boy coming up. My umbilical cord is buried in this sand. There should be something inalienable in that. But they never call me Bahamian and mean it; the word is always couched in inverted commas.

Mother's family had been here for centuries. They

helped build the cathedral in town, and a cousin served in the House. There's deep history in my veins on my mother's side. But none of that's any use as I don't carry her last name. On this rock, where you were born and our matriarchal lineage don't count. The law says that a child takes the citizenship of the father.

It's official. I'm a Cracker by law. When they were cutting up the lines of demography in the heady ascent to Independence my people were left out on the wrong side. My father couldn't get status, not even a work permit. No surprise really, since my mother's people had always been strong Opposition supporters. The Government made sure such families were denied the papers they needed. My father had to return to Florida to find work. After a while his visits became less frequent and then he stopped coming. I fancy people of the Government's ilk got great satisfaction in seeing families like mine broken up. They liked to whittle down the numbers of those they fancied did not belong, those who opposed them politically. They saw no distinction between nationality and their nationalist party. Everyone else was suspect.

Its not that being a white Bahamian is any better in the world's social estimation than being a white Floridian. In fact, here in the islands they call the native whites Conchy Joes, a name some will tell you has the same emotional force as nigger. They say it's because the native whites, struggling to uphold their liberties, declared they'd rather eat a poor diet of conch and be free than dine on the King's meat. There is an element of pride associated with the name.

Still, on my return journey to take up Thesinger's yacht job I still didn't have my citizenship papers. I couldn't vote. I couldn't hold a job legally. I couldn't stay in my own country longer than the time allotted on a tourist visa. You can apply for your papers when you're eighteen and cross your fingers.

But it's degrading to have to ask for what should be yours by right. They don't have to give it to you. Everything's a matter of discretion. And when your eighteen you're angry and passionate, you do things out of principle. So just to show them what I thought of their fucking papers, I didn't even apply.

I changed the circumstances by changing my surroundings. I left the island and after university joined the throng of backpackers and their counter-culture. There was no destination, only escape and experience. I was hungry. I wanted to put the world into my mouth and see what it tasted like. Hemingway gave me my central idea. I wanted to be an expatriate. There was something deeply romantic about the overt celebration of loss that appealed to me.

It was a vivid and varied life, measured not in days or weeks, but in terms of train schedules and time zones, in languages spoken and boarders crossed. The Backpackers banded together in hostels in Lamu, Hoi An and on Santorini, in so-called British pubs the world over. We sought each other out, looked for the ragged hair, the cargo pants, bandanas, the blazing eyes, we listened for the English words above the babble and languid jostling of marketplaces. Always we stood apart from the tourists. We were a different tribe. We travelers were authentic, while the tourists were people still-born to the world. They had homes, families and investments to return to. Their ability to experience was judged by us to be defined and diminished by their ridged lives. We sat on flat rooftops and made fun of them, burned patchouli incense, drank the warm local lager, Saigon Export, Tusker, and gazed out over the interior hotbeds of vegetation and immeasurable squalor.

Such fleeting moments were the basis for friendships and for love. From the very beginning love was always about loss. I had to demonstrate my virility to these traveler girls because it was all I had. But they weren't seeking someone with a job, money, or home. They wanted memories to look back on years later from their suburban marriages, when they would sigh and think of the plain room in the Plaka, the cheep wine, the endless quality of time and the loud cafes downstairs on Kydathineon street, the lean young man who wanted nothing from them but their sex. I was real. Then we were divided by different train schedules, by the very romantic sense of loss that had initiated matters.

Somehow I was more authentic than any other traveler. They were taking years off, spending trusts or exorcising a liberal sense of guilt that they were raised in Greenwich, Connecticut or Hempstead Garden Suburb rather than on the mudflats of Bangladesh. I got extra cache for claiming to be stateless, a purity which the others aspired to.

Together we developed a peculiar code of rootlessness and isolation. There were corkboards in every hostel with messages left of dates and destinations. Each scrap of paper a pinned hope. We observed local customs, learnt the sayings and the slang, we ate the local food and drank the water. We got as close to the tribal peoples of any territory as we could. We slept in their huts and tried their dances.

But I came to feel I had been taken out of context at a very early age. Even my features were out of place. Yet I was known by these features. When my apparently endless travels took me to the Far East I was know as the Frang in Vietnam and in Japan as Gai-Jin. In Kenya I was Mazunga. For years I wondered in the delirious heat where the shadows skate, where things lurked, where people hustled me and tried on their scams. I went through the rottenness, the twisted towns where filth triumphs, Nairobi, Lima, festering, where the law's grip was relaxed, and everything was tolerated but nothing achieved. I built up a inventory of jokes and party anecdotes, but I was no longer sympathetic.

I didn't want to become a doped out, aging traveler. Always the foreign devil. Never the hometown boy. And in the dark nights under the open skies of molasses I longed to be the boy the local crowd cheered for. I suffered from a basic animal need. I wanted a home. One thing I had gained from the adventure was a measure of confidence. I decided to return to my island, stake my claim, and push for my citizenship papers.

After coming through the tourist line I sought out work on a yacht because being on the sea was steeped in local lore and history, because it allowed me to immerse myself in that culture, in what I wanted to be recognized as. In some burst of wild insecurity I felt that swabbing decks would lend me a local authenticity that being born here apparently did not. But while it was at once among the most islandy of occupations, it was also one of the only lines of work legally open to me. The Bahamian ship registry is a flag of convenience and that means that under law you don't have to be a national to crew on a boat flying the Bahamian flag. That suited my particular circumstances neatly.

Of course, standing there on the piazza of *Bangalay* I told Thesinger none of this. Instead I emphasized my mother's maiden name. Unfortunately she had had no brothers, the name died out with my grandfather's critical genealogical failure and so lost currency. Thesinger had nodded, but I think he had been uncertain about the surname, his eyes searched as his mind tried to slot it into the local social arithmetic and failed.

Now, my people are nobody really. Not so as it matters here. But I was a native boy and I would impose myself upon them as was my right. Instead I told Thesinger of the savage anecdotes of travel and thereby hoped to both impress and divert.

IV

Thesinger encircled my shoulder with an arm and walked me down the steps from the piazza toward the bar. Tensing because of his gesture, I felt the open space of my traveler years being squeezed.

"I'd love to hear more travel stories," he said as he led me through a knot of men. "I've been to a few places myself. Have a drink." The bar's white tablecloth was soaking wet from the rain and the bottles of liquor were beaded with moisture. He made an offering sweep over them. "What's your poison?"

Before I could answer "cold beer" he picked up a pitcher, gave it a stir and then poured me out a glass. "Try this."

Feeling obliged, I sipped. It was cool and sweet with the tangy taste of lime and, unmistakably, of mint.

"Mojito," Thesinger grinned, perhaps in response to my quizzical expression. "A Cuban drink. Cool and refreshin', hey? Man, you need that with this heat, somethin' cool and refreshin'."

"Nice." I swallowed it down, thinking of warm beer drunk with great chunks of hay-covered river ice along the Mekong Delta. How barely there so many of those places were, tenuously holding on to the human present, one twist of fate away from slipping back into the murk of prehistory. Everything about Thesinger's homestead and the evening's affair seemed staged to exude a timeless authority, a permanence, as if we had stepped above nature. Except for the rolling sea that continued to erode.

"Here. Have another." He took my half-full glass and topped it up. "Cheers!" he said, and made one for himself. His Rolex glinted in the ambient lighting.

"Look," he admitted, shaking the keys in his trouser pocket with the hand buried there. "I'd love to talk more about Europe and Africa but I have to entertain. I hope you understand..."

"I'm so sorry! I could come back tomorrow if it's more convenient..."

"No! No! Really! Stay and enjoy the party. Tonight's a fund raiser, you know."

"What's the cause?"

"The Junkanoo, man," he grinned, referring to the Bahamian carnival, and with that one word I was taken back to my childhood, to New Year's night, sitting on my father's shoulders, pressing up against the barricades that lined the street and held the crowd back. We watched thousands of dancers and music makers in bright costumes move to the irresistible Afro-Bahamian beat.

"We're helpin' out a new group raise the funds it needs for costumes," he continued. "You wouldn't believe the sums they need for those crazy get ups. Myself, I feel Junkanoo has drifted too far from its roots. I want to bring it back. Roots are important. But culture costs money. So, I'm goin' to get these people well oiled and then maybe they'll free up on their wallets, hey?" He laughed, his bright face telling me his outrage was all a joke. "I'm afraid you'll have to wait about until the end, unless you got somthin' I could squeeze?"

"I don't want to intrude," I tried not to sneer, finding the talk of money both crass and out of my league, wondering why he didn't just donate his own cash.

"Nonsense. Look. Hang about. Have a drink. I'll take

you down to The Creek after the party."

"All right," I said, feeling awkward, but also starting to warm to my new situation, enjoying being in the heart of a cultural event on The Eastern Road, somehow feeling closer to my idea of home.

"I'll catch up with you later." Thesinger smiled and started off, then turned. "I've got it. Your mother's people. They're from Harbour Island originally before movin' down to Nassau, right? One of your ancestor's names is up on the plaque in the Cathedral honorin' those who built it. Yes, that's it. Good family." Then he strode off, leaving me standing there by the bar, quite taken back.

I felt somewhat less of a gatecrasher now that Thesinger had remembered my family tree, even if this was not my social set. I was a long way from the hostels and campsites of the backpacking world. But bars are always places of refuge for unattached men, so I loitered for the security it offered, a kind of social camouflage. I played out the act of connoisseurship, of something weighty hidden between men among the bottles and the measures of spirits and wondered at this Shangri-La.

Above me a tall, thin coconut tree arched skyward, the points of each of its fronds pearled with raindrops. Bamboo tikki lamps burned kerosene at strategic points about the lawn, more for affect than illumination. Seashell chimes clinked together on strings hanging below the piazza roof and halved coconut husks served for ashtrays. The barbecue grill smoked where the rain had hit the hot coals and I could smell the scent of hickory chips. The music was bongos and mambo. What a show.

Jacob Thesinger made the rounds, touching his guests for a "couple dollars". He slapped the guys on the back, grinned the widest and laughed the loudest. He kissed the girls carelessly. Of all the company his off-white tux jacket fit the best. Clearly bespoke. His hair was short, his frame restless. He strode, bounded amid his friends. He made funny faces and they laughed and spoke boisterously, fortified by alcohol, so it was impossible not to overhear them.

"Man, Jacob," one of his guests was saying, "why'd you have to go and set your big party for that date?"

"Well, that's the beginnin' of the season, m'boy, and we want a big bash to kick it off. Right?"

"But a sea dog like you should remember that that's the night the mutton fish will be runnin'. Every fisherman worth his salt will be out on the bank hand linin' the drop-off."

"Then I know you comin'?" Thesinger joked and his audience howled appreciatively.

"My wife won't let me skip it. But I'll be missin' some good mutton fishin'. You know that's the night of the moon. Boy they'll be breedin' with that moon."

"Now you want a little skinny mutton snapper or you want some fat lobster tail with butter and lemon?" Thesinger taunted him, talking large. "Succulent lobster tail, I tell you. Fresh. Me, Dock here and Clint over there, and maybe my new boy Gavin are headin' down to the cays to haul m'traps…"

Another loud circle of people moved between us, and I could no longer hear Thesinger. So I turned and gazed again over his view. It was black now, and the sea was a body that moved terribly. The sky was studded with stars and with isolated thunderheads. The distant storms pulsed with white lightning and moments latter the thunder volleyed in. The lights from the house shone on the crests of the waves and illuminated the little fishing boat in a ghostly pale.

I inhaled with deep satisfaction. So I had the job. Things might just work out after all. I thought about being out there in the expanse of the sea behind the helm on this crawfishing trip. I thought about the blond boy, Caleb, launching his boat at the ramp, and smiled despite my earlier anger. It was okay now. I knew he had something I wanted.

A couple of the men were blending booze so I joined them and fixed myself another. There was a bowl of conch salad on the bar and I spooned myself a serving into a cup and mixed in goat pepper to give it some spice. For the first time in many years I savored the local dish. It was an excellent blend of raw conch, onion, tomato and green pepper.

"That's a fine salad," I said to a guy who was trying it.

"Yes, boy. Tastes like there's some sour orange squeezed in," he replied, sampling it and scrutinizing me. "You Gavin, right?" He questioned, working his chops. "You doin' a stint down there by Jacob's boat?"

"Will be from tonight," I nodded, glad to get onto ground I understood.

"I'm Clinton Knowles. Call me Clint," he said, chewing as he spoke and spooning more conch salad into his mouth. Under his tuxedo jacket he wore an untucked, spread-collar Cuban guayabera shirt with two panels of embroidery down the front. He sported Gucci slip-on shoes and a clipped goatee square on a face slightly yellow with a touch of what the islanders called "a lick", the result of an interracial union between distant ancestors. I wondered if this was the Clint whom Thesinger had mentioned a minute before in connection with the fishing trip. He didn't offer his hand.

"Man," he said, "if you're goin' to be livin' down there you better have a gun or somethin'!"

"A gun?" I asked, grinning, waiting for the punch line.

"You need somethin' to shoot 'em with. They been crawlin' all over that damn boat from day one like cockroach. Man, I wouldn't live down by that way if you paid me!"

I didn't know how seriously I should take this Clint Knowles. He struck me as the kind that pats, that lurks and feels. I imagined tentacles growing out of his head. I could see them, luminous. There was something dangerous there. He was some oozing insect ready to prick you with a serum that immobilizes, who would devour you when he's ready. I felt my good mood waver. I'd been dreaming of sunny days on the deck, of fishing, not of circling the wagons, not of holding until relieved.

"I could sell you a hand gun," he offered.

"A hand gun? But they're illegal."

"Not in particular."

"What?"

"Only in general."

I laughed politely at his liquored-up foolishness.

He gawked at me and we stood awkwardly for a moment. I didn't know what more to say. He rocked on the balls of his feet, chewed conch salad and gazed about.

"Nice house," he said at length.

"Sure."

"It has all the old moldin's and proportions. Not to mention this view." As his hands were full he gestured seaward by puckering his lips.

"Amazin' view," I said. "Must be old money."

"Ah! Now," he pointed his spoon at me, "there's no such thing as old money. No such thing. You always need new money. New money or new blood."

"How's that?"

"Inflation. The cost of livin'. Bureaucratic nonsense. That's why I can always get a good price off an old person. They might have been rollin' when they retired at sixty but twenty years and no new money later they're as poor as landscape niggers."

I blinked. It wasn't the kind of thing I expected to hear from a moneyed and cultured crowd.

"Especially with these hard times," he continued. "Trust me. I know these things. I'm in real estate." He gazed around the piazza. "I could do a lot with this house if I could get my hands on it."

"But isn't Mr. Thesinger a friend of yours?"

"Oh! Sure! Sure! Bosom! But you have to be ready. You never know when an opportunity will come up. Things change. You know. Why. Just yesterday I picked up waterfront property, ocean view, infinity pool, for, well, half price. Cash money. Got it from a brand new widow. Always read the obituaries," he advised. "She'd been held up at gunpoint in her bedroom in her negligée. Terrible! Terrible!" And then he winked at me. "You know," he shrugged, "sometimes the lion is fattest in times of drought." His spoon once again became an explanation mark.

I was saved from having to talk to Clinton Knowles further by a gust of wind that hit hard up off the ocean.

"Rain comin'!" someone called out.

We all pivoted seaward and saw the maroon weather coming. The first icy drops struck and the fancy crowd out on the lawn broke, clinched up bottles and dashed for cover. The tropical deluge swept in and we were sprinting through it, laughing and screaming at the great fun.

Under the piazza roof I was jammed between panting, soaked bodies with Jacob and Arial Thesinger nearby. I felt awkward so close to so many Eastern Road people, but the experience of the storm, however tenuous, gave us a common bond.

"That's just one little spry," Jacob shouted above the storm and all the faces, shiny wet, broke into toothfull grins.

The rain came down in a torrent. The heavy, mercurial drops streaked down, just beyond the shelter of the eave. It clobbered the roof, surged out the gutter shoes in streams that snaked their way through the grass. The gray silhouette of the tall coconut trees bent under the deluge, fronds drooping. The electric power dipped, causing lights to dull and the crowd groaned.

"It's a fine boat," I vaguely heard a baritone voice declare in my ear over the racket of the storm.

"Sorry?" I twisted about to give the big man packed in next to me my attention. I had to look up.

"Jacob's yacht. It's a fine hull. Comfortable," he shouted, a liquor-racked double bass twang plucking in his speech. His face glowed with rain and exhilaration. I felt it too, the primal surge of the weather. Of things.

"I'm lookin' forward to crewin' on her," I shouted back, sure that I recognized him. His complexion was very dark, his afro close cut, his face framed in actual turtle shell glasses and his Yoruba nose was bulbous from boozing, saving him from being pretty.

"I'm Dr. Geoffrey Roberts," he said, extending a large hand through the press of bodies. His handshake was limp. Of course, the physician. He was famous, or perhaps infamous would be more accurate. Everyone on the island knew he had earned the nickname "Dock" after performing surgery dockside to a propeller blade gash to some guy's arm while three sheets to the wind.

His poplin shirt was half-unbuttoned and his dark skin contrasted with a gold chain and sixteenth-century Spanish medallion. Roberts's thick fingers held a cocktail glass delicately. Pulped wedges of lime floated among the ice.

"She handles the open water beautifully," he went on, his hand sweeping before his eyes, the palm flat, drawing it out for me visually. "Jacob's damn proud of her. He's got a fine open fisherman, too. Hey, Jacob!" he hailed our host above the storm. "Jacob? Didn't you bring that twenty-eight over from Miami yourself the other day?"

"Yeah, Dock," Thesinger hollered back, grinning. "Me and Clint. I took Clint because he's supposed to know the way. You think he knew the way? He didn't know the first thing about which way to go."

"It's not my fault!" Clint Knowles called out, standing on tiptoes several bodies away.

"Now, I know his reputation as a pirate is deserved," Thesinger carried on, and he was carrying on bad, "but where did old Clint earn this nautical image?"

"Ah!" Dock tittered, "he probably just went along to see if there was any property on one of the islands along the way. Maybe he could talk some fool Out Island woman out of house and home."

"Boy, you lucky I can't get through this crowd! You lucky! Let me come by you and put one cut ass on your black hip!" Clint joked.

"This boy can't find his own head, never mind reef head!" Roberts jeered.

"Look, so I lost the maps overboard. How many times do y'all have to rip me over this?" Clint complained, a nerve clearly touched.

"Well, that water, that Gulf Stream, it could soon separate sheep from goat," Dock Roberts admitted in what I took to be an effort to soothe matters and bring the conversation back to an even keel.

"Ah now, she was gentle with us that time," Thesinger went on. "We was lucky. We didn't have weather like this. But our luck ran out. It ran right out. I tell you, Gavin," he said, turning to me now. "No sooner did I have that new boat tied up at the dock than some bitch steals it. Brand new outboards! Twin two-fifties! Gone! We found the hull beached, stripped of the engines. Boat's in a sling on dry dock gettin' a new fit now. You can brave the ocean but you can't survive the shore," Thesinger said, shaking his head. He polished off his drink.

So the conversation turned to crime as it inevitably does at these social gatherings.

"Come boy! You've got to carry a gun!" Dock exclaimed to Jacob. "Man, these boats go through all kind of fool places where the bastards will chap you. I tellin' you! You need to get ready because when they come they don't stop. That's a little preventative prescription from your physician. Just remember, in the long run there's damn all I can do for yinna."

"I'd probably shoot some innocent bystander my mistake," Thesinger joked.

We were still wedged together under the piazza's shelter, protected from the drumming rain but not from a thin mist risen up of the ground from the torrent's impact that floated in under the eave. The pitcher of Mojitos was being circulated over our heads, the limes and the mint leaves quaking with the ice. We all poured another glass and everyone shouted to be heard.

"Y'all remember that story?" Arial spoke up, her wet hair bedraggled, her long arms shining with mist. "That one about the American couple down that way boatin'? I think it was in the Exuma Cays? Anyway, these men, they said they were fishermen, but you know, they'll say anythin'. They come right up alongside, which is one thing, but next thing you know they are climbin' up into the boat. Can you believe it?" she asked, touching the nape of her neck. "They were on board! That little boat! And only the man there and his wife! I would have been scared for my life!"

"They must have wanted it to run drugs," someone said.

"So anyway," Arial resumed. "The husband, thank goodness, he had a pistol and so he shot 'em dead!"

"True! True!" Dock leant in, "You gotta be outwardly fearless. You must never give ground."

"They're not responsible," Arial agreed with him. "You're put in those situations and you're just not responsible."

I felt a chill as I saw their heads turn in unison to look out into the night, their eyes white and seeking.

"The bitches!" Clint Knowles cursed and everyone laughed at the outrage of it and at the release. They laughed big. You could hear them over the thunder. They laughed "ha-HAAA!" Which is something the first time you hear it.

V

The thunderhead's massif rolled inland beyond the ridge and passed out of sight. The naked yaw of sky exposed the multitude of stars, which appeared small and insignificant in the open-ended reach of space. The cicadas called and the air was laden with seaweed and pungent night jasmine.

The guests drifted away as the night entered its deepest hours. Eventually I was alone outside on the piazza with Jacob and Arial Thesinger. The August humidity weighed on me. Everything dripped; the bowed trees and the gutters, my skin in the heat. Sweat tickled under my soggy collar as I stewed. Candles shimmered and turned in the light breeze that barely cooled.

Calypso music played and despite the heat my body responded to the addictive groove. With my topsiders off, my bare feet perched on a rattan ottoman, my toes tapped to the tempo.

The heat polished Arial to a shine. She was poised at the fringe of her seat, her arms extended in flamenco custom, the fingers slowly clicking to the calypso rhythm, her lips puckered. In the glare of candlelight, the muscles of her erect back shimmered with perspiration as she moved precisely to the music. I realized that this was a style she had mastered.

Thesinger watched her, his face fat with pride and possession. His white dinner jacket was draped across a chair arm, the black silk tongues of his bow tie hung loose about his spread collar, and his shirt, damp with sweat, was unbuttoned, the tails hanging over his Bermudas.

I was fading and felt it was the hour to bring the curtain down on the evening. I looked over at Thesinger to catch his eye.

"Well, honey," he said to Arial, evidently feeling as I did. "We've done our bit for culture and charity, hey? Gavin, m'boy, what you think? A nightcap? Then I can run you down to The Creek and we can get you settled in on board *Orion*."

I thought: damn your bloody cocktail. I couldn't face another, but I couldn't refuse him. In these parts a man is supposed to be bloody drunk and holding it. "Sure," I said. "One more won't hurt."

"Ha! One for the road it is then," he replied and went into the house, swinging the empty chrome ice bucket.

I wasn't prepared to be alone with Arial. I had to find something to fill the moment so I lent forward and picked a seashell out of a basket on the coffee table. It was smooth and white with a pink mouth.

"Do you like shells?" she asked in her soft, singsong island voice, watching me.

"Oh, I like to look at 'em."

"Do you collect?" she asked, suddenly eager.

"Goodness, no," I said quickly, and she seemed disappointed.

"I love shells. Shells are part of my life. I don't know what I would do if I didn't have my shells." She gently turned several specimens over in the basket to reveal their different sides and colors. "I study 'em. They are so pretty. Even these common shells are works of art to me. I pick 'em up beach combin'. My favorite shells, the rare ones, I have inside."

I raised an eyebrow.

"I have a rare Tiger Triton. It's a lovely, cream-colored shell with dark brown tiger stripes on its lips. I dove it up as a girl when I went boatin' with Jacob. It could go for quite a few dollars in the market."

I wished she had not mentioned the market. Thinking about my earlier experience made my skin prickle. I might have nearly died that afternoon. What if I'd not braked in time? What if I'd piled into that trailer at speed? Perhaps it's inevitable that these things color us. I told myself not to dwell on it, to think instead of the market, its vibrancy and grace, the local charm and the certainty of men working the native produce. There was lore there, the traditions handed on from fathers to sons, a wealth of local knowledge. I remembered too the image of the fisherman Caleb, standing on the deck of his boat with all the sea before him, coiling his rope in the sun. I wondered if he were more authentic than Jacob Thesinger was.

"Do you buy shells at the fish market?" I asked.

Her eyes went white and big and with a rupture of loose hair she turned to see if Thesinger had returned. He hadn't.

I went on, "I think I saw some lovely shells there this afternoon."

"Oh! Let's not discuss the market."

"But you mentioned…"

"Please! Don't!"

Something in her tone made me uncomfortable.

"O-kay," I said slowly, to tell her that I had not said anything inappropriate. "I suppose you can dive up all you want. You must swim like a fish." I tossed the shell I was holding back into the basket.

After a beat she replied, "I don't skin dive anymore."

I was about to ask her why when Thesinger reappeared with the replenished ice bucket, cutting off my question. "Last call for alcohol," he merrily announced, his face stretching into a broad grin.

I wondered how to avoid the drink. Get me out of here, I begged silently, hating the heat, feeling trapped in Thesinger's pretension and longing for something simpler.

"That's it," Arial called out, with too much glee. "Let's all have another one."

"I think you've had enough," he chided.

"Oh, but let's all have another," she giggled and smiled at him and then shot me a guarded look. I knew to be silent, but wasn't sure where I'd trespassed, what secret garden of hers I had disturbed. Or maybe I was just drunk.

Thesinger grabbed my glass and furnished it with new ice that immediately began to wilt in the evening's heat. He was all movement despite the temperature. Perspiration dotted his temples and darkened the back of his shirt as he danced to the calypso and measured out my drink. He never spilt a drop. I felt terribly drunk and envied his steady hands.

"Darlin', I'm so glad Mr. Blake here's goin' to help you out on the boat," Arial said to him, clasping her sweet vermouth.

"Call me Gavin, please."

"Well, Gavin," she said, turning to me, "you see, it will

free Jacob up to help me plan our party."

"We've got one hell of a bash lined up to kick off the season," Thesinger disclosed, looking up from his liquor ministrations. "It'll be the event. It's goin' to rival any of those parties you hear stories about from the good old days. As grand as anythin' my father Charlie threw."

"I overheard some people talkin' about it tonight," I said, sitting forward to listen.

"The word is out. I've grand designs," he cradled his cocktail in his open palm and swept it before him in a gesture that encompassed the future, pinned it down as a known and comfortable quality. "Wild hog will be shot in the bush and roasted evenly over a wood fire. A boat trip down to the cays is planned to stock up on crawfish tail and a full bar will be laid on. Mojitos. Margaritas. Martinis. I tell you, I have the band practicin' the songs I want. There will be a lot of old-time stuff. Meringue and samba. It's goin' to be down at the *Creek Cabana* where I keep *Orion*. Strings of lights will be strung up between the palms, a dance floor placed in the palm grove and tikki lamps burnin' everywhere, everywhere I tell you."

"Sounds like the real thing, all right," I said, trying to muster some enthusiasm. I looked out over the view and tried unsuccessfully to imagine tonight's party on a far grander scale.

Over the harbor, another storm was advancing up from the northeast. The view was disappearing. Already the little fishing boat was invisible. A down blast blew back the fronds of the palms and the tall, slender trunks leaned. Chilled air scraped against my face and cooled my sweaty skin. The candle flames tore and spat wax, both fueled and frustrated by the wind.

"Bloody hell!" Thesinger said. "Not another squall?"

We watched it come until it was upon us, pummeling

the roof of the piazza. It was tremendous, one of the last storms of the heavy, late-summer wet season.

The Rottweilers bounded out of the dark onto the piazza to get out of the rain, heads down submissively, whining. Their fur was wet and covered with the detritus of decomposing leaves and dirt from where they had rolled under the bushes. They left dirty black paw prints on the tile. Realizing I had gone tense at their arrival, I willed myself to relax.

"Poonkies!" Arial called to them sweetly. Their faces lit up and they started panting and trotted over to her. She cuddled their massive heads and cooed, "My two wet little beasts."

The dogs shook themselves and we all moaned as water shot off their backs in a blur. Their thick pink tongues lolled, dripping saliva as they flopped down against the wall and gazed out at the storm.

Suddenly the electricity failed, leaving only the candlelight. I would come to expect this in such weather. I'd greeted such power outages in the Third World countries of my travels with humor. But as *Bangalay* descended into darkness, I felt undermined.

"Oh hell!" Thesinger cursed.

"I hope the power don't go out durin' your party," I said and I knew I'd said the wrong thing.

"Man, don't put mouth on it," Thesinger laughed nervously.

"I'll leave you boys," Arial said, setting her glass down, she lifted a candle and rose. "Jacob, honey? Can you turn the generator on and lock up? I'm goin' to head off to bed."

"Sure, darlin'. I'll take Gavin here down to the Creek later. We'll wait out this storm and then head down."

"Do be careful, the roads are dangerous."

"I own those roads," he grinned. Arial rolled her eyes

and extended her hand to me.

"It was a pleasure to meet you, Gavin. Goodnight," she said and turned. In the candlelight I saw the naked skin of her back patterned with the embossed print of the rattan and goose bumps from the storm's sudden cold. I stood. I couldn't help myself. I felt stupid immediately and sat down. But the ceremony of the evening seemed to require it. She exited through the twisting curtains, limping slightly.

Carrying gas for the generator, Thesinger and I went around the side of *Bangalay* to the shed. He stomped through the storm as raindrops strobed and streaked through his torchlight. Instinctively I hunched over to take the force of the gale on my back. Heavy raindrops pelted, stinging my skin. My bare feet were cold and I trod carefully to avoid stones. The dogs trotted and panted at our heels, soaked immediately. I could smell their fur. Palm fronds and coconuts, torn free by the squall, lay scattered across the lawn. The tikki lamp flames had been extinguished, and the raindrops hit the lid of the barbecue with a tin tapping. Rivulets carved by rushing water ran down the ridge toward the sea, eroding the land, carrying it off forever.

"Around here you have to be self-sufficient," Thesinger called back. I wondered if that had been my family's crucial failing. I relied on to many things, on the Government to grant me my papers, on Thesinger's pay packet in the meantime. I scoffed at the notion that he might think a little generator would rescue him.

He pulled open the shed door and aimed the flashlight beam inside. We hunched into the small space out of the rain. It was dry inside and smelt musty. Gripping the wall, a large-eyed Madagascar gecko froze in the unexpected illumination. Trails of wood ants worked their way across the roof trusses and snails clung to the walls.

"You know," he chuckled as he leaned into the humid shed, "I think I'm goin' to just stop payin' taxes. What's the fuckin' point? They can't even keep the power on. I tell you, man, just a little rain. Boy, if a bird takes a piss on the electric cable the power knocks out. And the roads? Don't get me started on these here potholed roads. And the police? There are two abandoned stations in this area alone. No wonder Robert's is always on at me about a gun. Now, I don't mind havin' to do things myself. I can make it on my own you see. But don't make me pay such high fuckin' taxes for nothin'!"

He hung the torch from a nail in the ceiling and the light shone down onto the small generator.

"You should declare your independence. Make your own country of one," I joked sarcastically, knowing that this was a route that had not worked for me.

"Sure, get those trains runnin' on time. I have my plans. I already have my own power company right here in this shed. Eastern Road Power & Light Limited."

"Closed mouth don't catch no fly," I cautioned him with the old island saying and he nodded.

"That's right. Let's see if this old banger even works."

His practiced grip was steady as he poured gas into the tank without spilling a drop. He flicked on the choke, hunched forward, grabbed the handle and pulled the starter string to the motor. It coughed. Taking the choke off he pulled again. It fired up, shaking fiercely and clamoring in our ears before settling into a loud purr.

He plugged the electric cord into the generator to feed power to the house and stood back from his work and nodded to me. How simply he seemed to set his life right. But it was easy for him. He had the money.

We left the door to the shed ajar so that the engine

could get the air it needed, and hurriedly walked back to the house with the dogs through the clinging turbulence.

We entered the den. Thesinger slid the iron bolts to secure the French door behind us. Metal struck stone with a bone knocking chill and he padlocked them, closing out the storm and the Rottweilers. The first thing I saw was a handsome and impressive lion head. The trophy had a shaggy gold mane and terrible, yellow, grooved teeth. It hung square above the wet bar at the back of the intimate room. Large seashells were displayed upon the bar and the shelves behind it were stacked high with old phonograph records in worn cardboard sleeves.

"I call this the Bahama Room," Thesinger said proudly, indicating where I should sit. The den was filled with sunken leather club chairs, Burgundy and British racing green.

The thickly-plastered limestone walls were decorated with a mural. The watercolor was primitive, yet idyllic. Underwater scenes of colorful sea gardens teeming with tropical fish rose from floor to ceiling. A silver barracuda hung in the dim over the reef, surveying its territory and large crawfish peeked out of every rock ledge. There were portraits of laughing pirates sprawled upon chests filled with plunder, drinking rum from large mugs. A seaplane, a Grumman, cut a white wake as it broke the water coming into an isolated island harbor. Stacked crates of Prohibition liquor, bound for thirsty Americans, lined one wall. A sloop and its small crew endured a terrible sea on another. The sloop, painted black, stole through the night, bathed in the thin blue light from a gibbous moon, the mate stared fixedly forward at the bow holding a lantern at arms length. The final scene depicted what I recognized at once to be the view of the harbor outside Thesinger's home, but empty of any boats and without anything built upon the barrier islands.

"It's quite a paintin'! Don't you think?" Thesinger boasted. "It's all there, our history, our land."

I pushed my wet hair back, rubbed my wet legs down with a towel and admired the mural. Like some strange geological artifact, or the concentric rings of a fallen tree, the images peeled back the past. It seemed to sum up so much of who we were or, more complicatedly, who we would want to be.

He placed a Dewer's and soda on a bamboo side table, but I'd had enough and I didn't touch it. He spun himself another cocktail. I could hear the clear bell of ice dropping into crystal.

Then the crackling of a needle placed on old vinyl. That odd, archaic sound felt eerie. The music was an original Louis Armstrong side. Thesinger twirled the LP dust jacket between his palms. Next to the turntable was an extensive, certainly irreplaceable collection of other LPs and 78s.

"I like this stuff," Thesinger smiled. "It was my father Charlie's collection, and some of it belonged to my grandfather J. T. I made a point of holdin' on to it after my father passed. These recordin's are from a bygone era. Civilized. I feel obliged to look after 'em."

I tapped my feet to the music, heard the squall pick up outside.

"Well, we'll just wait it out here," he sighed, coming over and sinking into one of the club chairs, "then I'll take you down to the Creek."

I sipped my Dewer's and soda after all, revitalized by the rain and the Louis Armstrong. My gaze fell on the wonderful shaggy lion's head. It dominated the room, wide-eyed and full of murderous intent, the roar permanent.

Thesinger saw my admiration and said, "My grandfather

J. T. shot that. It was his lion. He tracked it in British East Africa. What a landscape that is, with its barren, dry valleys and dusty kopjes. It's somethin' to shoot there."

We were quiet then and I leaned back, relaxing into the soft, creased leather, chewing the blended scotch, the muffled rain and wind somehow deeply appealing, mood setting. I thought about the lonely landscape and the tracking of the lion, weighing the hunter's considerations of light and wind direction, weather, the season, afternoon or morning. Long hot days in the sand under acacia trees, frightening nights in the open of the Rift, coming up painfully on the predator, outwitting it in its natural habitat, then the kill.

I remembered shooting hog. The big boars could be dangerous, especially to a boy. My father showed me how to handle the gun, how to nestle it in the shoulder, to aim a little low, and to take the recoil in the arm. My first hog I hit square in the flesh of its rump. It dropped squealing, pulling itself in a circle around its wound with its front legs.

My daydreaming was interrupted when I became aware of the absence of the storm. All I could hear was the drip-dripping outside and the song of the cicadas.

"Well!" Thesinger said, standing and clearing our glasses away. "Closing time, gentlemen. Time for the booze-cruise down to the *Creek Cabana* before another shower comes through. You can get your trans in the mornin'. Time to meet your new mistress, my little yacht *Orion*, and your ocean-going sleepin' berth."

Even as we shut the metal security bars fast across the French doors and bolted them into place, even as I felt the excitement of seeing the yacht for the first time, I wasn't ready to leave the Bahama Room. It was a private clubhouse of sorts, and I had been extended the privilege of membership. My initial prejudices about Thesinger had mellowed. He was deeper than I had first thought.

I was drawn to his mural and this room. The raw paint on the wall, the images, the soft and pliable leather, it was what had been saved. A pictorial history of sorts, a representation in color and brush strokes kept safe from the ravages of intent and circumstance. A remembrance, dignified and obligatory, which weighed upon me.

VI

We barreled up The Eastern Road in Thesinger's '61 Lincoln Continental with the windows down and the cool night air rippling across our faces pungent and humid. The sedan was a classic marque. I liked its distinctive razor front end and the fact that the back doors were rear hinged. He played Afro-Cuban jazz and we shook our bare feet, nodded our heads to the Latin rhythm as the car splashed through the puddles. His hand lay lazily on the steering wheel and the wide body of the car drifted out to the center of the road before he wrenched it back. At the straight Thesinger accelerated and my stomach lurched. Reaching for the seatbelt, I found there was none.

My backpack, which I'd thrown in the rear, bounced on the bench seat next to a pile of fireworks on long polls. The cardboard casings were covered in cartoon stars and bursting rocket trails. The lightweight wood rattled, the car's suspension being inadequate to deal with the frequent potholes.

"Damn! That's a lot of firepower," I commented.

"Boy hey!" Thesinger grinned. "I told you my party was

goin' to be decent. I don't play, you see."

"You could shoot the moon."

His high beams illuminated the road immediately ahead in twin cones of light. The road beyond was dark, the electric power still out and the streetlights standing impotently. The properties behind the continuous walls were invisible and mysterious. Squinting, I leaned forward in my seat to try and make out the road beyond the lights. It was impossible. I felt I was driving into the past.

"Don't worry. I know this road. Every damn turn and rise."

"We're goin' a bit fast."

"Maybe we need to see better where we're headed, hey?"

While he drove he reached behind onto the rear seat and came back with a rocket. I was startled to see the pointed shape of it and hear the grains of gunpowder pouring about inside.

"Gavin man, it has to be done," he winked.

"What?"

"Catch a fire."

He leaned out the window extending the pole before him, tilted, lancing into the future, the rocket's conical nose vibrating in the on-rushing air. He couldn't be serious. But he pulled out his Cartier lighter and put flame to fuse.

"Wait!" I called. "The police station's 'round the corner!"

I was too late. The firework's tail hissed, the cab filled with sparks and the stench of burned powder as the rocket flew off its launch pole. The blindingly bright nucleus left behind a snaking comet trail of smoke. It cut a hot, spiraling path down the open road, went beyond the headlights, illuminating the winding street and the parallel walls, the shadows of the trees momentarily definite, and exploded ahead. I saw the expanding blue lights before I heard the delayed report. A second later we drove through remnants of cindered powder and airborne paper, the last hot embers on the tar vanishing under the chassis.

"Wooooo!" He hollered.

"Christ! You'll get us arrested!"

We rounded the corner to the local police station. It too was dark. The headlights revealed the peeling mint green paint of colonial service covered with explicit, looping graffiti. The wood columns at the front door had split and the portico sagged. I was surprised to see it abandoned, silent, without explanation. It had been in use before I'd left the island and it took me a moment to register the implications. When I did, I felt loss.

We sped on. Branches from the giant tropical trees draped out over the road and the vines dropped wildly. Rainwater still dripped off them into the long puddles along the roadside.

Jacob reached behind the seat and got another rocket. I realized we were free to do this. No one would stop us. No one could ever stop us. The understanding filled me with giddy pleasure. I touched upon a freedom I'd not known before. Excited, I grinned at the insanity of it.

The pole went out the window, the fuse sparkled and the rocket launched. The burn multiplied many times in the reflective surfaces of the long puddles where the explosion repeated in a splintered cascade of arching trails of red. We rammed through the drifting smoke and took the corner.

Another car came around the bend at us. I pushed myself down into the bucket seat, closed my eyes and, for the second time that day, braced for impact. The two vehicles passed, the sound of rubber screamed in my ears as our car was buffeted by the air between.

"Oh, what a friend we have in Jesus," Thesinger sang, pressing on the brake pedal, pulling up the hand brake lever and turning the wheel. I thought we were out of control. But the car spun to a stop in a narrow driveway just off The Eastern Road. I braced myself with a hand on the dash to stop my body being thrown forward.

There was no collision. We just stopped. For a moment I stared at the name Continental written in looping script on the glove compartment in front of me. When I finally did look up I saw a closed gate and a familiar length of varnished driftwood with "*Creek Cabana*" burnt into it. We'd arrived. The gate's aluminum work shone in the headlights and the dark garden lurked beyond. The car idled and Thesinger killed the music. After the peal of rubber and the pounding of the fireworks, the silence throbbed.

"Hey, killer. Open the gate, man," Thesinger said.

I sat for a beat, the salty scent of the ocean mixed with the burnt smell of tires in my nostrils.

"Chief," he said, "what happen? Let's go."

I fumbled with the door handle and managed to open it. My legs moved automatically. Slowly I swung out and somehow stood. Then, inexplicably, I spun around and stared out at the road. Thesinger also looked over his shoulder, his angular features strained. A car streaked passed out on The Road with a loud Va-Voom! A fine cloud of mist hung in the air where its tires had kicked up the water off the tar. Other than that the road was empty. My heart pounded.

We looked at each other. Thesinger chuckled knowingly but I was disturbed by my own reflexive action, disappointed by it.

"Jesus!" I said, steadying myself. "I'm drunk."

"Don't let go of that door," he grinned.

"I'm finished."

"You're drunk all right. You know how I know? Because it takes one to know one and I'm a drunk fool," he said.

We looked at each other and burst out laughing. I couldn't stop. I sat down laughing on the wet gravel drive in the open car door with the white wall of the front tire luminescent in the dark.

"Listen. Get the gate. Open the damn gate."

"I can get the gate," I laughed.

"That's right."

I pulled myself up and went off toward the gate. I let myself fall forward slightly to induce motion and hoped I'd stay on my feet.

"Boy, you tackin' hard," he joked.

Hinges squeaked as I opened the gate, rainwater spilling off and I thought it was quite a funny gate.

He drove through and I closed up behind and got back in the car for the short drive down the gravel path to the Cabana. The entire grounds seemed to be covered in a dense grove of coconut trees, except for a clearing at the end of the drive where the *Creek Cabana* stood. It was a quaint, one-bedroom island cottage by the water. He cut the lights as we approached and the small, wet stones made that nice tearing sound under the tires as we went.

"I just use this place for entertainin'," Thesinger said, pulling out his key ring. I thought of the grand party he intended to stage here. "And for keepin' *Orion*," he added.

The masonry work around the Cabana front door was inlaid with seashells, a rustic touch that made me think of Arial's collection. Thesinger unlocked the door and we went in. He flipped the light switch out of habit and miraculously the power was back on. He raised his eyebrows at me in a "Well, what do you know" expression.

The room was simple, furnished beach house style. There were old photos in bamboo frames, one, unmistakably, of Thesinger's grandfather standing astride his prize lion. Beyond the sliding glass doors Thesinger switched on the landscape lighting and I thought I could just make out the lines of the yacht. I was keen, peering, trying to get a look at her.

Before I could make her out there was a clatter in the next room. I flinched.

"Who's there?" Thesinger demanded.

I heard the pop of a light bulb breaking. We dashed to the cramped doorframe. Steadying myself against it I blinked, adjusting my eyes. I could see that a window was shattered and some of the furniture was in a shambles. But the room seemed empty, which confused me. Then I saw a man's reflection in the mirror across the room. It took a moment to work it out, first that I was looking at a reflection, the image of a man in a mask hidden behind an open closet door and then that this louvered closet door was the one immediately next to me. I could tell by his tense stance that he'd been about to flee. Now we'd trapped him.

"Here!" I shouted and shoved Thesinger aside as I saw the swing. "Knife!" I called, spun out of the way and watched the sickening blur of the blade cutting the air.

"Stop where you are!" Thesinger barked.

"Fuck you!" The man spat, the teeth protruding from the ragged burled cotton of his mask.

"Don't you threaten me in my house!"

"I man!" The man shouted.

I was the closer target. He swung crossways, aiming for my gut. His blade was a machete, inches thick with a hooked point. I sucked my stomach in, realized that the blow was short and I was safe. I could see the razor flash of his eyes through the mask's twin holes and thought I glimpsed his fear.

"I goin' to chap you right up, bitch!" he screamed.

Driven backwards by his cuts, I stumbled and almost fell. His blade came down on the floor tile, jarring, chipping off a hard ceramic wedge that hit me on the cheek.

I saw a barracuda mounted on a plaque on the wall. I grabbed the trophy, held it up to shield against his onslaught. He came on. I clutched my shield and his stroke struck the fish square. The force shook my hands to the bone. The barracuda was split in two and the plaque fell from my stunned hands.

Thesinger got the intruder from behind. He had both his arms wrapped around the other man's, pinning them at his sides.

"Punch him!" Thesinger called.

"But?"

"Punch him, damn it!"

The head under the horror-showmask was faceless; only the eyes betrayed life. I slammed my fist into the man's mouth. It hurt my fingers awfully and I came away with stars in my eyes and doubled over from the shock and pain. Through it I realized the man was screaming and kicking and Thesinger was yelling to hit him again.

The masked man jumped on top of Thesinger and they collapsed together. The machete was dropped and disappeared among the upturned furniture. Both men came up scrambling stupidly, trying to be the first to get a hold.

Seeing Thesinger's Rolex, the eyes behind the mask went white and wide. He latched onto Thesinger's wrist with both hands and tried to pry the watch off, clawing at the clasp. Thesinger punched short jabs into the man's face, but he wouldn't let go of the Rolex. Thesinger grabbed the man's face through the knit mask, squeezed it and pushed his head up. The mask stretched comically across the dome of the man's head. Thesinger got his weight on top and pinned the intruder. I heard the clasp on the Rolex come loose and the jewelry on the watch's face flashed.

"You bastard!" Thesinger spat, groping in among the furniture and retrieving the machete. Lifting the blade high above his head, point down, he got ready to stab. The intruder let go of the watch and grabbed Thesinger's armed hand. The machete quivered with the power of the opposing tensions. Both men gasped as they got both hands and everything they had behind their struggle. The loose Rolex dangled from Thesinger's wrist, flashing a spot of reflected light across the intruder's face.

"Boy, fuck you!" he spat as he got his full weight in against Thesinger. But the blade didn't move and he squeaked. "Please!" He whimpered and with that word the scales tipped. The status of victim fell from Thesinger, he was in control.

"Mr. Thesinger?" I called softly.

Their wrists and hands were shaking from the tension.

"Thesinger?"

A knee thrust into Thesinger's groin. The force somersaulted him over the intruder's head and he hammered onto the tile. The man jumped up, pulling at his ski mask to align the eyeholes. He dove at me. Still holding my throbbing fist, I yelped and tumbled aside shouting, "get off me", but he wasn't on me.

When I turned, the man was half out the window where he got stuck. Thesinger went wild. One hand holding his crotch, he got up, charged across the room and assaulted the man's leg. I got in there and grabbed hold of an ankle and we tried to pull him in. The man's eyes rolled back at us. His teeth through the little mouth hole were grouted with blood where I'd hurt him. He kicked hard and I was launched off and lost my balance. Stomach acid stung my mouth and suddenly I was on the floor. Picking up a broken table lamp I smashed the intruder's knee with the fired clay base again and again.

The masked man howled and struggled to get free. He was pulling himself out all right and soon he had most of his leg out and just his foot to go. Somehow his sneaker came off and Thesinger grabbed the man's naked foot with one hand and the shoe with the other. I knew Thesinger couldn't hold him for long. As a final act Thesinger bit the man's big toe, his top incisors rimmed with blood and the man screamed, wrenched his foot out of Thesinger's mouth and vanished.

"Outside!" Thesinger ordered. In a frenzy, we tore off toward the front door. I kicked the fly screen open and we rushed out onto the wet gravel path by Thesinger's car and searched in the darkness. How could we find a masked man in black clothes at night? And what would we do with him if we did?

I saw movement, a man limping between the palms.

"There!" I pointed.

Two eyes looked back at us and we both sprinted toward them. I picked up a coconut from the grass and hurled it. The husk crashed down in the dark. The eyes had gone.

We stood there panting, chests heaving, my hand still hurting. The rain was coming in again and I felt the first drops spit in my face. Thesinger was holding one white, muddied sneaker, his bottom lip moist with another man's blood. I felt exposed all of a sudden, vulnerable. I felt violated and scared.

"Damn it!" Thesinger seethed. "God damn it to hell!"

"Let's get back inside," I said.

There was a roll of thunder and I knew it was about to break.

Thesinger stared out at the black.

"I want that son-of-a-bitch!" he yelled into the night. Then he tried to tear the old shoe apart as his fury crested, his face screwing up and his arms pulling at it, but he couldn't. The material was too strong. He just looked silly.

"Let's get on inside," I said.

"My God, I mean, I'd his toe in my mouth. What was I thinkin'?" Thesinger asked with nervous humor.

We laughed at it. We were inside with fresh drinks and the music on. We'd been sure to bolt up the door and lock down the windows. The rain was hitting hard and in sheets upon the roof and the windowpanes. The lightning lit the world outside a fantastic blue.

The fan rotated, ticking as it turned, and cooled down our sweating bodies. From the record player an old Calypsonian began her song.

Let me live and let me die,
For I heard that lullaby,
There beneath the moonlit sky,
My Bahama Lullaby.

Even while feeling ill from the kick to my stomach, shaky but sobered from the episode, my body couldn't help but move to her crooning.

Thesinger was sitting on what looked like pool furniture, with the destroyed plaque of the barracuda between his legs. There was a great big gash down the middle of the fish where the blow had landed but its head was still awful and fierce, now comic given the exposed stuffed torso.

"Maybe I have a disease!" Thesinger continued, wiping the intruder's blood from his lips with a handkerchief. "Wait until old Dock hears this. Boy! You need to pack heat. You need to unload into the bastards. That's the best prescription.

Damn." He swallowed a mouthful of rum and soda. Lightning bolted across the glass.

"You know, they won't let me put up a higher wall along The Eastern Road," he went on, all animation. "That's Government people for you. I'm worried about safety. They say it's too high. Too high? Can you believe it?"

"There's the Buildin' Code…" I said.

"To hell with their Buildin' Code! You think they follow any code? Code!" he rankled. "You know they do whatever they please. No one checks. Not like you mean. Not like your university ideas."

That hurt me.

"Sorry, but you'll learn. The law is what they say when they say it. Tomorrow they say the next t'ing and the law is the next t'ing. You 'okay' only so long as you 'okay'."

"Surely not."

"Man, they ain't for you. Not unless you influence things properly. You need to facilitate. They say, now boss, you know the engine don't run with no oil. But hey, I won't do that. I can't buy stock in that. So they turned the plans down. Rejected it."

I looked at him, wondering what the hell I'd do about my citizenship papers if he were right.

He sucked his teeth and took a swallow from his glass. "After tonight I think I'd better just go ahead and build my high wall anyway. Maybe it's the right thing to do."

"There must be someone to talk to? An official?"

"I'm through with talkin'. Always talkin'. Talkin' for years. I can't wait 'till I get chop-up or shot down dead. Let 'em come here and tell me stop. Let 'em come, I say. Boy, this is my land. My land! I'll tell 'em about my ass." He was shaking a bit and I was impressed by his passion. He looked down at the barracuda absurdly laid open upon the wood of the plaque.

"I remember catchin' this."

Then he was quiet and he looked far off.

"That bitch was in my house," he said at last.

"I know," I said quietly.

"Well, I sure am glad you were here. I tell you. That was somethin', hey? What a shock! You know. Thanks."

"Its nothin'," I said. But I was sure shaky.

"I think I'll get this sneaker mounted and hang it in the Bahama Room," he said, weighing the dirty shoe up in his hand.

"Except you didn't get him."

"No, I didn't, did I."

"We saw him out, though."

"You know, all things considered, I think that killin' him would have been fine under the circumstances."

"Mr. Thesinger," I said. "Have a drink."

"I could wring his neck."

"Just a glass to take the edge off," I said.

VII

Orion's hull was the perfect size for Thesinger's stage in life. She sat tied up at the dock, glittering in the bulkhead lights. Exquisitely built with a white sculptured profile, she was a masterpiece of Italian design. The black, teardrop-shaped salon window curved back aerodynamically, giving the impression of speed. The aft section was open, with teak flooring and furnished with deck chairs. Yet there was something at bit seedy about her. There were patches of black mildew, the gloss to the fiberglass had faded and part of the canvas sunshade was ripped and fluttered in the breeze. None of that mattered, though. I thought back to my days working on yachts in dry dock at Sweeting's basin, and now I licked my lips at the chance to crew on one.

"Pretty, isn't she?" Thesinger boasted, all pride now.

"Sure. What does she do?" I asked, trying to forget the fight, to shake off the nervousness that we were being watched, and to think instead about yachting and what was expected of me.

"Oh, a fair clip. I can squeeze a top speed of around 36 knots out of her. She cruses at 32. I can't take it any slower."

"What's under the hood? Twin Caterpillar diesels?

"The best in German engineerin'. Twin MTUs. Two thousand horse power each. I'll show you."

The rain had ceased and we could hear the drip-dripping from the trees tap-tapping down the garden and from over-hanging limbs into the oily-flat waters of the creek.

"Permission to board?" I asked, fatigued, wanting to find my place and settle in.

"Permission granted."

I shouldered my backpack and followed my skipper as we stepped up the plank onto the stern deck. The teak decking was cool and clean, speckled with rain.

I gazed aft out at the Creek. It was difficult to see. Only Thesinger's bulkhead lights and those of a couple other properties worked. From its mouth, which led out to the bay, the creek curved inland, the edge bulkheaded in concrete and the land on either bank subdivided. The lots with bulkhead lights were neatly kept with cabanas, but the dark lots were vacant and overgrown. The branches of the trees on the property next door reached out over the creek and roots had broken through the bulkhead in places, cracking the concrete. I thought that there must be untold places to hide, and I suddenly felt Clint's reservations about living down here. I wasn't sure I wanted Thesinger to leave me alone.

Other than *Orion*, there were only two small runabouts tied up in the creek, and further down, a half submerged wood-frame boat. The curving edge of the harbor, stained with weeping rust marks from the bolts in the tie backs, looked naked without the yachts that should have lined it. I wondered at such expensive real estate going to seed.

"Damn," I muttered. "I would have thought this place would be hoppin' with yachts."

"Yes, well. Some just can't afford the upkeep these days. You know, with things being tight. You're lucky to get this job…besides, there are issues."

He didn't elaborate and I continued to take in the view. We were further east and nearer the barrier islands that framed the harbor. We were also closer to the little fishing boat I'd spotted earlier at *Bangalay*. It lay off out beyond the inlet, anchored on a shallow sandbank.

"Grand, isn't it?" Thesinger raised a single eyebrow, gazing with propriety upon the fair grace of his vista. And it was true, even with the vacant properties and the all but empty creek. It was all very grand. "On the evening of my party, I want to take *Orion* out there, into the depths of Montagu Bay and shoot fireworks off. I want a show."

I imagined the mad light, the acrid smell of powder, the shimmering color and the pandemonium that would ensue. I envisioned the multiple whistling of the rockets and guessed it would be one hell of a party.

"We just have to be careful when we take her out," he continued. "There's a sandbar buildin' up at the mouth, siltin' us in. That's the other reason the creek's not a popular moorin'. The Property Association's been tryin' for years to get a permit to have it dredged. Can't get one from Government. Just like my wall." He sighed long and smooth. The sigh itself a comment. It was practiced. An expression that told me he expected nothing less from the forces he struggled against. But also, that he intended to win.

I nodded. The creek was beautiful and worth restoring.

"But a good captain can still negotiate it," he perked up, smiling self-consciously. He unlocked the tinted glass salon doors. Inside, the icy air-conditioning hit me. Thesinger locked the door fast behind. The salon was an intimate space paneled in cherry with a well-worn carpet and a glass-topped coffee table full of seashells. On the walls were framed prints of large mollusks.

Thesinger followed my eye. "My wife's collection. We used to go down to the cays for the weekend and she'd dive 'em up," he said, and guided me forward.

The galley was adjacent to spiral stairs that led up to the flybridge wheelhouse.

"My family always had boats," he remarked as we toured. "Sometimes a number, you know, for business. It's sort of in the blood. Wait till you see the bridge. I've got every gadget in the world."

We climbed the spiral stairs, but it wasn't the computers and electronics that caught my attention as I stepped out onto the bridge. Mounted in the center of the deck stood an old wooden ship's wheel with brass fittings.

"Wow!" I said, staring. "You steer with this?"

"No! No! It's just decoration. An old wheel from one of my grandfather's boats. You know, we used to ship spirits into the States during the Prohibition years. This is the wheel from his lucky boat. He used to say that so long as he had this

GARTH BUCKNER

wheel he was untouchable."

I imagined a night with no moon and one of J.T.'s boats running the blockade with a cargo of spirits. Thesinger didn't seem to feel any shame in his family's past. He was open, even proud of it. I wondered idly where his money came from now, the "new money" that Clint Knowles had advised me was so vital.

We went below decks and Thesinger showed me the full-beam stateroom and the guest cabins.

"We'll have more time tomorrow to go through it all and get into the nuts and bolts," he said. "It's too late now and I'm bone tired. Anyway, here's your digs, kid." Thesinger tapped open a varnished louvered door with his foot. "Home, sweet home."

The crew cabin was a narrow rectangle, wood paneled with a single bunk built against the starboard. Though small it had its own head, a porthole and a compact desk built against the larboard wall.

"Great! Hey, thanks Mr. Thesinger!" I said, and slung my gear on the bed.

"Gavin, about tonight. Well, there's a good reason I want you for this job. Sure, I need an extra hand and there'll be plenty of work. But security is also an issue. You know how it is."

Thesinger looked at me, embarrassed. Perhaps he felt that after tonight's violent episode I might question whether the lifestyle he felt he had to maintain, the objects he felt obliged to keep, might not be safe in his hands. His facial features had formed around that kind of pleading embarrassment.

"I wish I could tell you that tonight's events were unheard of," he said. "But, to be frank, some fuckers tried to steal her a little while back. Oh, they didn't get away with it.

But they certainly did some damage. I guess that's another reason why the creek's not the anchorage it once was. But I don't think there would be any trouble if she was manned."

"Why not get a guard? Professional security?"

"What? Oh, no! Half those bitches are thieves and the next half will go to sleep on you," he chuckled cynically. "No. I need someone I can trust. Hell, the meek are havin' their turn, I guess. I feel better with you here already." He paused a moment, then said, "Listen, I've given the captain some holiday he had comin'. So, it's just you on board for the rest of the season. I don't plan on takin' her out for a while."

I felt the dream of charting out to sea evaporate with those words. I was trapped in that little empty creek. The boat strained on the mooring lines outside and the squealing took on a personal quality.

"There's no watch while we're in dock," Thesinger continued, "but you'll have duties. There are some repairs I need done on top of the regular maintenance. The chrome needs a solid work over and a good rubdown. Anyway, enough time for all that tomorrow afternoon. Hey! I don't want you to be overly concerned. This job's fun. Plenty of sunshine. Don't worry." He said goodnight and made his way out. I heard him locking up.

I was alone. This was the first place I could call my own that I'd been in for years. But it didn't feel like home. It was more than the newness, the sense of the unfamiliar.

After tossing my cap on the bunk, I put away my topsiders and other things. I only had a few items, Gore-Tex and khaki shorts, my foul-weather gear, bucket hat, sports sunglasses and extra deck shoes.

Then there was nothing to do but sit on the bunk. I remembered the evening's trouble, Clint talking about the bitches crawling over the yacht like cockroaches, and Dock's baritone saying you've got to pack heat. This is not what I'd expected. I wondered if I needed this trouble. Maybe I should quit. Except I had no other choice. It was this job or deportation.

I decided to go up on the bridge. Maybe if I looked at all that gleaming brass, the instrumentation, the hanging charts, the view over the sloping nose of the yacht, maybe if I touched the machinery it would calm me. I needed to think matters through. Putting my fears aside and proving myself to Thesinger was the best thing to do if I was going to keep this job and the weekly pay envelope while I waited on my papers to be approved. How long would that take? A Year? More? What about all that talk of bribes? This was supposed to be a Christian country. I had to believe my application would come through.

I made a deal with myself. I'd give the whole show a year. If my citizenship didn't come through by then I'd leave and never come back.

Topside, everything was still and dim. The faint green of stand-by lighting illuminated the console. The windshield was streaked and beaded from the earlier rain. I stood behind the old ship's wheel and gripped it in both hands. I set my legs apart in the stance of a sailor, and imagined riding the seas. I gazed out, down the creek to the horizon. A brightly-lit yacht, elegant and shining, was crossing southeastward on course for the Exuma cays. I needed to be out there. To be free.

I was surprised to see Thesinger standing at the end of his property where the creek's mouth met the sea. I thought he had gone home. He was gazing out at the tropical view. His white jacket was draped over one shoulder with his finger holding it under the collar, his loose black bow tie hung unevenly across his chest and his untucked shirttails covered his Bermudas. From my vantage I could just make out his face. He stood there staring. His mouth open, hungry looking, as if me might swallow the sea entire, devour the very earth. I was fascinated. As much as I can read faces, I would say his held first the look of romantic longing and then of growing, animal rage.

He moved so suddenly that I instinctively ducked below the bridge glass. I saw him hurl his cocktail glass out to sea with savage, brute power. The liquor curled clear and strange in the bulkhead light. The glass shattered against something. I followed the sound with my eyes and saw that it had hit the small yellow and white wood fishing boat anchored on the sandbar. I reckoned he must have hit it by accident and wondered what had prompted him.

When I turned back Thesinger was gone.

I locked all the doors and portals before I climbed into my new billet. I was kept awake by the drumming of a small, outdated diesel engine that was lurking somewhere offshore.

I turned in my bunk thinking of Thesinger's act.

The violence.

VIII

Bribe money was not something I'd counted on. I hoped Thesinger was wrong. Perhaps they were just the bitter prejudices of a man whose family had fallen from power. In his mind, everything new must be rotten. It has to be, to dignify the past.

I have a birthright, I won't have to bribe anyone, I

thought as I strode into the Immigration Building. Plucking up my courage, I told myself I was simply coming for my things.

A few hours later, still sitting in the waiting room, I began to get nervous. I was the only white among a crowd of Haitians. They were poor and the body odor was terrible. All the plastic chairs were taken and one lime-green wall was lined with people leaning against it, with a dark band of dirt at back level.

The immensely fat female immigration officer sat at her station chatting to a friend on the phone. She took great pride in her press-on extension nails that were dipped in pink glitter and her face sagged with the authority of a Roman emperor.

When I'd picked up the citizenship application forms from her desk her eyes had swelled and her head rolled. Perhaps my presence was startling, different from the Haitian dogs she dealt with daily. Clearly I must be treated separately, but not so as to reduce her authority. At first I thought her refusal to acknowledge me beyond a sucking of her teeth was the height of rudeness, until I saw how she bossed the Haitians around.

"What you does want?"

"An application for citizenship please."

"Why?"

"Eh…because I want to regularize my status…"

"You does want to what?"

"Regular…I was born here."

Then the teeth sucking. A great show was made of looking for the form, as if my request were unique and she was going to some trouble. When she finally held up the papers, rather than extending her arm toward me, she let them drop upon her desk. She pointed a fat finger to the waiting room and went back to talking on the phone.

Carefully I picked up the form and read it over.

"Excuse me," I spoke up.

She kept talking sip-sip on the phone about her baby's daddy who wasn't checking and her eyes boggled at me.

"Sorry. Just one question."

"Eh?"

"The form mentions a fee, but doesn't give the figure."

"The who?"

"The amount. Of the fee. How much?"

Then she was all sweetness and sugar.

"Darlin'! How much you does want to pay?"

"What?"

"Hold on Nikki, I got a customer. Okay, love. Don't you worry about that form. No one does check 'em anyhow. Now. I got one son, and his daddy ain't no good. And this boy needs one operation. In Havana. I know you want to help me. You could sponsor him."

"Your son?"

"That's just one couple dollar to you."

"I'm afraid I don't have the money…"

"The waitin' room over there. Sorry Nikki. Just one foreign man. That's true, hey!" She looked me up and down, confirming her friend's amusing comment.

I sat in the lime green room and waited. It was very hot and I was sweating. The Haitians sat still, unfocused, as if stepping outside time until their names were finally called. Thereby they might save all the lengthy portions of their lives lived in lines. I hadn't learned such patience and I fidgeted and thought of sweeping policy changes Government should make, new acts of parliament, reform of the civil service. I thought of the fine speeches I would deliver at the political rallies when I had my papers. I'd sort things out.

But I was not sure what I was waiting for. No one came into the room to meet any of us. No numbers or names were called. We just sat.

"What happens next?" I asked the Haitian man next me.

He had a large yellow grin, but did not answer my question. Perhaps he didn't speak English.

Taking my completed form up to the fat officer with the extension nails, I decided to find out.

"Excuse me…"

"Waitin' Room!"

"Its just that…"

"Am I talkin' for just myself?"

I waited. But no one came. No one official. Other men and women arrived to wait, all Haitians, except one other white man, he looked English, patrician, and armed with his belief in queues he positioned himself at the end of a group of Haitians who happened to look like they were standing neatly in an official line.

IX

Those first weeks at the Creek were peaceful, the days sunny. In goggles and fins I scrubbed the slimy hull underwater. I polished the dull chrome to a high sheen, oiled the parched teak floorboards and laid down a new nonstick coat to the faded fiberglass decking. Sometimes *Orion* seemed more an old mother tub than an elegant yacht. Perhaps Thesinger was just a foolish romantic to want to keep such a thing. But the work felt good. Soon I was deeply tanned, and my hair became tinged with blond.

Mostly I was alone. A few guys came around looking for boat work and I sent them away. Thesinger came rarely, and only then to show me what he wanted done on the boat. As the season approached, he appeared in the itchy heat with caterers and suppliers to plan his big party. I never got a chance to know him during that time. I never saw Arial. I lived in the sun and slept with the ocean breeze cooling my naked body.

Even the first evening's alarming episode took on a distant quality. I felt it had happened in another life. The days coasted one into the next and I never left the Creek. When I ran out of work, I'd take to the sundeck to watch the day end. There was always a bottle of rum and Thesinger had an ice machine. I'd sit there and look down the lonely creek out to sea, and fidget as I thought about my citizenship.

My travels became wrapped in the warm clock of rum-emboldened reminiscing. Those distant experiences seemed richer than anything on offer here. My nostalgia was heightened when I went with a traveler girl. She was working her way through the islands and I stowed her away out of sight on *Orion*, watching her swim in the day and making love to her lean body in the dark. She possessed nothing but an elaborate Asian tattoo in which she invested mystical significance, and the crucial freedom to move on. Eventually she did. The creek seemed that much emptier then and I contemplated quitting.

A few days before Thesinger's crawfishing trip down to the Exuma Cays, he told me Sweeting's Boat Basin had patched up his openfisherman and he asked me to pilot her back to her mooring alongside *Orion* in the creek.

As I drove my truck west along the shore the heat

folded the air and cooked me. The parched sky was a sheer dome with distance but no perspective. Out to sea, the pleasure boats headed over the shallow, aquamarine banks to the white beaches or the sea gardens. A bulbous-nosed seaplane from Miami came straight into the wind, down to the harbor and a flock of seagulls circled and dropped, fighting beak to beak over the fisherman's slop from the illegal market. Things hovered.

I'd not been back to Sweeting's Boat Basin for years but not much had changed. The shop floor smelled of marine-grade grease and anti-fouling paint. Fiberglass hulls hung from hydraulic hoists, with great webbed straps cast under their streamlined bellies. The yard was only half packed with boats racked on blocks or in trailers; glass bottom tourist boats, go-fast speedboats painted black with four engines and other, simpler, fiberglass designs. But there were a lot of empty trailers, too.

I set out walking with a wide, street-smart slouch. I thought of watching old Sweeting building boats under the lean-to in his yard, working only by eye and with hand tools, no power and no plans. When I'd worked in the yard, he had always cursed his hard, grooved, thick-skinned hands. He had said he had poor man's hands. But to me, they were instruments of creation.

I passed an old mixed-race man with long, platted hair painting varnish slowly onto a sailboat's bleached teak rail with long, smooth strokes. There was a stillness to the basin, a feeling of inertia. I suppose that was to be expected with the economy being down.

I was delighted to find Abner Sweeting still there. I spied him down by the crane hauling a gleaming new cabin cruiser. The boat was sitting half submerged at the bulkhead edge. As the chains lifted it, seawater poured from a gash in the fiberglass below the waterline. Sweeting was directing the operator, a man with long, natty dreads tinted blond from time in the sun, when he spotted me coming down the line of dry docked craft.

"Lordy! Lordy! Gavin Blake as I live and breathe!"

"Papa Sweetin'!" I called out and we embraced. He was stocky and wore a blue short-sleeve shirt with an open, spread collar and gray flannel pants. His hair was slicked back with pomade and his face was framed in a pair of thick black glasses from the 1950s.

"Chilly! Watch that thin' don't spin!" he called up to the hoist operator. Then he looked back at me. "Boy, it's been years. All this time and just me one to manage things. Truth is there's not much to manage right now, even for me. I'm glad to see this boat. Now look at this here boat. These rich foreign bitches buy up these fancy boats and they ain't know how to captain one! Don't know about the sea! Just blaze out there full throttle like nothin' in this world could stop 'em." He spat tobacco juice on the concrete floor. "Thank God for foreign bitches them!"

Oily water poured out of the boat. The hoist operator had the craft suspended over the surface and was letting it drain before he brought it on dry dock.

"Still," Sweeting continued, "they soon does learn, hey? They soon does learn. Serves 'em right. These rich bitches have no business being out on the sea. They out there with all that tackle and computer and they clcanin' it right out. It's gettin' so the poor man can't keep up. They done brought up the whole waterfront down this way so we can't get to the sea," he laughed. "Now they buyin' up all the island out there. Puttin' in airstrip and generator, dredgin' marina. I'm sort of glad this one get bust up. Hey? ha-HAAA!"

Sweeting spat again. The boat had rotated in the

hoist and the twin inboards were exposed to us now. An inexperienced driver must have run her up on a reef, shredded the fiberglass down one side.

"I make sure my sons learn about the sea," Sweeting went on. "I pass on the tradition, make sure they understand things. That's our way," he said simply and I envied him that.

"So Gavin, you lookin' for work? I wish I could help you."

"Thanks Papa, but I've already got a job. I'm workin' for Mr. Thesinger on his yacht up by the creek."

"Thesinger. Know the family. My pa used to manage old Jessie's yard here before he sold out to us an' my uncle was his election general. We do all their boat work."

"Yeah, well, I'm thinkin' about quitin'. Movin' on."

"How's that?"

"It's not what I'd thought. You know. I never get to sea," I shrugged, trying to oversimplify my frustrations.

"His openfisherman's ready to roll."

"He sent me to fetch her."

"Well."

I didn't say a thing.

"Look. . . Gavin. Think it over, boy. Ain't a thing goin' on and you're lucky to have the work. 'Sides, the Thesinger's are old school. You'll get a taste of their world. Maybe you'll learn their secret," he laughed. "Ah! Let me show you where this openfisherman's at before you roll off and wake up half way around the world on God's backside. Right down the dock, boy."

Sweeting pulled a set of boat keys that were dangling from his pocket on a red foam float chain and pointed down the yard to the dock. I followed him to the main concrete pier, which was covered in the white splashes of laughing gull feces with the hot sun on our shoulders.

We stepped down onto a floating section where a sleek openfisherman was tied up. The design was aerodynamic, purposeful, the bow tapering to a fine point. This was the boat that had been stolen and stripped. The one Thesinger had found smashed up on the rocks. It looked like Sweeting had done a decent job. The anti-fouling paint was fresh and the hull gleamed. New twin outboard two-fifty horsepower engines were mounted side by side and stood tilted and trimmed out of the water. She had a fighting chair at the stern and a teal canvas T-top on a stainless steel frame. She had been lovingly restored and you would never know of her desecration by looking at her.

Sweeting handed the bundle of keys over to me as I stepped down onto the white fiberglass deck. At the center console I slid both keys into the twin ignition switches, put my finger on the trim button and pressed down to tilt the outboards into the water. Nothing happened, no wine of hydraulics, no movement. I looked back and the engines were still and broke into a small sweat as I pressed the button again. Sweeting stood watching.

"Shit," I said under my breath.

"Eh," Sweeting said helpfully, "we turned the battery off."

"Well, why didn't you say so," I complained, wondering where the battery was, trying to fight through the mental mud of years to a time when I'd actually understood these things. I figured it had to be right under the main console for easy accessibility. I squatted and opened the console hatch and thankfully the battery switch was there.

Trimming the two engines down, I felt my leg shake a little. I hated being scrutinized. The truth was, I'd not driven a boat since going off to university years ago. I felt eyes on me from the dock waiting to see what kind of a boy I was. I had to show them I was a salty dog. Turning the ignition over separately for each outboard they both coughed, spewed out black exhaust as old fuel was burnt off, shook as they fired up and then settled down into idle.

Sweeting smiled at his boat basin's work. "Okay Gavin boy. Good to see you. Don't be a stranger, hear!"

Giving him the thumbs up I cast off the stern line and went forward to get the bow rope.

"Watch that current now," he called.

That made me angry. The implication that I didn't understand such local things wounded my pride. But when I cast off the bow rope to his waiting hands, the boat instantly began to drift backwards. The two outboards were only feet away from the concrete pier. In a moment their plastic covers would hit. Flushing, I jumped behind the console and grasped the controls. Throwing the twin throttles forward the boat jolted into gear, perhaps too fast, and the backward drift stopped. And then I was moving forward.

I turned down the channel between the two rows of docked boats and headed her toward the harbor. Halfway out, I turned back to look for Sweeting. He stood on the dock watching me go. Behind him there rose a line of muscular, gleaming, white boat hulls. The marine fuel and oil banners cracked in the breeze, their colors bright in the sunlight. I gave him the upward nod and he returned the gesture, the lenses of his glasses glinting. Suddenly he waved both arms wildly and I wondered what was up.

"Oh sweet Lord!" He shouted.

I looked forward and saw another boat coming right at me. Her captain was already hauling hard on the wheel to turn his boat and avert a collision. My heart raced. I couldn't afford to smash up Mr. Thesinger's boat and I punched the reverse.

Luckily, the other boat turned. She was bright yellow with heavy diesel smoke hovering above the water behind the prop. Her captain stood behind the center console and worked the gears. He was shirtless, thin, with long white-blond hair. I realized with a cold shock that it was the same boy, Caleb, who had almost caused an accident on The Eastern Road. I was safe, but Caleb had to work the gears to prevent hitting the docked boats. He gave up and rushed to the gunwale to hold himself off.

"Asshole!" He shouted back at me as he leaned his full weight against a dock pole. I don't think he recognized me.

"Dread, you need to watch where the fuck you goin', hear!" I cussed him in my best vernacular. "You need to move your stupid self so you don't get up in people's way!"

I didn't look back for fear he would recognize me, and kept going with a nervous snicker.

Careful with the current, I touched her forward, then to starboard and out toward Montagu Bay. My hands trembled and my eyes darted across the water on the lookout for driftwood and shallow spots. I was afraid I might hear an engine rev up in pursuit. My back was to Sweeting's Boat Basin and I made an effort to be easy for the benefit of those who watched.

The sun was gorgeous and the ride smooth. I pulled my T-shirt off and slid my shades on. Opening her up full throttle down the harbor, I got the hull high on a plane, splitting the emerald water in two, leaving a white tear of wake behind. I trimmed the props to bring the lower unit someway out of the water, reducing drag, and squeezed a few more knots out of her. My hair was blown back and water teared from my eyes. I slid in a Bob Marley disc into the onboard CD system, cranked up the volume and cruised to the cool reggae on my way back to the creek.

I watched out for the sandbar when I came up on its mouth. There was a deeper cut inshore and I took this and slowed until she was running with no wake as the concrete bulkhead passed on either side. To port was the point of Thesinger's property with its gazebo and small beach. The edge curved inland with *Orion* moored smartly against it, her bow facing the entrance.

I took the opernfisherman passed the yacht to tie up at her stern, and for the first time got a good waterside view of the neighboring property. From Thesinger's place it was too overgrown to see. But from this vantage, I saw through the jungle of vegetation a planted garden gone wild, and just made out the skeletal timbers of a roof frame above the tree canopy where the cedar shingles had rotted and fallen through. It was a harsh tale of abandonment, of human giving up and giving in. I imagined I could smell the musk of past generations and it made me shiver, a ghosting history encircled the ruin, an insistence. The ruin had passed out of the present like my mother's maiden name. I wondered why no one wanted to embrace its proportion and the joy of bringing it back?

X

I was sharpening knifes for gutting and filleting fish. I picked up each blade one at a time and honed its edge the way my father had taught me when I'd been a boy and he still lived on the island.

Gray-blue reefs of cloud raked the sky and the eastern horizon beyond the Creek mouth was brightening and touched with that hint of the dirty gold that precedes the sun.

It looked like a good day to fish and, feeling more generous now that we were even on the crashing score, I bade Caleb good luck. The sea was open and flat, matte purple before the dawn. I hankered to get out there and gave a snorting chuckle at the thought that *Cuda* might clear out the coral heads before we even made wake.

Thesinger wanted to be underway soon after sunrise, so I had to have everything shipshape and ready. He'd asked me to wait here for him. I was making an extra effort because this was my first trip out with my boss and I wanted to leave him with a favorable impression.

He required a good stock of crawfish tail to cater his big bash. These crawfish are not what people up east at my old university ate, not the small fresh water variety sucked down in bars. These were large, spiny lobsters and great to eat. Thesinger had set the traps down last season. The plan was to haul them up, pack the coolers with crawfish tail and be back that evening.

It sounded easy and fine and a good way to spend a day in the sun. Some of Thesinger's buddies were coming down for the ride, so it promised to be a cruise. The ocean was glass early that morning and it looked like a good clear run down to the cays. I wanted to get out there and cross the horizon.

As I was washing the blades with the hose, I looked up and saw a girl coming up the Cabana's little beach. The sun was just peaking over the horizon and immediately it was scorching. The globe rose behind her and it lit up the thin scrim of her wrap. Her body showed in curved shadow and line. Every now and then she squatted down and raked the sand and the seaweed with her fingers. I thought my traveler girl had returned, but by the barely noticeable limp I knew it must be Arial.

"Hullo there!" I called.

"Why, hullo Gavin. I didn't see you."

"Did you lose somethin'?"

"What's that?"

"Are you lookin' for somethin'?"

"Shells," she said, and I remembered her collection. She sauntered up the beach toward me, just limping. She sported a bikini underneath a colorful wrap about her waist. I could just smell the salt on her and some kind of fruit scent from her hair, maybe her shampoo. Her hair fell down each side of her chest, which was speckled with grains of sand. I don't know how aware of her own sensuality she was, but it was a force that caused my throat to thicken.

"You comin' down to the cays?" I asked.

"Oh no," she replied, and I was relieved. "I don't boat anymore. I'm just walkin'. There are so many lovely shells on the beach if you know where to look."

She opened her sandy palm to reveal several small shells. She smiled up at me and picked at them one by one with her other hand, turning each over for inspection.

"Here, this little pointy guy is a trumpet, he's rather colorful. And this little pastel chap here is a type of cone. They're dead of course. I never collect live shells. That wouldn't be cricket, hey?"

"They're rather pretty."

"I don't just gather little ones. I have some big fellas too. I used to love to dive, and see what I could find on the reef."

"Sure," I said, wondering what had stopped her but not feeling comfortable enough to ask. "When I was a kid I once found a Spanish coin on the sea floor. You know, one of those old doubloons, or whatever they're called, from a galleon."

"How romantic."

"I got it put on a chain and I wear it round my neck."

"So you do," she said, looking at it hanging at my collarbone. She reached up and touched it. I could feel her fingers on my skin, my chest hairs being tickled. "Why, it's lovely, Gavin. Like the pirates used to wear. I didn't know you were so sentimental."

I'd worn the coin on all my travels. The weight of it reminded me of this place. It told me who I was, despite my claims to statelessness.

"When I was a girl, I once made a necklace of shells with a sand dollar at the center. But, you know, the sand dollar broke. They're such fragile things, aren't they? I cried and cried. Silly to want to keep and show off such fragile things."

We stood silently for a moment, regarding one another. I wondered if I could have her, then told myself to forget it.

"So," she said, "you gettin' things set for Jacob's big trip."

"I guess."

"Yeah, well, Jacob has been plannin' this for so long. Gosh how I hear about those traps of his. I hope there's somethin' in 'em."

"I'm sure there will be," I chuckled, thinking how impossible it would be for them to be empty.

"I've asked Jacob to keep an eye out for shells while you boys are out there. But I know how you men go, he'll probably forget."

I smiled because what she said was true.

"Boy hey!" she carried on, "I'm glad he's not the only one I rely on for shells. I have other places I can get 'em. You want to come with me and see? We'll go down by the fish market. There's a fisherman there, who said he would look for shells for me. You know, rare ones, big ones, while he's out there."

"Have you got things from him before?" I asked, surprised by her mention of the market.

"No. Usually I collect 'em myself. But, you know, I was down to the market for some fresh seafood and I met him there. I told him I would come see him and give him a couple dollars, if he would find me some good ones. I mean to go this mornin'. Would you drive me?"

"Well. Thesinger asked me to stay right here till he comes."

"Can't you go where you want?" she asked, all innocence.

"He's payin'."

"I'm sorry. Of course. But don't you think he'd want you to help me, Gavin?"

I looked at her body in the wrap.

"I'll drive you," I told her.

"Oh!" She said, suddenly looking up at me wide-eyed, "but you mustn't tell Jacob that I went. It must be our secret. You understand? He doesn't like me to go there. It's not just that it's a bit rough, this girl can handle herself, it's more a sort of political thing."

I looked at her quizzically as we walked up toward my truck.

"Well, it's like, that market is illegal and it's filthy. It's a health hazard and it undermines our property value. Jacob says no one wants to pay top dollar and live next to that stinkin' place and he has been tryin' for ages to get it moved or cleaned up. Either that or at least get our property tax down to reflect the lower value. But he can't win. Government won't listen. They don't give a damn, do they? It upsets Jacob and he doesn't want me to go there. But I have to get my shells. So what's a girl to do?"

I pulled my truck out of the crush of roadway metal, exhaust, and away from the tempers of the drivers. We opened our doors to the noise and energy of the restless market. The high pitch of boat engines being revved tingled up my backbone and reggae blared from multiple cars, assaulting my ears. After the cacophony came the smells, a powerful scent of gut slop cooked by the sun and of shells piled at the tide line. A dried out fish stink that thickens the palate, that gets the teeth combing the tongue's fur in revulsion.

"This way," Arial inclined her head as we made off through the press of bodies.

There were wood and wire cages filled with crabs ahead of us. Some of the vendors didn't have baskets to keep their's in and so they had cut off the legs and claws and set the live bodies out in a pattern on the concrete. The claws were piled neatly to the side and the prices were reasonable. We stepped over the dismembered crabs and their eye-stalks moved and looked.

Everywhere fishermen washed their catch with water toted up in plastic buckets from the sea. Fish heads littered the cracked concrete. Crawfish were laid out prominently for drivers of passing cars to size up and select.

Arial looked back to make sure I was following. I gave her a wink and we pressed on. She made for a fishing stall farther down the ramp, where a man in a wide-brimmed straw hat was working at a red snapper with his blade. He slit into the fish's belly and pulled out the innards with his big hands. Two small boys at his side were helping.

"That's him," she pointed, smiling over her shoulder to me as she negotiated the crowd. "That's the man who said he'd dive my shells."

We wove our way between the crowd. It was breakfast time and the lunch ladies sold meals of grits, tuna fish and potato bread in tin foil from the trunks of their cars. Farther down, the eroded bathing beach formed a slumped crescent moon and at its western extremity stood the old stone fort with its rusted canon which had once guarded the eastern mouth of the harbor.

I could see a baptism underway out in the water off the beach. Or perhaps it was an exorcism. Women dressed in heavy smocks wailed and held their hands up while the preacher dunked the subject's head under the water. He lifted it back up and thrust it under again while the water beyond blazed with quicksilver that scorched the eye.

"Mornin'," Arial called to the fishmonger. "Remember me?"

The fisherman's broad-brimmed straw hat flopped forward over his face. His sun-blotched hands continued to fillet the fish and the shoulder material of his tee shirt was dark with sweat and a vanilla-scented cigarillo drooped from his lips.

"Oh yes, miss, I remember you," he said glancing up, raising a white eyebrow. It was Caleb.

"How you do today?" Arial smiled.

"Oh, thank God for life. I right here in His hands until He want me. I got my health." He gave her body the once over. "Despite everythin', I got that."

"Caleb, this is my friend Gavin Blake. Gavin this is Caleb," she introduced us.

"How are you?" I asked, wondering if I should be wary.

"Not as good as you, Mr. Gavin," he replied and I considered if it was a complement or an insult. Then I realized he was referring to Arial, that he assumed things and this pleased me.

Caleb's two boys stared up at me with unblinking eyes.

"What y'all doin'!" Caleb snapped at them, gesturing with the vanilla cigarillo between two fingers. "Boy, get me one next fish and don't look people in the eye." He turned back to Arial. "You want to buy some fish, miss?" He asked, carving off the head of the snapper his sons handed up to him and throwing it into the sea. If Caleb remembered me from the narrowly averted traffic accident or from our near miss at the marina, he showed no sign.

"I want to buy shells," Arial corrected him.

"Conch salad you want miss?"

"No. Shells."

"Conch shells, hey? You want to take it home with you? Souvenir?"

I realized with a flush that he thought we were tourists. He hadn't recognized me because he didn't even see me. That was how it had been on my travels. If Arial noticed his presumption she wasn't fazed by it.

"Boys!" Caleb said. "Go buy Billy them and get some conch shell, hear!" And the two boys started off through the crowd.

"No, no, no," Arial said. "Call 'em back." But the boys had disappeared in the press of people. "I don't want conch shells. I'm lookin' for pretty shells," she told Caleb, "interestin' shells, colorful ones. The kind you might see when you are out there divin'. Do you see shells when you are divin' for fish?"

"Oh yes, plenty shells. Plenty. The whole bottom down there's covered in shells."

"Yes. Well. Do you think you could get some for me if you see any you think might be special?"

Then the two little boys were back, pulling at Arial's hand and each holding up a small, rough conch shell. Each had a broken hole where the fishermen had bashed through it to get the meat out.

I was getting impatient.

"Missy! Missy! Ten dollar! Ten dollar!"

"Oh, aren't they sweet," she cooed at them and said, "no thank you. I don't want conch shells."

"Five dollar," one of the boys bargained.

Arial laughed and the boy looked at his pa all confused.

"You know the shells I mean?" She asked Caleb.

"Well, I don't usually do that. I'm a fisherman. But considerin' things is slow I guess I could do that. For a couple dollars I'll do that."

"Okay then. But I don't want any livin' ones."

"All right then. I'll yuck 'em out, clean 'em up, bleach 'em and have 'em all nice for you so they don't get all stink up for when you go home."

I wanted to interject that he had it all wrong, that we were from right here.

"No, no. I just want dead ones. Leave any livin' ones on the reef. Only take dead ones. And please don't clean 'em or bleach 'em out. I want 'em natural."

"Whatever you say I go do," Caleb said, shaking his head, the blond wispy hair blowing. "Now the only t'ing is how you goin' to pay me?"

They talked price and I tried to relax while I watched the market. There were a couple of leaning shacks hawking all manner of odd items; toys and tiers, hair-dryers. There were stalls laid out with bananas and mangos in cardboard boxes. The vendor women stood about and laughed and argued in large-print dresses with hands on their hips and their hair tied back with headscarves. A boy toted Tribunes on his head and a rastaman in on oversized tam held up small paper bags full of roasted peanuts and called out "Ire nut" to the stuck traffic.

I'm conscious now of how out of place I must have seemed then. My cloths were collegiate, preppy, my accent was transatlantic, clipped. It was no wonder they took me for a foreigner. It should have been no surprise to me that Caleb had tried to sell us cheap tourist trinkets. But I never saw it that way. Instead I noticed the vendors selling crawfish and I wondered why Thesinger didn't just purchase what he needed.

XI

"Man," Thesinger called as I arrived back at the Cabana and ambled down from my truck to the creek. "Where you been?"

A crawling sensation ran up my neck. Arial had asked me not to tell. I'd dropped her home on the way and hoped I'd get back and finish stocking up for the trip before Thesinger showed.

"Sorry, chief. I'd a couple of errands to run. She's ready to roll."

"Boy, when I want to roll out at daybreak, then I want to roll out at daybreak. Follow?" He was drinking coffee and standing on the lip of the dock in his shorts with no shirt and the sun bronzing his lean back. I couldn't see his eyes through his thick black, plastic shades. "Still, it would help if my God damn friends showed on time."

I felt relief as the blame shifted to others.

"Well," he continued, "the weather's fine. We should have a good run down to the cays. Though the satellite image shows it might kick up. There's a front comin' on later."

"I can handle a little weather."

"Yeah man," he winked, sipping from his mug. "That's the spirit. You sound like a real island boy."

I jumped down to the deck of the openfisherman and quickly stowed the gear. Thesinger stood on the concrete edge above and watched.

"Boss?" I called. "Wanna take some kit for spearin'?"

"We hallin' traps, not jookin'."

"But if the traps got caught we would need to skin dive down to free 'em up"

"Sort it out."

I stashed enough masks and fins for everyone. I spat on the glass and rubbed the spittle about with two fingers to get the hard film of salt and muck loose before hosing them down. The wet rubber smelled good. I took down spears and Hawaiian slings and I hoped that if we had to spear, I could make some account of myself.

Thesinger was pacing. "Maybe I should call these lazy bitches on my cell. It's time to go fishin'," he muttered. "Let's blaze out there where there's no one and let's put 'em in the boat, I say."

"Amen, boss," we suddenly heard from behind. It gave me a shock and Thesinger nearly jumped into the creek. We turned about and saw his friends, Dock Roberts and Clint Knowles.

"Fellas!" Thesinger hailed them, grinning. Then he tapped the face of his Rolex and held it to his ear as if there was something wrong with the mechanism.

They laughed like they didn't give a damn. They were ready for sport. They were carrying cases of beer and coolers full of ice for packing crawfish tails. They wore sun hats, shades and flip-flops. Clint Knowles was smoking the butt end of a Cuban stogie and he had applied stripes of zinc suntan cream under his eyes, which reminded me of ritual war paint.

Dock Roberts wore a shiny, tight, Speedo swimsuit and we all laughed at it. His shirt was off and his heavyset chest was lighter in tone than his black arms.

"What's that?" Thesinger called out to him, indicating the choice of swimwear.

"This is how I express myself," Roberts replied and he was certainly proud of it.

"Well now, I hope it don't get expressive," Clint rolled his eyes.

"Since y'all is such big men, get in this boat and get ready," Thesinger said, jumping down from the bulkhead onto the deck. He went back behind the center console and put both keys in the ignition, switched on the batteries, pressed the tilt button on the throttle and trimmed the outboards down into the water. He spun the two keys and each engine in turn fired up with great belches of fumes and bubbles seething in the water. The outboards rattled for a moment and settled into idle. Thesinger glanced at me and cast his eye proudly over his reworked boat.

The guys handed their stuff down and I stowed everything except for the coolers, which I lined up at the stern.

"Jacob?" Clint called, apparently seeing me for the first time, "You bringin' your boy along, hey?"

I immediately felt my social position ratchet down a notch.

"So, big man," he said, peering down at me from the bulkhead, "how's livin' down this way? You keepin' the place cockroach-free?" He laughed, winked at Roberts. "Man, Dock, I see it in my mind's eye like one horror movie. All them roach massin' out of the bush with their machetes to chap up University Boy here. Hey, University Boy, stow this."

I hated the way he said it, hated that I couldn't retort because I was the employee.

Clint flung his tote bag at me. When it landed the top fell open, and I could see the black handle and trigger of a handgun buried in a towel. All the firearms I'd seen had been official. Boarder guards. Military police. Carbinera. Never had I seen such private force. Clint shrugged and spread out his hands in a what-can-a-man-do gesture.

"Just in case. So we're ready," he said, his eyes narrowing above the tribal stripes of suntan cream.

"Ready for what?"

"Roach!" He laughed again and swung himself over the guardrail and onto the deck. He gave me a slap on the back and another grin.

Surely the gun didn't matter? It was an affectation, an indulgence, not a weapon. Clint had gone over to Jacob and Dock and the three of them were standing around the console looking at sun-damaged laminated charts. The other boys had not seen the gun and I chose not mention it. Attending to my duties, I stashed Clint's bag and then went to the cooler and fished through the ice for the three coldest beers. I popped the caps and served them, unsure if I should take one for myself.

"Cheers fellas." Jacob said and raised his bottle. "I hope all yinna ready to roll."

"Who? Watch out!" they boasted. "We're goin' to jook all the crawfish. Plenty crawfish. We're goin' to clear it right out."

Thesinger grinned and threw down the gauntlet, "Talk cheap. Money buy land."

"Now," called out Clint. "Talkin' about ownership, I just want to make it clear that any crawfish I jook is my own."

That took the smile off Thesinger's face.

"That's not the plan chief," he said.

"It's my plan."

"Listen, boss,"Thesinger said patiently. "The whole idea of this boat trip is to haul m'traps and bring home the crawfish for m'party. All the crawfish are for m'party."

"Not mine. I jook 'em, I eat 'em."

"Not this time. If you want to come for the ride that's cool but the law is that all the crawfish are for the party."

"Now I told yinna," Dock broke in, looking clever, "I told yinna not to bring his red ass. This one is the worst of these red white bitches. All they do is steal. Your people ain't bring you up, they drag you up."

"You ain't used to being in the sun," Clint said to Dock. "You got a touch of the sun."

"You the one with the touch, my brother." Dock was laughing.

"Man! Get on yinna donkey and ride out of town!"

"Oh Lord!"Thesinger moaned. "Y'all stale fools been at the bottle already? And the sun only just clean. Now look here, we goin', we goin' out and we're comin' back with plenty crawfish. And every one of them hithertobefore mentioned crawfish both severally and jointly must be delivered up for Jacob Thesinger's party without deduction or offset time being of the essence. Breach of this agreement will result in keel haulin'. Amen! Let's roll."

As we powered out of the empty creek, the colorful fishing boat loomed directly in our path. It struck me then for the first time what a stupid place it was to moor a boat.

XII

Making thirty knots, we went out into the tinted sea on a compass heading of one twenty degrees. Open water lay before us, brushed, stained and blotted with pink and silver and teal. The boat ripped the surface. Above, the cloud's sublime calligraphy hovered in and out eliminating line so that fact became secondary to spectacle.

Crossing over the shoals of the Yellow Banks, Thesinger slalomed the boat deftly between the coral heads that scratched at and fingered the surface. Occasional solitary, long-beaked Houndfish leaped in alarm ahead of the bow and javelined away at right angles, and before us flying fish fluttered in the momentary silver brilliance of their haste.

The bluff at Ship Channel was our first landfall hovering up upon the horizon, and then also visible were the high hilltops of Highborne Cay southward on our starboard. The cays came floating above the sea on the blue shimmer of heat that ringed the horizon, appearing only wishful and indefinite. Closer they solidified into humped limestone formations covered in low scrub, ringed in thin exquisite beaches and moving sandbanks carved out by the current that empties the flat banks through the cuts of fast flowing water that churn out into the sound.

"We reach," I cheered, feeling the seascape imprinted within me. I turned and grinned at Thesinger, feeling something fraternal, and rode the boat's motion comfortably.

"Set us up with a round of ice cold brew and get one for yourself," Thesinger grinned.

The gold liquid went down cold and crisp, the white

foam bubbled over and the green world sparkled in the light while the sun burnt through the ozone and patterned freckles on my back.

Pleasure boats rode everywhere. Brilliant white Haterases out of the Carolinas with high tuna towers ploughed the ocean, their outriggers trailing lines baited for billfish. Sailing sloops flying the Quebec flag lay at anchor in snug bays. Other openfishermen with Nassau registrations tore along, their engines at full throttle. We passed a small Zodiac with a man in a bucket hat whose Labrador panted at the bow. A seaplane with fat pontoons swooped down in an arch and dropped over a ridge on its landing approach. Nearer at hand, the sandbanks swelled up to run ribbed just beneath the surface of the invisible water and covered in the streaking orange forms of starfish.

"All we need now is some tunes," Clint said, appraising the landscape with an unlit cigar in his mouth.

"I got some good old stuff here. Classic calypso," Thesinger beamed from behind the console. He reached down to his bag.

"Why don't you get with it, man. Nobody wants to hear those scratchy negro tings," Clint laughed.

"But these are classics!" Thesinger protested, holding up the disc.

"I don't want to hear it. I came out on this party for fun, not to be bored dead by pappy's songs of yesteryear."

"You know, Clint," Roberts joked him. "Yinna ain't got no culture. No broughtupcy. You may be Joe Bucks real estate but you still a red bitch."

"Better nouveau riche than no riche at all. But seriously here, Jacob. Yinna need to clean out all that old crap and come up to this century. Yinna need to catch up yinna backward self."

"I wouldn't waste somethin' of taste on you," Thesinger laughed, putting the disc away. "Besides. This ain't no cruise. We came here to fish and I'm goin' to put your crass ass to work."

"Me? You got your boat bitch for that," Clint pointed the cigar at me and laughed ha-HAAA.

He winked, perhaps knowing how neatly he had bookended me between on the one hand, my insecure desire to be native and on the other, the white trash Conchy Joeness that would inescapable follow success. I told myself his vacuous anecdotes and graceless hilarity were a practiced cover for his own oily shortcomings. But it was Thesinger who unintentionally tore me down.

"Clint, lay off Gavin, man. You can't expect him to know how to do all the things we need to get done."

We went out through Ship Channel in silence with the Sail Rocks and South Sail Rocks to the north and with Beacon Cay to starboard. Beyond the cut, the shallows descended gradually away and then chasmicly so from forty or fifty feet straight down to over a thousand along the underwater wall's edge. To one side of us was the aquamarine of the bank and to the other the dark blue of the Sound. We angled sharply to port and chased the string of small cays northward until they faded to the south and we left the depths behind and crossed over into shallow waters known as the Middle Ground.

A wall of cumulonimbus advanced upon us from the north-east, towering into the Tropopause with a wispy anvil of cloud suspended before it, and sank to the sea where the rainstorm looked misleadingly small and impotent as it crested the curve of the earth. The water before us was still and flat. The sun climbed up on its mid-morning arc just clear of the clouds. We studied the front and I understood that it would come upon us and give us a bit of stick.

"Small craft warnin'," I announced.

"That's an affirmative," Dock Roberts nodded.

"Y'all! Let's haul these here crawfish cages and make wake,"Thesinger said, sizing up the threat.

He slowed the boat and turned on his GPS. The openfisherman came off its plain and sank softly forward. With the rush of air from the forward motion of the boat gone we felt the first natural wind. It had the cool temperature of an imminent downblast.

I noticed another openfisherman stopped off our stern, with a powder blue hull and racing lines. They seemed to be sizing up the storm. I felt safety in numbers.

It took a few moments to triangulate the GPS with the satellites and find our position. After we had a fix, it was easy to program in the locations of Thesinger's crawfish traps. We headed for them on a rumb line to the northwest at an angle slightly away from the storm, skirting the Middle Ground's maze of reefs. The powder blue boat was also moving.

We came up on the first trap location, but GPS is not a precise tool and it only gave us a rough idea of where the pot was.

"Okay! Listen up,"Thesinger said. "We're lookin' for a patch of sand, about thirty to thirty-five foot depth, with a long grass bed to the north and a couple of isolated heads to the south."

I sat astride the bow and the other guys took up their watches while Thesinger tapped the engines forward dead slow. He angled the boat so that the sun was behind lighting the floor of the sea. I felt the cool air from the thunderstorm on my back and it felt good after the strong heat of the day.

The sea grass was suddenly ahead of me. I called it out. Thesinger put the engines in neutral while we all scanned for the heads. Roberts scoped them just to port and we turned that way.

"Just about here,"Thesinger decided. "Someone get the water glass and have a looksie. It's gotta be down there."

I placed the old wood bucket with the glass bottom on the surface and pressed the glass down an inch or two under the water. In the rush, no one seamed to notice that I was the one doing the job. Leaning over the gunwale I could see clearly to the ocean floor. His trap was down there a good thirty-five feet on the sand. It was very obvious with the corrugated metal roof gray against the white bottom.

"Its right here," I said. "Hey? Don't you bother to cover your trap roofs with sand to hide 'em?"

"Sure. Why?"

"Well, this here trap don't have any sand on top of it and it looks pretty visible down there."

"Current must'a swept the sand off," Thesinger shrugged. "Anyways, let's pull she up and see how many tail we got."

I put a pole with a hook in the water. Dock held the glass to guide me as I angled the hook toward the trap. It was tough work in the current. Dock called to Thesinger to go back and forth on the throttle. The sweat broke on my forehead.

"Don't fuss the boy, Dock," Clint said, changing his tack. "He was born to this work." I knew he didn't mean it as a compliment and I considered letting the pole slip and whack him. But I was already fighting the current and one fight was enough.

A vibration up the shaft told me the end was tapping against the trap. Concentrating through the glass, I guided my hook onto the deadeye attached to the top. It took a few passes, but I hooked it.

"All right," I instructed them, and Dock and Thesinger hauled on the rope. I felt it come free and I could see the rope go taut and then the trap launched off the seafloor in a small, slow-motion cloud of particles.

They worked hand over hand until the cage was up by the gunwale. I got in there and helped them lift it up and over onto the deck. Water gushed from it and rushed back where it collected in the bilge. Seaweed and a fine gray mud spread about the deck.

There was nothing inside. Not even cowhide.

"It can't be," Thesinger said, perplexed. "There should at least be a couple in there."

"Hey, no worries. Maybe it's just a bad spot. You know. Let's go pull another."

"But this is my drop! I've got plenty right here before."

"Maybe you kill it last time," Clint said between his bitten stogie.

"Oh, come on, man!"

"Look, let's roll and get these pots in the boat before this storm is on us and we're the one's in the trap," Dock reasoned, hands on hips and his unfortunate swimwear on pointed display. We all nodded and I got the pole up and laid it down along the deck. Thesinger shook his head, entered the next point into the GPS, and we were off again.

As we rolled I saw the powder blue boat behind us pick up speed. It seemed to be pacing us.

Perhaps they were lost? All they had to do was come alongside and ask for assistance. But I couldn't help think of Arial's story of the couple boating down here in the Cays getting boarded and the husband having to shoot the pirates dead.

The next location held the same story. The trap was clean. Empty even of the cowhide.

"Looks like the crawfish checked out of your hotel, man," said Clint Knowles. "They didn't like the service."

"Hey, maybe someone put New York sirloin steak in

their own, and those crawly bugs just turned their nose up at your stink Conchy Joe cowhide," Dock was laughing.

"And how about that?"Thesinger demanded, frustrated. "Where's the cowhide? It didn't walk out of this here trap. I mean, that cowhide was dead when I got it from the store and it was dead when I put it down in the ocean."

"That's somethin'," Roberts admitted.

"Maybe little minnows ate it," Clint giggled. I noticed the suntan cream stripes under his eyes were dribbling and he didn't look quite so terrible now.

"Oh shut up, Clint, its not funny, man,"Thesinger bit back.

"Hey guys," I said. "Have any of y'all noticed this boat? The one behind us? Powder blue. It's like it's been shadowin' us since we came up by the traps."

The guys all turned and studied the boat in silence.

"It's just another openfisherman," Dock said.

"It was with us when we stopped to look at the storm and at the first trap. Now here it is again."

"You mean like he's watchin' us?" Clint asked.

"It's just kind of strange."

The weather was starting to come in. The sun burnt a white circle behind the first high up clouds. The temperature quickly got colder and the sea kicked up with little whitecaps rolling across the surface as we made way. Now it was just the business of hauling the last trap. We were not drinking beer anymore, and I was nagged by the worry that we might get skunked and have to go home empty-handed in the middle of a cut-ass storm.

We kept our eyes on the powder blue boat behind us. It matched our velocity off our stern to the port side. None of us wanted to be obvious about looking at it. But we all knew. Clint had removed his tote bag out of the hatch and had it between his feet.

At the last trap, the waves knocked the boat and pushed us off target. Silt swirled up in the water and even with the glass bucket it was difficult to mark my target. But I got it in the cross fades, hooked it clean and gave the thumbs-up to Thesinger and Dock Roberts.

"Hey Clint," Thesinger called. "You just goin' to stand there?"

"No, I'm goin' to get another beer as your deck swab is busy."

"Boy, get on this work."

"I got the weakness."

"I thought you came to fish," Thesinger said.

"You told me not to."

"Come again?"

"You said they was all your own so I'm leavin' it to you."

"You're a bitch."

"True. But I ain't freein' up for you," he laughed, drinking a fresh beer and playing with the zip on his tote bag.

They pulled away on the line and brought that trap topside. But it was empty just like the others. I couldn't understand it. At least one of these traps should have had some tail in it. The drops looked like good choices and spiny lobster should be spilling out across the deck.

"Robbed!" Thesinger spat.

"It's a job, all right," Clint signed. "They must have followed you when you sunk these traps. Maybe they made it look like they was trollin' or conchin' or somethin' and then they came back just before the season and fished you right out."

"I worked so hard on this!"

"At least they left you yinna traps."

"I don't need traps. What the hell I goin' to do, feed traps to m' guests at m' party?"

"I just said it's good you have your traps is all."

"Maybe my guests can lick the chicken wire on these here traps."

"Settle down, man."

"God damn it!" Thesinger cursed. He picked up one of the traps and threw it overboard. It sieved the water between the wire mesh and then vanished. "They're too fuckin' lazy to work it out for themselves. Too slack! I kill myself out!"

"Maybe this boat followin' us knows somethin' about it?" Dock said, lifting his head in an upward nod toward the powder blue boat.

"Hey," Clint leaned in. "Could be they took your t'ings?"

"I bet they did," Dock nodded.

"It's just a boat," I shrugged.

"They're followin' us, dread! What you think? All this ocean and they're like white on rice. It ain't right! Use your head!"

"Boy, let's check 'em out." Thesinger banged his hand down on the console and threw the throttles forward. Our boat kicked into gear and powered off. All three of us stumbled about and reached for a hold.

As soon as I'd checked myself I saw us speeding up on the openfisherman. It was insane. We would get up on them and they would be lost, or hoping we'd found a good reef to spear on or something. Now we were riding them down.

But as we got closer I started to look for a weapon. What if this was for real? What if they were Runners? They might be armed. Clint had his gun but the rest of us were unarmed. I looked for my cleaning knifes. I could be pretty good with a blade. And the spears. It would only take me seconds to load one.

The powder blue boat powered up and it was off, the engines trimmed up to leave as little drag as possible, the bow slapping down and rising up, howling off south toward the Sound. A sane voice inside my head said we'd put the fear of God into regular people and now they were fleeing for their lives. Another voice told me they wouldn't be running if they weren't guilty.

XIII

We pursued the openfisherman south at speed and the storm front battered hard out of the northeast. The sun cast sky ladders down between the heavy clouds before these closed together and the day turned abysmal, the sky's ceiling slung low and obscuring the sun. The islands withered and faded, made small by the torrent, and they became unknown navigation dangers that suddenly loomed and passed in our reckless chase. Beyond the cut and the relative safety of the banks, the ocean was up and coming in heavily. The chill air set my teeth chattering and my muscles into involuntary twitches.

"Keep 'em hot! Keep 'em hot!" Dock's exhilarated call marshaled us through the clamoring gale.

Our hull slapped and jarred on ragged waves. The blue boat struggled to keep her distance. Great walls of white spray launched out either side as she dug into each wave crest and trembled out.

Rain fired down and stung in undulating curtains, making us move together under the limited shelter of the t-top. Water slopped off the canvas, drenched us, made our course next to impossible. It sliced and the hull jarred and slapped upon the waves. The sea spray hit us in the face and we spat out mouthfuls of it and the salt raked our eyes and our vision blurred. The openfisherman became a gray outline, an afterimage of the mind, and then it vanished. Visibility collapsed. Thesinger pulled back on the throttle and we all peered ahead intently to spy the boat and any reef heads, before it was too late.

"Can't see a thing," Thesinger whispered. "Where's she at? Can y'all make her out?"

"No, boss," I said, searching.

"She'll have had to slow down. No way she could navigate in this," Roberts reasoned.

"Goin' fast is craziness," Clint said. I could see goose bumps up all down his naked legs.

"Shhh!" Thesinger said quietly. "Listen."

I strained my ears to catch sounds other than the wind, the rain pelting the sea and the babble of our own motor. If they were smart they would cut their engines altogether and just sit and let us pass. But it was hard to hear with the storm howling and I didn't see how they could stop in it. It was too much. My hands were locked, cold, my jaw was clenched shut and already aching, my sunglasses were speckled with spray. I knew that we would never even see the reefs if we came upon them. It would be the same for the powder blue boat. They would have to seek shelter.

"There's no way." Thesinger shook his head, his upper lip hard from the cold. "Just no way to track 'em down in this. Maybe we can still head home. There's just time before dark."

We turned back.

The upper unit of one of the two outboards shook and failed causing the boat to lose momentum and wallow. Thesinger pulled the throttle back to neutral and turned the key to restart the motor. The engine fired, belched, but cut out again. He spun the ignition a second time and the exhaust coughed black smoke, but did not catch. He choked it and twisted the key once more. This time there was a loud snarl, then silence and the engine was still.

"Gas?" I asked.

"Gage says we're fine," Thesinger said, tapping it.

"Women and children first," Clint joked, his face tight.

"This is nothin'," I shrugged. But I bit my lip.

"If this is nothin', then fix it!" Roberts spat back, gray faced.

"That's right, University Boy!" Clint cussed. "I tired of this!"

Thesinger grinned the grin of a devil and sang out the old islander's saying. "Boys, if y'all can't sail, cut bait…" And we all looked up grinning, even Clint, and completed the saying in a chorus. "… and if y'all can't cut bait then get the hell out the boat!"

"Gavin." Thesinger turned to me. "Check the fuel line's open."

I negotiated my way across the pitching deck to the stern where a plastic hatch opened to the fuel and oil lines that fed the twin outboards. I stretched down through the water collecting in the stern to open it. More water poured into the shallow hold and I could hear the machinery of the bilge pumping it out. Leaning in, I felt along the greasy gas lines until I found the valves. Both were open. I gave Thesinger a thumbs-up.

"Pump the ball," he ordered over his shoulder, spinning the wheel to line the boat up into the swells.

I clasped the rubber of the gas line ball and squeezed it to hand pump the gas into the engine. I pumped until the ball went hard and my hand went stiff. Now, I thought, come on and work. You had better work. Please start, I thought. I felt all eyes on me, Clint looking hang-dog and I cursed Sweeting's.

"OK! It's hard. Try it."

Thesinger tried the ignition and the motor fired, shook, ran and then died.

For God's sake, I thought, I only just picked up the bloody boat from the basin. It should work. But I should have checked the engine out after we'd got the boat back. Sometimes those fellas could break two or three things while they try to fix one.

Surges rolled under us and I steadied myself. Falling into the vacant space between two waves, the boat impacted the surface and another jolt racked my spine. Thesinger spun the wheel to head us square with the next set of swells.

"I'll take the engine cover off and check it." I braced myself, one leg under the gunwale and the other hard up against the fighting chair. I thought, please God do not let me be thrown over. Reaching about the outboard I undid the latches and struggled with the boat's movement while I lifted the domed plastic cover off. The naked workings of the engine stood out, exposed and intricate.

"Turn it over so I can check it," I ordered, authority passing naturally to me. The engine fired and stopped. There was no problem with the starter and the flywheel span smoothly. So I looked back down into the hatch and checked the fuel flitters.

"Oh man, your filter's all bunged up," I called out.

"That explains things," he said curtly, Sweeting's Boat Basin's poor maintenance exposed.

"I can fix it," I said.

"Fix it," he said, and I quickly removed the filter. The mesh was plugged up with a gooey filth. I couldn't believe that the boat could come back from the marina with a dirty filter like that. Still, I was being paid to check these things. I scrubbed the filter clean with my nails and washed it in the sea. I'd this vision of dropping the filter, but I held on tightly and gave it a good rinse. Securing the top back on the engine, I pumped the gas line ball hard, then closed the hatch.

"That should do the trick," I said.

The second engine shook, belched smoke and gave a good kick as Thesinger pushed the throttle into gear. It worked. We all raised our fists and yelled in triumph and relief.

A little spry was all that was left of the rain. The main body of the storm had passed over us and stood ahead to the west along the path we had to take. If we ran home we would catch it up. Going slowly, it would be a rough ride with the last hours spent in the dark.

"Where to?" I hollered over the noise of wind and waves. I knew we weren't going home.

Thesinger lifted his head to imply the distance and as his hands were firmly on the wheel he pointed with his lips. A long cay lay north-to-south off our port bow. The weather was out of the northeast and I reasoned that the western lee of the island would be sheltered, the waters there dead calm.

"Camp out?" I asked, and Thesinger nodded.

"But we got no tents," Clint said, incredulous, "and no sleepin' bag. Why we don't try and outrun this storm?"

"We ain't takin' a cut hip in the dark in this weather on the way back to harbor with a lame engine. No sir," Thesinger replied.

"Man, forget that, hey?" Clint said. "Head north and skirt the storm. This ain't nothin' but a little local system.

You could shoot for Douglas Channel, north by northwest, turn west along the north side of Rose Island and then home one time. Full throttle we could beat this storm home and be chillin' in the air-condition tonight!"

"You want me to run right back over the Middle Ground and I can't hardly see?" Thesinger mocked.

"So?"

"Boy, Clint, the tide goin' out, man! I ain't runnin' those reefs!"

"That's only a couple little heads."

"Look! We got crawfishin' to do in the mornin'," Thesinger said.

"What?" Clint couldn't believe it. "You want me to sleep out in this rain with all these mosquitoes, nippers and no bed?"

"No surrender," Dock smiled in a manner not unlike that of my father before Immigration drove him off. Clint sucked his teeth. He didn't like it at all.

"Boy, Jacob, why you don't just head home and go down to that fish market by you in the mornin' and buy up a string of crawfish tail? They got it all right there and all you got to do is pay. That's it, just go down there and pay!"

"Clint…!" Thesinger started, then bit it off and grinned. "Man, I don't buy retail. I don't want one little string when I could get me the whole kit. Where's your sense of adventure?"

Personally, I wanted to set up a fishing ranch fast. A beach was as good a campsite as we could hope for with that storm riding in. Soft sand would be a creature comfort.

Thesinger made for his cay through the slaking rain. It was a tough run with the swells coming in fat and then dropping. The boat climbed their faces slowly and sped down the far side.

Behind the submerged barrier reef that stretched out off the island's northern tip, the waves became mushy and infirm and finally the waters went still. Thesinger thrust the throttle down and we picked up speed across the glass-smooth bay. The twin two-fifties sent vibrations through the hull. The speed and stability were exhilarating.

"Well, I guess we're just doin' whatever you want, hey Jacob," Clint sneered sarcastically.

Thesinger ignored him and began a gentle turn into a small bay. A high, white bluff buttressed one end of a placid beach that stretched between the scrub-topped, hills. The tidal-plain of sand sat quietly and still with the moan of the weather muffled beyond. He trimmed the engines up to make it over the banks and turned the stern toward the beach. I ran forward up on the bow, knelt, coiled the sand anchor rope and hurled it. It held and I called back to Thesinger that it was set. Then he gave a signal with a slight toss of his head to Dock at the stern, who threw the smaller anchor up onto the beach and pulled the rope taut. We tied ourselves off and the boat sat still and calm as Thesinger killed the engines and tilted them until the props came dripping clear out of the salt water.

Jacob reached into the console hatch and took out his cell phone, dialed, held the handset to his ear and looked up at the sky. "Sweetness? It's me…We got skunked…I don't know…Some ass found the traps and cleaned me out… Bastards is right. That was my drop. Anyway. Look. There's a wicked blow comin' down in the next few minuets and we've had engine problems…No, everythin's okay. It's just we're not goin' to make it back tonight like I planned…I guess we'll just hunker down here. Camp out…Don't worry. We know how to rough it…Be careful. Lock up tight….Love you too." He thumbed "off" and stared at the phone for a moment, perhaps feeling the loss of the connection, before stuffing it back in its waterproof bag.

"Oh, come on, man," Clint complained about camping. "Don't you care about how the rest of us feel?"

"Buddy, you're either captain or you're crew. I'm captain." Jacob stared Clint down. "You got a problem with that?"

XIV

Foreign bitches like me should carry they stink ass, Caleb had screeched and I'd had to hold myself back from laying him out.

I'd been hanging out on the fish market ramp earlier that morning, waiting for Arial to arrange for Caleb to dive up her shells, when our confrontation began. I'd been in a dreamscape of color, watching the sun float into the yellow tinged air, envisioning the adventure ahead and thinking that I'd finally arrived.

"Hey, boss," someone spoke up.

"Hum?" I mumbled, twisting about to see Caleb beaming at me.

"Boss. You want me to take you fishin'?"

"Sorry?" I asked, leaning toward him with my arms folded across my chest, coming out of my daydreaming.

"For a couple dollars I could take you and the missy out and show you the sights. I don't usually like to do it, but I'd do it for you. Take you to the bathin' beach and the sea garden. I could take you snorkelin'. See m' boat right there?" He pointed a sun-blotched finger at the little fishing boat hauled up on the edge of the ramp. It was the yellow and white boat that moored just off the Thesinger property, the one I'd almost crashed my truck into. "I call her *Cuda* and she could take you wherever you want to go. Hey, Captain? Where you want to go?"

"That's all right. Thanks." I smiled, hoping to look like I appreciated the offer but hating the hassle.

"Okay then. How about some night fishin' then, boss?"

I flashed the ivory, wondering where Arial was. I spotted her peering at a large heap of conch shells piled up at the tide line where the fishermen had discarded them after yucking the mollusks out.

"Hey, Boss? The full moon soon out and then the mutton fish will run. I tell you, nothin' like being out there on that sea at night and catchin' mutton fish when they runnin'. I would never miss that. No, sir, never, I tell you. I'll be right out in my boat. I could take you."

"Look. Thanks. But my friends already have a boat. We're already goin' out with some friends," I said, trying not to be annoyed. He was just trying to raise some business, but it embarrassed me.

"I guess I don't mind goin' along," he compromised.

"You don't mind goin' along?" I repeated in surprise.

"Y'all need a guide," he insisted. "Y'all don't know where to go. I'll go with you Captain and show you where to go," he smiled and patted me on the shoulder.

"No, no, we don't need a guide." I shook my head, wanting to get away, wanting to be blazing down to the cays.

"Now, boss, there's plenty of reefs out there, sharks and all kind of trouble and you need one local guide to show you what's what."

I stood blinking at him, wondering if we were living in the same world. I was turned off by the patronizing use of "boss", wondering if he could even see who I truly was. I was reminded of the square at Marrakech from my travels and its impromptu guides with their scams and come-ons. Caleb's red-headed son gaped up at me, his face scrunched up in the sunlight, the freckles bright, a look of solid incomprehension about him.

"Plenty rocks!" Caleb said seriously, almost threateningly.

"Don't you worry about me, papa," I said, laying the accent on thick. "I know the sea."

"Humph!" he snorted. "You must be jokin' with me. Tryin' to get me to go with you for cheap. How you t'ink you could fool me? You think I fool? How you could know this sea?"

"What!"

"You best let me come before y'all get lost or smash up on the rocks them and drown. Be serious!"

"That's all right, bulla," I told him, "we're goin' fishin' and we know the way."

He sucked his teeth and picked up his machete to carve another snapper. He spat onto the ground, wiped the sweat that shone on his face and looked me up and down.

"Who?" he said. "Man, y'all don't know nothin'!"

"Nothin'? I don't know nothin'?"

Caleb was chuckling now, the dramatic chortle of having scored some decisive point, but also the sound of nerves being touched and a mind running out of things to say.

"This is my home!" I spat. "I know all about these things!"

"What? Don't try that. You'll foreign bitches think you could buy up the place and call it your own. It ain't yours. Carry your stink ass!"

XV

Nestled high up above the tide line in the lee of the wind there was a good campsite in a clearing between several tall casurarina trees. The great bowed and kinky tree limbs looked like they sheltered the barren spot from the storms that loomed over the island. While above us the low pulsing sun shone full force on the thunderheads, revealing them in Biblical proportion, wrathful and without remedy, like some place from Thesinger's mural.

"Well, let's get unloaded and set up before this rain pounds," Jacob said, "start passin' gear, hear."

They hefted the coolers full of ice and beer across the deck, I jumped from the stern platform into the waist-deep shallows, and they lowered them over.

"How are we to keep dry when the rain comes?" Clint moaned.

I studied the fat clouds that were rolling in but I didn't bother answering. Nobody answered. Clint didn't even need to ask. To the east, the thunderhead pressed down upon the world and a purple band of rain pelted out. The down blast swept over my face and rooted out small chittering birds from their roosts in the cay's blacklands who dove quickly back among the darkening coppice.

"Hey, check this," Thesinger called, and I looked back to see him holding up two large, mildewed beach umbrellas.

"Oh great," Clint sneered, "five star."

"Man, Clint," Dock said, "Why you don't go stay at someone else's hotel? I'm not sure there's any room at this inn."

"That's right, where the rest of us fellas goin' to sleep when your fat self is curled up under both those umbrellas?" Clint shot back. Then he sighed sarcastically. "Well, I hope this beach inn is better than Jacob's crawfish hotels."

"I think we can all fit under the umbrellas," I ventured hopefully.

"You?" Clint said. "No boy, boat bitches sleep onboard."

"A few tents could have been stowed in the hold easily enough," Jacob suddenly complained to me.

"I thought we'd be back by now," I pleaded.

"You should have considered the possibility of getting stuck," Jacob shrugged.

But I'd not thought of it. And I should have taken better care of Thesinger's boat. A bloody fouled up filter was no way to account for myself. But why should I account for myself? Because, a voice inside said, this is your only chance. Muck this up and you're back on the traveler's road.

"Ha, yinna wait," Dock laughed, "this story is going to enjoy a long life on the cocktail gossip rounds."

"I'm off for firewood before this light goes," I announced and pushed off into the bushland.

I was angry and I went fast. Bloody hell, I thought, and my argument with Caleb hadn't been smart. Maybe he could thwart my citizenship application. It was a small island. All he had to do was walk into Immigration and complain.

I went through the seagrape and silver buttonwood that grew among the saw grass along the shoreline. I passed the curly-tail lizard's foot-tracks that ran through the powdery sand, and the large land crab holes that went down to the water table and passed the small hermit crabs that crawled in the richly-molded compost. I went bent over under thatch palms, over the dune and down through the whitelands, walking in the shadows to stay in the cool, watching out for swamps and deep banana holes.

The wood was no good in those swampy lowlands behind the sand dune, where everything was rotten and moist. I went up to the thick blackground coppice, kept clear of poisonwood, onto the hard, sharp ridge where the wood was petrified, where the stunted palmetto fronds trembled and yawed in the stormy, salted wind that ascended the hard-shaped rise and buffeted my face.

Dry thatch palm fronds made the best kindle. I tore up termite-infested barks, whole dead trees. My forearms became a mess of dark decomposing matter, bloody red scratches and inflamed mosquito bites. Little protected by my boat shoes, my ankles became a crisscross of scrapes from thorns and the sharp edges of dog tooth rocks. But with a hefty armload I trekked out and dumped it in the sand to the downwind side of our campsite. There we would build the fire. Large red carpenter ants scrambled over the split ends of branches. Sweating and panting from the labor, I turned back for more. We would need a big pile and I felt obliged to get on with the work. Only when we had a decent fuel depot did I drop my last armful.

"Boy, it's bonfire night tonight," Dock said.

"That's if we get it lit before this storm gives us a dousin'," Thesinger said, judging the east.

"Maybe if we light that we'll get rescued. Hey!" Clint joked. Clint always had a joke. I didn't need his jokes. But he was Thesinger's friend and it wasn't my place to say a damn thing.

I squatted and started to dig out a sandpit.

"Buildin' sand castles, University Boy?" Clint taunted while he mixed himself a drink on the cooler lid.

"We build the fire in the pit with the dug out sand as a

wind break," I said matter of fact.

"That's it," Thesinger nodded, squatting alongside and helping me carve out the pit. "It's an old technique."

"No doubt. Well, I'm sure glad the kid knows some tricks," Clint scoffed and then sauntered on down the beach a ways and surveyed the sea and the heavy weather with his drink poised.

"Clint's pissed at you because he's pissed off and he wants to be pissed at someone and not at 'things'," Thesinger shrugged, "I guess you can't cuss "things" out."

"I'm sorry about the boat," I admitted, liking him.

He patted some sand down on the windbreak by the fire pit.

"We need to rustle up somethin' to eat," he said at last.

There was no way we could take the boat back out there. Even if we could handle the storm, which had not even hit yet, we'd no fishing rods and the weather was too heavy for us to spear.

"We could swim the cut between us and the next cay. See if there's any conch in that cut. There might be some conch in a cut like that," I suggested.

"You could do that? Swim those cuts, with the current? And dive conch?"

"Sure," I said, like it was the most natural thing to expect. "We might even get a good shell to take back for Arial."

"Okay," he grinned, but he looked uncertain. "I guess we could give it a try. But let's get this fire goin'. Hey, Dock. Break up some of that kindlin' there while Gavin and me finish this pit."

Dock broke the big pieces across his knee and laid them out in order of size. Yelping suddenly, he staggered back, his arms backstroking, his fat fingers tense and spread.

"Jesus Christ!" He screeched, putting a hand to his mid-rib.

"Hey? What happed?" Thesinger jumped up.

"God damn snake… in the wood…scarred the daylights out of me." He was panting and bent over, his hands on his knees.

"A snake?" Thesinger asked.

"How big?" I asked.

"Hell yes, a snake! Huge! It was in the loose bark on one of the branches. The bark came off and suddenly this snake was comin' at me. Lord, what a fright!"

"What's up?" Clint demanded, sauntering back from the surf line, cocktail swilling in his hand, his hard tongue working the goatee hair on his upper lip.

"Old Dock here found a snake in the wood pile," Thesinger told him. We all peered though the gray light trying to see the snake. It must have slithered under something.

"That's not a good sign," Clint said with raised eyebrows.

"Maybe we should kill it," Dock said, sweat on his brow.

"Man, Dock, you always want to kill somethin'," Thesinger laughed.

"Listen, it scared the shit out of me!"

"Yeah," Clint said, pouring more booze into his cup and adding a handful of ice. "You have to be savage in the defense of your civilization. Let's kill it!"

"Don't you think we should get this fire started before this rain hits?" I asked, but only Thesinger seemed to listen.

"Hold on now, Gavin's right…" he started to say.

"Y'all just chill, man," Clint said. "I gettin' m'gun and we could blast that snake to Hades."

"Gun?" Thesinger said.

"Yes boy! You don't think I fool enough to come out this way without some protection against all these random bitches?"

We studied him as he traipsed across the beach to his duffel bag. Clint crouched, unzipped it and pulled out his handgun.

"Y'all," Clint called, showing it off. "Get ready."

He came over and we all stared into the woodpile and wondered where the snake was at. I was excited, wanting to see what would happen. Clint took up a wide stance with the gun held in both hands pointing at the ground between his legs. He nodded at the woodpile and grinned through his goatee.

"The Bible tells us that the snake is the enemy of the Lord, so prepare to die," he said to the woodpile. "Man, y'all slack bitches, kick that dead wood aside and just give me one clean shot."

The rest of us were about to kick the pile apart when we were caught short by a raport and a flash that seared my retinas. A portion of the woodpile explode in spinning fragments of bark and I smelled rancid gunpowder.

"Man, what happen?" Dock yelped as Thesinger and I jumped clear in strange kangaroo postures.

"I saw it move! I saw it move!" Clint shouted, hopping.

"Clint, that ain't nothin' but wood ants, hey!" Thesinger shouted.

They were all rowing and there was a bell pealing in my head.

"I tellin' you! I saw it move!"

"Look! See? Ants! Scurryin' all about that log you shot up! Boy you shootin' at ants!

"Well, move the damn wood then!"

The three of us loosed the pile with a bit of footwork,

exposing the sand bellow. The snake was coiled among the debris of bark.

"See!" Dock declared. "Man, look at that snake!"

"That's the smallest fuckin' snake I ever saw," Thesinger said.

"It's still the enemy of God," Clint barked and started firing. The handgun bucked. The sand smacked up in small impact explosions by the lugs, and I had to hold my hands up to stop getting the granular shrapnel in my eyes.

When Clint finished firing I looked at the ground. The snake had been shot to bits.

"Well," Clint said. "That was fun. Who wants to spin up a brew for the cavalry?"

He and Roberts went over by the cooler with the liquor. I looked at Thesinger and we chuckled and went back to our work at the fire pit. When we had the sand in the pit nicely patted down we built the fire. I always enjoyed that, there's something very satisfying about that type of work. We placed the palmetto fronds in the center and built the kindling around it in the shape of a pitched tent. We left spaces in the stack of wood for the fire to breathe.

"Hey, Clint," Thesinger called down the beach. "Boy, bring your lighter here so we can get this thing burnin'."

"I could shoot it a fire."

"Put that gun away, hey. Just bring your lighter."

Clint stuffed his handgun back into the duffel bag, sauntered up and handed over his butane lighter. I went around to the windward side of the pit to add my body to the firebreak. Thesinger crouched close and got the lighter's flame in to the palmetto kindle. The flame leapt up from the dry fronds and it burned quickly. Too quickly. I was afraid the palmetto would roast away before the wood kindling caught. Thesinger got in there and blew on the flame. The fire flared, the bark began to singe and flames licked up the splits in the wood.

"Dock. Get bigger logs,"Thesinger told him.

Dock selected a couple and Thesinger built them diagonally into the fire's pitched structure. He was sweating now and leaned back from his work. For a moment we all stared into the flames. The fire was leaping up and a good trail of smoke drifted westward on the wind. I breathed a sigh of relief.

"What about food?" Clint asked, rubbing his goatee.

"There's no food," Dock told him.

"But I'm hungry."

I sighed, shook my head and gazed off down the beach. I didn't want to look Clint in the eye.

Thesinger studied me before responding to his friend. "I'm goin' to go down to the cut and see if there're any conch. Gavin's comin' too.

"Gavin?" Clint asked.

"That's what I said. Maybe we can have conch dinner. You chaps tend the fire. If this rain comes down, throw all the wood on top so it don't go out."

At the end of the cay, a spit of beach ran ahead of the cut. At the water's edge we stripped to our shorts and donned fins and masks, shivering as rain ran over our naked shoulder blades, and stood in the wet sand that had been made smooth and hard under the torrent. The storm pulsed over the ridge. My hair lay flattened against my skull and my jaw was clenched from the cold.

"You don't have to come. I can do this alone,"Thesinger said through chattering teeth.

"I can dive conch."

"Boy, you been away too long. You lost it. I bet I clean it right out and you get nada."

"You're on."

I didn't wait for him. I jumped right into the stream. Near the sand spit the water was either still or eddying back and I swam hard through it. Thesinger dove in and we raced out to the middle of the stream where the current caught us. Even through I knew it would be strong I was surprised when it grabbed us and sent us swirling toward the rocky, narrow cut.

Between the cays I could see through the rain to the rough waters of the Sound, where a thunderhead's low bulb swept in toward us.

He measured me, his eyes bright and his brow cleft creased in challenge. Then he was off, arm over arm, doing the crawl, and I was after him. We were jockeying for position and he pushed me as I got too close. When the current was at its fastest we stopped swimming and drifted. I focused on a single spot on the bottom a short distance ahead. It was the distance I figured the current would sweep me in the time it took to dive down, kicking hard the whole way. It was a bit difficult to see between the churned up water of particles and dimming light, trying to pick out the conch shells grown invisible with barnacles and sea grass on the sea floor.

On my first dive I had to check myself midway down because of the pressure. Pain stabbed through my sinuses. I felt foolish not to have anticipated it. By the time I'd held my nose to equalize I'd been swept past my shell. On the way to the surface I saw Thesinger swimming powerfully along the bottom, grabbing a conch.

On my second decent I remembered the pressure and cleared it as I went down. But the shell I picked was empty. I kicked back to the surface and breathed in deep and hard. Everything had gone still and calm and the down blast that proceeded the storm had passed. Now came on the storm itself. Iron rain drilled down. The drops bounced across the flat ocean surface, each a perfect sphere, holding a momentary, miniature reflection of the world entire.

Measuring the speed of the current, I judged that I'd one dive left before I'd be swept out. I kicked with my fins, propelling myself to the bottom, hoping something would be down there. I saw only one, and when I pulled the shell from the grass the conch retreated inside.

My chest burned for air. Shoulders back, I kicked off from the ocean floor, and beat at the water with my fins until I broke the surface. I couldn't make out the shore through the rain.

"Jacob?" I called, wanting to tell him we were one-one.

There was only the quaking of the rifled thunder.

"Jacob?"

Treading water in that tiny mercury world, I waited for a response. None came. I told myself that it didn't matter. Maybe he was diving and couldn't hear.

I guessed where land would be and swam toward it. It was a long swim and I felt relief as the white beach shone luminescent in the purple air through the pelting rain. As I waded out of the surf the sea tugged my feet and the sand slipped. My skin crawled and I convulsed with cold in the rain. Carrying my conch, I quickly jogged the sandy path over to the inside shore and out on the opposite beach. Jacob was about to step down the sand spit to swim the cut once more.

"How'd you do?" he called, shouting over the storm.

"We're even," I declared, holding up my conch. But he only laughed and pointed to two shells by his feet.

"I'm up on you, Blake. I'm half fish and you're half foreign bitch. Ha-HAAA!"

"Current's fast and this rain's somethin'."

"It's about gettin' conch, man."

"I guess the light's good for one more, hey?"

The red, mushroom-shaped sun scrimmed through the storm clouds sitting upon the molten run westward sea as we ran and dove in again. This time, I had the distances right and I didn't forget about the pressure. I gathered four conchs, two on each dive. I wanted to be first back. I wanted to beat Thesinger. So I swam hard and staggered up on to the shore. He followed. We leaned over, hands on our knees, wheezing with the rain pouring over our backs and looked sideways at each other.

"A good haul I reckon," I panted, showing him mine.

"Four, hey? Same as me. But that still puts me one ahead. Looks like I got you beat. But good effort."

"Now those conchs are pretty small," I said, looking at his haul. "Why don't you throw 'em back? I think you should just chuck 'em."

"Up yours. These are keepers."

We took the path back to where we had left our things and squatted to clean our catch.

"Do you want me to show you how to get the conch out the shell?" Jacob asked.

But I'd already placed a chisel's sharp end on the point in the shell where the animal held on, and I grinned at him in answer as I hammered down on the handle with a stone. The blow punched through and the conch slid out. I held up the lump of moist white meat, the entire body shrinking back on itself, and showed it to Jacob. I saw him measuring up my conchs with admiration.

"Yeah Blake, I guess you got the daddy-os."

It pleased me enormously to hear him say it. We both grinned. Then we set to work slicing off the orange skirt, the eyes, innards and the claw of each conch and threw them into the surf. Soon the water throbbed with the spirited movement of feeding jacks.

The second storm was passing. The rain let up and the ocean was calming. Out to sea where the rain was now slight and the world visible again the shifting spectrum of final light played upon the sky and the waters. The somber palette of evening, touched with the vaporous colors of tenebrous browns, deep maroon, and plum wrapped the western sky of towering cloud, whose heads were further illuminated by their own hot interior flaring. Jupiter, at its perihelion, shone large and alone in the dusk until darkness revealed the fantastic pale cloud of the Milky Way like the very backbone of all things.

XVI

The boys set the coolers in a circle about the fire so each man could have a gabby bench. The first of the rains had passed on and I'd pulled out some dry cloths from the chilly box we were using for a waterproof chest.

I watched the old, clear sky and the multitude of stars fixed and falling. I thought of my forebears on my mother's side gathered about the same beach bonfires, weary from their works of fishing or sponging. I looked at Jacob and remembered the Bahama Room mural of the bootlegger holding forth a lantern, making his silent night blockade run in a sloop painted black, weighing his own invisibility against the need to see, a fine balance between two dangers.

Looking at the weather-rough faces that shone within the pale perimeter of fire I think that in that first quiet moment we all felt let down. Clinton, his stubble growing in, blurring the clean definition of his goatee, smoked a slender, Cuban cigarillo self-consciously. The pungent tobacco mixed with the wood smoke. The wind shifted and I shut my eyes tight against the sting. Dock Robert's bald, ebony pate shone in the firelight, the lenses on his turtle shell glasses silvered, he sat in a crumpled linen shirt. My own floppy hair blew in the breeze that tore the fire, and made it pop and spark. Jacob stoked the burning pile, rearranging the fuel. Deep shadows darkened his dimpled chin and the mid-brow cleft. We all slapped at the nippers that bit and stung, smearing their black bodies across our skin, becoming streaked with our own blood. Our disappointment was measurable. But we were half-cut now and talking fuck.

"Man," said Dock, his glasses flashing. "I wonder what happen'? To those fellas in the blue openfisherman?"

"I ready for 'em when they come." Clint's eyes came alight, the coal end of the thin stogie glaring as some warning signal of terrible things to come. "I fully loaded. Primed. On station. I'll shoot 'em up."

"Cut the thieves down," Dock laughed.

"That's right," Clint grinned, "then take they t'ings."

"We'll leave it to you, Clint," Jacob said, producing a pigskin case. " 'Cos when t'ief t'ief from t'ief God laugh."

"Boy, fuck you."

"Clint. You're genuinely disingenuous."

We chuckled at Knowles's expense and Jacob unzipped the pig skin case and showed us a neatly segmented glass cocktail kit, with a miniature shaker and small tumbler glasses strapped to the underside of the tan lid.

"Mojitos?" he asked.

We all laughed.

"Where did you get that?" I asked, meaning where had

he been hiding it all this time.

"Jermyn Street," he said, cocking a self-mocking eyebrow.

"Very refined," Dock's baritone shook.

"No other way to travel," Jacob smiled, removing the shaker from the kit and filling it with ice cubes. The kit also contained a little pack of sugar and loose mint leaves, and he put these in the mixer on top of the ice. Then he got the white rum bottle and upended it into the ice. The clear liquor filled two-thirds of the container before he twisted the tin cap back on.

"Man," he said to me, "dig up a couple cold cans of soda water, hey."

I reached into one of the coolers and found a couple of cans loose among the ice and handed them over. He popped the tops, poured the fizzy soda and stirred the cocktail with a chrome twizzle stick.

"Presto," he announced, pouring the drink evenly into four small tumblers loaded with ice.

"Sir," said Dock, raising his cup, "you're a don." And we toasted that and drank the cocktails right back.

After the apéritif we ate the conch from plastic cups with our fingers. The meat was chewy and tough and we had to work at it. The quantity wasn't sufficient and none of us were satisfied. When the conch was gone, we sat restlessly about on the coolers and looked about. Clint was digging a hole in the sand with his toes.

"Man, I could eat steak."

"I think there's a petty shop up yonder," Dock smirked.

"Boy, Jacob, if you had set your traps right we'd have plenty crawfish tail right now," Clint pointed the cigarillo at him.

"What'd you mean 'set my traps right'?"

"I'm just sayin' you was skunked is all."

"I was robbed!"

"How you know that? Maybe there never was any crawlers in any of 'em pots! Maybe they was just sittin' there empty this whole time and you're just makin' excuses for yourself."

"Excuses for m'self?"

"Fellas!" Dock cut in. "Let's mix up another round and play some dominos."

"Clint's talkin' shit! I set m'traps right! I was robbed! Clint! I tired of your fuckin' lazy self. What do you do, hey?"

"I just settin' out the fact that you was skunked is all. You was skunked and you need to keep that in mind when you tell whole parties of people that I lose charts overboard, hear!"

"Christ!" Jacob ran a hand through his short, sharp hair.

They quieted and we played dominos on a cooler lid, smacking the tiles down, trying to figure out what "cards" the others had. Dock proved the best player. He could guess our hands by watching what we played. He was able to block my moves and I admired that. Often I had to rap my knuckles on the cooler lid to indicate that I'd no card to play.

"Boy, I'm glad you got that filter clean," Dock Roberts said to me. "I wouldn't want to still be out there, or capsized. Hey, Clint. What would you have done if that boat had capsized, hey?"

"Man, I don't care. It ain't my boat," Clint grinned through his goatee, his eyes on the small black dominos in his big hands.

"That's okay, you laugh now in the dry with food in you," Dock said, slapping down a card.

"Call that food?"

"I'd like to see you laugh swimmin' out there now with all kind of shark snackin' on yinna hip and t'ing."

"Shark? If that did happen I would just make sure Jacob here knew it was all his own fault."

"Nothin' to do with you?" Jacob joined in.

"Not if I met it like that."

"You would blame me for the boat sinkin'?"

"I blame you for everythin'. Now, whose fault is that?"

"ha-HAAA! I knew you was one of them fabric softener bitches," Dock laughed, spinning his last domino upside down on the table, telling us that his next move would win him the game.

"Boy, Roberts, let me tell you about my ass," Clint said, slapping down his own card. Dock groaned and rapped the lid with his knuckles. He was blocked and his last card went unplayed. Clint had kept the game alive for another round.

"Well," Dock carried on, poking his last domino impatiently, "if the sharks did go to work on Clint here, I must say I'm not sure I could do anythin' about it."

"I ain't know what shark would want with my skinny-bones-no-crawfish-in-my-belly shelf," Clint said, puffing cigarillo smoke.

"Maybe I could stuff sand in his wound or bandage it with palm leaves, a stick shoved between his teeth for anesthetic."

"You're always such a cheery bastard," Jacob laughed.

"I'm just lettin' you in on the ship doctor's expertise. You need to know the standard of service on board. I'm tellin' you, you may as well feed yourself on Scotch than come to me. You may as well have red meat. 'Cos in the long run, bulla, there's precious little I can do for you." The Dock was animated and agile, ready to win when the game came back to him, and then he went stock still.

"Hear that?" he said.

"I didn't hear a thing, but I'm down wind of you so if it was a roaster I'll know it soon enough," Clint joked.

"I'm serious."

We went quiet. I heard nothing but the sea and the weather. Then a metallic purring tickled my eardrums. It was the signature of an outboard. We all searched seaward but there was no sign of a boat out there in the dark.

"Must be runnin' without lights," Jacob said.

"No," Dock said. "I don't think its out there."

"Now where else does Dr. Geoffrey Roberts think a boat would be than out there on the wide open sea?" Clint asked sarcastically.

"Cut it out, Clint. I'm sayin' it's not right out there."

The sound ricocheted off the curving bluff and came from different angles, making it difficult to get a good directional fix. Suddenly the sound was immediately to our left. We all looked down the beach. The propeller was loud, but the boat was invisible in the dark. The customary red and green running lights that were required by law had been extinguished.

I squinted, saw by starlight a white line on the water. It was the wake at the prow of a boat I still couldn't see. Then the engine pitch decreased and I knew the boat had slowed down. My skin tingled and my fingers went icy.

I looked at the others. Clint grabbed his tote bag and extinguished his stogie in the sand. Jacob looked at me, the cleft in his brow deep and long, his lips open, the angular features of his face exaggerated, lit up red and brilliant by the flame. The fire felt hot but I caught a chill, realized we were sitting in its blazing light.

We sprang up and dashed for the dark, cutting out

at different angles. I passed the place we'd left the spears, grabbed one and began threading the shaft through the Hawaiian sling. A voice in my head said, be calm, walk, do not run. Demonstrate control. I was sprinting. At first my vision spun with bright spots with the change from the firelight to the opaque beyond and I couldn't see.

Barefoot, I ran out onto the beach, fumbling with the spear. My nervous fingers got the shaft of the spear notched into the sling, and I pulled back on the rubber and aimed the point toward the sound of the engine. The boat was idling just offshore. But where? Blinking in the dark, my eyes slowly adjusted. I could see the stars now, the dark purple of the bushland behind. And I could just make the shoreline. I squatted to make myself a smaller target and kept my guard up, ready to shoot the spear.

They could be anyone. They might not be dangerous at all. Maybe they needed assistance. Geoffrey was a medical doctor. But I kept my mouth shut. I remembered what my mother had always said; 'Closed mouth don't catch no fly'. I focused on the engine noise and made the form of a small, openfisherman laying off there. Was it the powder blue boat? Had it found us? What would they do? Or was it drug runners or pirates? I couldn't tell if it was the blue boat. I couldn't see Thesinger or the others, which was a good thing, it meant others couldn't see me.

"Okay," called a voice from the boat. It wasn't a question or a salutation. Rather it was a simple, cold acknowledgement that we all knew the situation.

"All right," I heard Jacob answer.

I stayed silent so as not to reveal myself. Now we knew their position but they didn't know ours. The boat idled for a beat. I kept the spear tightly drawn, my shoulder aching against its pull.

"Okay then," came the final reply.

"All right then," Jacob said.

The conversation completed the engine of the dark boat went into gear and slowly accelerated its way up the beach.

I hunkered there in the dark as the motor passed and quieted. Suddenly I looked behind me, unwilling to relax my grip on the harpoon. I watched the folds of shadow for someone there. I couldn't see anybody, but determined to keep watch.

A more subdued crowd gathered about the fire. We didn't say a thing, but looked to each other, eye to eye, and I felt the tension, the anxiety and the unanswered questions. Jacob put a sandaled foot into the fire, kicked the logs apart and the fire died down to devil-eyed coals and the occasional lick of flame from the under side of a solitary log. In the red glow I could see Clint holding his tote bag in one clenched fist and his revolver in the other.

"Cockroaches," he whispered to me, but he didn't smile.

"It's probably nothin'," Jacob said unconvincingly. "Probably just fisherman out for a night catch."

"They don't have any business comin' and watchin' us like that," Dock complained.

Jacob spat. He was shaking as he crouched down by the embers and for the first time I saw his pigskin cocktail kit lying in the sand. It must have been knocked over during our flight. Several of the glass segments were smashed.

"Blast," he said, gathering up the bits.

"I guess it's a question of trust," Dock continued. "You just can't trust people."

Jacob was looking up at the gun in Clint's hand.

"You know how to use that?"

"Sure. Point and shoot."

"Somethin' tells me its not that simple."

"We should have a plan," I said.

"That's it," said Dock, "we have to be ready in case they come."

I looked over my shoulder, gripping the spear shaft.

"Look," Jacob said, "if they come back, we run from the fire and crouch behind the dune line there, layin' down. I'll fire the boat's flare gun out over the water. That'll scare the shit out off 'em. It'll also give us a clear sight of 'em and what they're about. If we need to shoot 'em Clint will have good light to take aim. They will be exposed out there on the water and it should be a clear shot."

"All I need is a clear shot," Clint said.

"Why not try and shoot the gas tank? You could blow 'em sky high," Dock suggested.

"Can you do that?" I asked. "I mean blow up a boat with a gunshot like you said?"

"How do you know where the tank's at?" Jacob asked. "Boy, I wouldn't try that. Aim for 'em and aim for their chests because that's the biggest target area. Don't try for anythin' fancy, just plug 'em and be done with it, I say."

"Maybe they won't come back," I said.

"But they might," said Clint.

"I don't know what they would come back for. We got nothin'," Dock said, trying to reason it out.

"They might kill us for the boat," Jacob figured. "They might need the boat to run drugs or smuggle people, or maybe they think we have a heap of money on us, or maybe they will just kill us because they didn't like our attitude."

"Or maybe they was just fishin'," I said.

"And maybe they was just fishin'," Jacob nodded, and then we all fell silent, squatting there by the embers.

More thunder rolled down and the scent of the air became thick and rich with coming rain.

"Well, these embers won't survive another dousin'," Jacob grunted, looking at our spread out fire.

"If I bury 'em with sand, the coals might keep 'til the mornin'," I ventured.

"You do that and we'll try and set these two umbrellas up into some kind of sleepin' arrangement," Jacob said. I thought I'd better make sure I got a place there.

"Hey, where are the topless Polynesian beauties with the flower necklaces? I could just do with a little coochy," Clint joked, still carrying his bag with the hidden handgun. I found I was thankful for his humor. It eased my tension. I raked the embers into a pile and the combined heat caused them to combust. Quickly pushing sand over I buried them.

My eyes slowly adjusted. The beach lay deserted. Our boat stood proudly just offshore, the anchor lines tort. I looked for our unwelcome guests but the entire world was empty. Behind me, the guys were getting a makeshift camp together. The adjustable portion of the beach umbrella poles had been detached so that the pole was now half its normal height. They stuck these in the sand and overlapped the umbrellas to form a sort of roof.

A bony hand of white lightning grabbed downward, imaging our faces in electric blue. The thunder racked the ridge top.

"Let's get undercover quick," Dock yelled.

They spread towels under the beach umbrellas. Dock went up the sandbank behind our spot and dug a drain channel to divert any water that might flow down the beach away from us. The first fat raindrops thudded into the sand and I got up and went to our shelter.

We all got under it, which was a bit awkward and a

bit of a laugh, with four grown men bedding down so close together. We bumped into each other and jostled for room. To my relief, I found a space.

The lightning torched and cut, the storm moved overhead and the thunder walloped. The umbrellas rocked but held true and rain poured in sheets off the plastic edges in a rhythmic torrent, but we stayed dry. I snuggled into my arrangement of towels, thankful for the warmth of the others next to me. I saw that Clint had his gun by his pillow, and I thought that that was a good idea.

XVII

I woke in the dark. Shuddered. The rain had halted and the camp was quiet. Water dripped from the umbrellas and from the trees in the bush. Soft waves lapped at the sand and our boat's anchor ropes squealed as they strained and then relaxed. Lying there holding my breath, I wondered what had woken me.

I couldn't hear a boat motor, or anyone approaching from the bush. Only the mosquitoes' whine scratched at my ears as the sweat tickled down my skin. It all got me edgy when the wind lulled. My stomach growled with hunger and my mind whirled. Would I ever get my papers sorted out? Why should a birthright be so hard to claim? It was no good. I sat up and looked about. Clint and Dock Roberts were asleep beside me, but Jacob's place was empty.

I crawled out and stretched. Jacob stood alone by the water's edge. He looked alert. Maybe he was afraid the blue boat might return. Or maybe he couldn't sleep because of his failure to catch any crawfish. The boat had been jinxed and the weather no good and he could make all these excuses. But the truth was Clint was right, Jacob got skunked and it was a downer. He had nothing to show. We would go back in the morning. It's terrible luck to go back so empty-handed.

I felt comradeship in our separate senses of loss and went down to where he was watching strange green phosphorescence glow momentarily in the beating surf.

"Look at that," he whispered as I came abreast and we both watched it in silence for some time. "I just came down to check on the boat. You know, make sure the lines were well set."

"I already made sure of that," I replied, slightly hurt.

"Oh. I just couldn't sleep," he said quickly, embarrassed.

"Me neither."

"The bugs drove me nuts," he was scratching himself.

"I've got bites all over my ankles."

He looked up, craning his neck, and I followed his gaze. The sky arched steep and black with the light of stars nailed stainless above and beyond us forever and, I imagined, harboring about them other worlds of colors and sizes and orbits and atmospheres the imagination of which curdles the brain.

"What d'you know about that sky?" Jacob asked me, meaning all that lay beyond.

"Looks like it's clearin'," I said.

He nodded.

"Well," he said, "the tide's goin' out and I think the boat's a bit close to shore. I want to set her out a ways."

We waded out together, loosened the anchor lines, swam the boat out a few more yards, and reset the bow and stern lines to his satisfaction.

"We got to get out there and try spear us somethin' when mornin' comes," Jacob said as we sat together on the bow.

"Amen, brother," I agreed, watching the stars.

He squatted on his haunches, rubbing the day's growth of beard and looking fixedly out to sea. "The thing is, the location of the traps was no good. We got a cut ass and no crawfish. So where to go?"

"I reckon we head due west across the bank," I suggested, "and out to the edge of the Tongue of the Ocean, north of Green Cay and work the wall north toward the White Bank. We could look for a good head to spear on and hope we get lucky. Nobody goes down that way. That whole country down there's empty, waitin' just for us."

He considered it, nodding his head gently as he mulled it over.

"Well, we've got the gas. Yeah. It's a plan."

The thick wedge of a gibbous moon was setting, casting its paper-lantern light, and I realized that Venus, the morning star, was up. So it was very late indeed. I wondered if I should even bother turning in. But Jacob wanted to talk.

"Arial and I practically used to live down here," he continued in a voice just above a whisper, a voice of reverence. "Divin'. Campin' out. Skinny-dippin'," he chuckled. "Boy, it was somethin' watchin' her. She was so sleek, so quick. Always fishin' up shells. None of this crap like tonight. You did good, Gavin. You're a real island boy."

"I'm not really from here."

"What? Don't talk fool."

"No. Honestly."

"But you were born here. Your mother's family."

"That doesn't matter, does it? I mean, my dad was from Florida, so I got no papers, no citizenship," I blurted out.

"Shit, Gavin. I didn't think about that."

"I've applied."

"You better bribe someone quick before they loose your stuff. That's how it is. It's not like my wall. When you're straight you tell them to carry they ass. But you, you need to grease that wheel. That's all those cocksuckers understand; power and money. And they trade the first for the last. It's the business they're in."

"But it's my right. Surely. I mean, being born here…"

"Whatever," he said dismissively and did not meet my eye. "Well," he continued in a more labored voice, "this trip wasn't what I'd hoped for. Not like it used to be. Not like me and Arial. I think I'm goin' to make some changes. I have to be frank with you, Gavin. You've been a tremendous help. Really. Thing is, to be up front, well, holdin' on to *Orion*'s not fun like it used to be. Not with the creek siltin' in and the problems with robbers. Haven't taken her out in an age. She just sits there. I'm just not into it any more. I'm sorry, man, but you know. Hell. This guy from up in New York gave me a ring. He's lookin' for somethin' secondhand. He's got his heart set on this hull. Made me an offer. I've been puttin' him off but now I think I've made my mind up to just accept. It might be different if we could get permission to dredge the creek. But what can you do? It's all politics. So. Looks like the night of the party, when I take *Orion* out to set off the fireworks, that's going to be her last cruise. I'm sorry, Gavin. After what you just told me I know this kind of drops you in it."

XVIII

When I'd been a boy I thought nothing of just wading out into the sea and spearing a fish or a crawfish on the first coral head I came to. It was no longer like that. Now the reefs close in to shore are empty. If I skin dive those reefs, I see nothing but little colorful fish darting among the sea fans and anemones. But there's nothing to eat. Too much engine oil and effluent. Too many fishermen with fish finders and GPS. So we just go further out.

With the sun behind us, the sea ahead was a-sparkle and hard to judge. The sunlight daggered the water in jagged white rays, narrowing down the line of perspective to the vanishing point. The weather had quieted. The front had passed. Only a pallet knife cut of cloud scraped before us as the sun burned off the early mist resultant laxity of form. With the throttle pushed full forward and the engines running at top speed, we progressed with force across the aluminum water. We left the cays behind and left behind the frequented waters, busy with pleasure craft and sailboats. We went out where there was no mainland or sign of human habitation above the horizon. Not even another boat out there, only the wide-open, empty sea. Eventually, I could make out the dark green shimmer of what must have been the high point of small Green Cay to the south.

We stopped where a good-sized patch of beige marked a reef. The sea fans and the brain coral heads lapped the surface in the wave troughs. Clint took the helm. The rest of us geared up.

"Right, boys," Thesinger said, standing on the gunwale kitted out in his frogman getup, spear held upward. "This is it. Let's go get us some crawfish."

He held his mask in place and stepped out into the sea, his flippers making quite a splash. Roberts and I followed. As I hit the water, bubbles exploded about me and sodium tingled on my tongue. The ocean floor, more than thirty feet down, was tinted green through my goggle glass. The sand undulated softly in hillocks and rippled waves. Thick patches of sea grass stretched off in one direction as far as I could make out, and a solitary stingray swam above the grass, its long tail trailing behind. I could make out an old car tire covered in green moss half buried in the grass with a length of nylon rope floating upward by a couple of glass bottles.

Jacob kicked his fins and powered off toward the reef. I raced after him, my spear shaft probing ahead. Sea gardens loomed out of the darkness in ragged silhouette that contrasted with the bright waters above. The reef mounted from the sandy floor with towers of coral and sea fans, growing to within inches of the surface. The light play made it appear alien and foreboding. I made out yellow brain coral, orange elkhorn and, deeper down, the corals that grow flat in order to gather the sunlight rippling across the sea floor in swirls.

Inhaling deeply through my snorkel, I bent and dove. Pressure built, hammering my sinuses as I reached the bottom and pressed in on my temples, jaw, and cheeks. I equalized, felt my ears pop and the pain disappeared.

I swam slowly along the mounting edge of the sea gardens with Jacob reconnoitering ahead and Roberts behind. Purple sea fans waved gracefully in the current. I saw corals and anemones, sponges orange and yellow, sea urchins with their long black spines, beautiful fish and ugly fish, the terrible examples of brute creation. The inexplicable choreography of a school of small silversides bursting and imploding in strange and flashing splendor caught my eye. But I didn't see any crawfish.

After several dives Jacob motioned us to the surface.

"Reef's a dud. Not a crawfish here," Roberts said.

"Let's mount up and roll to the next," Jacob decided, and we waved Clint over with the boat. We pulled off our fins and threw them on board and then hauled ourselves in.

Jacob took the helm and we cruised north along the line of the wall, looking for the next reef. I was parched but enjoyed the sun booming on my shoulders and the sky above layered across the polaroid seascape with cloud.

"Relax," Jacob told me and handed Dock and I a beer. He didn't take one himself, just kept his eyes fixed on the surface until he found the next reef.

"All right." He cut the engines. "This is it."

We dove down to the coral head. At the base of the reef I scouted under ledges and into cracks and holes. With quickened heartbeat, I kept thinking I saw spiny antennae waving out from under a shelf. Excited, I coasted over, stayed up and behind the spot so that they wouldn't see me. I didn't want to frighten them. If I did they would move back deep into the ledge and it might make the work of killing them difficult. Steadying myself on the crown of a brain coral, I hauled my body over and, spear ready, gazed through my clouding mask and shimmering light into the dark shelf beneath the ledge. It was empty.

As we climbed back into the boat, Jacob spat his snorkel out.

"We gotta get somthin'," he exclaimed.

It was midday, and with the September sun high there was little escape from its substantial heat under the small t-top's shade. We pressed on up the edge of the drop off, scouting for another coral head.

"Christ!" Jacob gritted his teeth. "How are we going to spear enough crawfish in half a day to feed my guest list?"

"Maybe we'll come on the mother load," Dock shrugged.

"Or you could make the crawfish an appetizer," I ventured.

"Chief, I want boiled crawfish with garlic and butter in the shell for everyone. The proper deal. And these heads, they should have somethin' on 'em. We're not too far into the season. I can't believe they're cleaned out already."

We came on another reef in the series of sea gardens that bordered the edge of the drop off.

"Come on Gavin! Dock, what are you waitin' for? Get some kit on and get in the drink!" Jacob rushed us.

"All right, settle down man, we're movin'," Dock said irritably as we pulled the fins and masks on and slid back into the water. Roberts kicked frog style, his black body tinted beige by the light. I watched him survey around the head, my spear held ready, waiting to see what he'd find. The sun was charring my back now and I wished we had some cream. The only movement was Jacob, Dock and I circling the reef, and the sea grass on the sandy bottom trailing in the current.

"You guys aren't lookin' hard enough," Jacob spat as we came up empty.

"What you sayin'?" Dock rounded on him. "Listen buddy, I could still spear circles around you..."

"Well, I'm not seein' it!"

"Shit! Where's your catch?"

Jacob, square-jawed, slapped his shades on and pushed the twin throttles down. The boat accelerated northward. He had us going flat out and I had to hold on tight to keep my balance. The sky was entirely clear now and the sun relentless.

The shallow shelf below extended west and at times we found ourselves crossing sandy shoals with inches to spare. Jacob spun the props and we headed back out to deep water. Other times the lay of the shelf turned eastward and the depth of the water changed the color to royal blue.

"Gavin! Watch where the edge is at, man!"

"Jeez! I'm sorry. The sun makes it hard to see."

"That's not good enough," he said and slammed the boat to starboard until we met the shallow edge. We ran alongside it again until we came upon another head.

"We're scorin'," Jacob said, spitting on his mask and cleaning it out as I dutifully sat beside him and prepared to dive. He rolled backward off the side and went straight down. I plunged in. Roberts followed. Clint sat chilling by the controls, his shades on, getting cut on beer. I thought he should take his turn, but Clint never moved.

Shaking slightly, I made sure my spear was notched and tested the tension on the sling. I went head first, beating my fins, my leg muscles screaming as I propelled myself to the bottom and scouted the ledge. I spun onto my back and scanned up under the rocks and outcroppings and the twisted forms of elkhorn coral. A moray eel gaped from a hole and an octopus worked its alien way through the fans. There were lots of pretty little aquarium-type fish, but no grouper fit for spearing and not a crawfish in sight.

I broke the surface, seeing stars. A nervous jolt shook me. My skin tingled and my face was numb from a lack of oxygen.

"Damn!" I muttered, shaking my head to make the spots vanish.

Behind us, Clint Knowles was bringing up the boat. He had that islander's way of approching way too fast with the engine trimmed up and the bow riding high and slapping

THINE IS THE KINGDOM

down, cutting the power at the last moment and the craft sinking to a stop perfectly next to you. The move sent a white wake over the three of us and we spat water.

"Stop screwin' around!" Roberts cussed Clint.

I held on to the side of the boat and felt cold.

"Well," said Clint, seeing our unused spears. "I guess that's it, hey? No more spear fishin' for today."

"Thanks for the newsflash," Dock replied sarcastically as he climbed up the stern ladder by the engines, throwing his fins onto the deck. "So much for the Feast of The Five Thousand."

The three of us sat about panting. The day was getting on and I hoped Jacob would call it quits. I knew it was a downer to get skunked like that, but after all, it was only crawfishing.

"I guess we go down to the Fish Market and buy the tails cleaned and packed in ice," Clint shrugged.

"Hell no!" Jacob shouted.

"Sorry to spoil your party, man," Clint curled his lip.

"I said no God damn way!"

"Listen, those poor bitches will practically give 'em to you with things being tight," Clint joked, but Jacob wasn't listening.

"There's got to be some down there," I shook my head in disbelief, trying to support Jacob even though I figured we were finished. He had to see sense. "They're just someplace else."

"Well they better be, because comin' here was your idea," Jacob gritted his teeth.

"Be reasonable," Dock said.

"We came out here to do a job," Jacob said and I could tell by the way his brow cleft deepened and his chin went rock solid that he meant to carry on.

"Count me out," Dock rubbed his face with a towel,

popped another beer and sat down heavily by Clint, his bald head beading with sweat and the gold of his chain flashing as his chest heaved.

"Well, Gavin." Jacob looked at me bright-eyed, as if we were the only true blues around. "I guess its up to us."

"Oh come on, man!" Clint threw his hands in the air. "Enough already, hey! Time to head in!"

"There's enough light to check one more," Jacob insisted.

"Man, I tired of this shit," Cling sneered.

"You tired?" Jacob mocked. "What you done all day? Listen, we need crawfish…"

"You need crawfish!"

"It's my trip and unless you want to swim you can shut up and go with the flow," Jacob snapped.

The sun trembled on the ocean in the west, turning everything to blood with New Providence a thin line on the northern horizon when we found our last reef and slipped back into the water. The ocean floor was purple from the lack of light. The reef loomed in dark silhouette and I wondered how I was supposed to find a thing. Jacob and I swam down side by side with our spears projecting forward to the sandy base of the reef and then began to circle in opposite directions. But it was no good. It was too dark.

I surfaced, heaved for air and hung on to the side of the boat as I tried to regain my strength. Hauling myself up on the platform, I sat while Dock took my flippers and mask. Resting there a moment, my naked feet kicking in the water, I was shaky, goose pimples were up down my arms.

The ocean was quiet, calm, the opposite of my beating heart. The sky beyond was marbled with cloud, yellow and lavender and gray. I shook the water from my ears and blew out my nostrils to clear the passages of salt and the sinus pain, climbed over the gunwale into the boat. A cold beer was handed to me and a towel thrown in my face. I pressed the rough material around my eyes to rub the salt and the feeling of the tight mask away. The beer cleared my throat, washed away the rubbery sensation. I knew I couldn't do it again.

Jacob pulled himself out of the water. It poured off his lean body and he strode across the deck to the center counsel. Clint moved aside for him. Jacob turned on the boat's running lights, an admission that nothing more was possible. I knew the day was over. Jacob never looked us in the eye. With chilly chests still empty, he gently slid the gears forward and turned the wheel to head for port.

Dock was huddled in a towel against the opposite gunwale, keeping a distance from Jacob. I followed suit. But Clint hung around and tried to engage Jacob in forced conversation.

"Clint! Just don't even talk to me," Jacob growled.

Above us, the free motion of twilit sky, the blotted borders and gobs of colors purple, brown, gold and cream, changed moment to moment, darkening. The first lights at the western end of the island winked in blue and white on the horizon in the mustard air. I drank beer and felt like hell. All I wanted was a hot shower to get the dirt, sand and salt out of my pores. I wanted my mattress in my little billet on board *Orion*, with the AC cranking. I loosened up my stance and let my legs move with the sea and settled in for the ride as we powered home.

XIX

We starred out at the sea and kept to ourselves without making eye contact as we raced the coming night back to harbor. Jacob jerked the throttles forward and wrenched the wheel forcefully, his upper lip hard. The empty coolers rattled on the fiberglass in the stern. Nothing more was said about the market.

With the offshore breeze of early evening in our faces and the stars littered out in the deep sky we turned into our home harbor and powered through from the west heading east. Jacob didn't slow down despite the no-wake law. We passed the tremendous cruise ships berthed at Prince George Wharf, and went under the arching concrete spans of the bridges to Paradise Island. The water was choppy from the comings and goings of so many craft, from smacks, barges, dive boats and container ships.

I was embarrassed passing so much maritime activity. I knew we were just one boat among many, indistinguishable, yet I somehow felt that everyone knew we'd failed. I was glad Jacob didn't let up on the speed. I wanted to get back fast and be alone.

We left the cacophony of the commercial area behind for the gentility of the residential eastern shores, where the bollard lights and the house lights sparkled loose and shimmering across the black water. Here the harbor lay quieted and the water stilled through engineering, and the homes stood along the shore perfect and fine. I found the dark spot of the abandoned police station and I tried to pick out *Bangalay* as we tore in and our boat wake slapped the bulkheads.

The quiet was broken by the noise of the fish market. As we headed towards it Jacob deftly slalomed around the couple of sunken fishing boats that lay just beneath the surface. The wrecks were not marked on any chart nor identified with buoys. They had been abandoned and you simply had to know where, or chance to see them in time, or run aground. Behind us our white wake curved serpentine neatly between the wrecks.

The market pulsed with activity. There was a party underway with people gathered around the boat ramp, where two go-fast cigarette boats with four outboards apiece stood. The hulls were newly waxed, the dark paint shimmering, one with a detail of a skull smoking a joint. I got the feeling the revelers were celebrating a successful drug run.

"Hey, Jacob," Clint joked. "I wonder if these boys have their equivalent of your Jessie Thesinger's lucky ship's wheel?"

Jacob looked shocked.

"Maybe you should get back into the racket. Run drugs instead of booze. Six of this. Half a dozen of that."

"Clint. Just stay on board when we reach and make sure none of the bitches them steels this boat. I couldn't stand 'em takin' it twice."

Grease laden smoke hung low and blue over the water from the cook out cauldrons and burnt the air. The offshore wind scattered the garbage and we streaked over floating fast-food wrappers. Music pounded from a system dominated by a bombastic bass. People danced and shouted.

Lacking any desire to visit this place, I wondered what they would think of us. Our boat was dirty with footprints and sand, the Plexiglas windshield that half wrapped the centre console was streaked with salt, and we were unshaven and rough. It was obvious we were coming in from a trip, and if we were buying produce, it meant we'd failed to provide it ourselves.

If I were Jacob I would have been acutely embarrassed. But he didn't try and sneak in. Instead, showing off, telling everyone here was a man who doesn't give a goddamn, he took the boat in on a plane and roared her up to the ramp.

The go-fast boat owners spotted us and waved frantically, their affected coolness gone in a rush of fright. Hugging the opposite side of the boat, I was ready to jump overboard. Jacob slapped the throttles back to neutral and the bow sank forward breaking our speed. He touched the reverse and the engines grabbed the sea and pulled us to a halt alongside the two cigarette boats. Dock and I ran forward to fend us off, and so did the owners of the go-fast boats. We all leant in, hands on each other's rub rails, pushing.

I starred into the jaundiced eyes of a very black man with a chiseled face and high cheekbones. His lips were puckered in fear and anger. A thick gold rope chain dangled at his chest and swung below his white undershirt.

"Muddo-fuck!" he spat, like it was war. "Stupid mother fucker!"

I looked at him stony-faced but knew he was right.

"Chill dread!" Dock said in a falsetto voice. "We just come to do we t'ings!"

The man threw his arms in the air, washing himself of us and cut us with his eye. He put on a show of coolness, moving to the dancehall music, holding his Guinness bottle aloft and bending his knees, dancing in front of his girls.

"Boy, tie she up," Jacob snapped and we cast out a small stern anchor because the tide was flowing in, and we needed a line to keep us from being swept up. Dock, Jacob and I slipped off the bow into the inches deep dirty water at the foot of the concrete ramp. I slipped on the green slime that grew in matted chunks along the cracked edge of the ramp. The go-fast boat owner watched us with is head angled back and his eyes reduced to slits, his arms folded in exaggerated threat. The smoke from the cook out cauldrons stung my eyes. I held a hand up to shield them and then thought that the gesture was somehow weak and dropped it and held my head tall.

Clint stayed on the boat with the engines running as much to guard against interlopers as to keep us neatly off the shore. People like to get on to show you that you can't keep them off. They'll climb in, lean against the rail and laugh, like what the fuck are you going to do.

Jacob sighed as the three of us pushed up the ramp through the throng of partying people who milled and danced. Some just stood to make you go around them, stood to make the ownership of that particular square footage clear.

The first stalls we came to were closed down and people were sitting on them or playing dominos. The people stared at us.

"What y'all doin'?" a fat guy boomed. "This a private party."

I didn't see how they could have a private party at a public place.

"We're just here to buy some crawfish tail," Jacob said, matter-of-fact. "This the public market, right?"

The fat man pointed up the ramp and we moved on to another stall, where the vendor there was packing up, her old station wagon hatch open and her coolers stowed inside. To my relief, she clearly had a good amount of crawfish. It would be enough for the party, and that might mollify Jacob's mood even if it wasn't how he wanted it. We could get the business done and get the hell out of there.

"Excuse me," Jacob called politely to her. "Could I buy some crawfish, please?"

"Close."

"I need rather a lot."

She sucked her teeth.

"I pretty much need everythin' you got there."

"Everythin'? Child, you can't afford that!"

"I ready to pay now."

"These here is too expensive. I need cash money!"

"Let me see," Jacob asked, and she made a show of slowly going to a cooler, bending over and opening the lid. It was full of white machine ice and neatly packed frozen crawfish tails. "All these coolers full up like that?"

"Mm-hum!"

"I'll take all!" he called over the racket of the party.

"All?" she sneered.

"Stop playin', woman! You want to sell 'em or not?" Jacob said, the cleft between his eyebrows deepening.

"Don't be talkin' to me like that! I don't have to sell nothin' to you, hear! I don't have to do nothin'!"

"Okay, fine. Please may I buy your crawfish."

"I ain't givin' you the coolers so how you ga get all these tail out from round here?"

"Do you have any bags?"

"This look like supermarket?"

"Forget it. Just the tails," Jacob said, taking out his billfold and then turning to me. "Hey, Gavin, boy check by those abandoned fruit stands and see if you can rustle up some boxes."

I went off through the press of bodies in the dark, with the scent of body odor and rum mingling with the charcoal burn and the pepper scent of jerk chicken. After being at sea, the street party with its loud intensity, its brash colors and closeness felt invasive. I focused on my objective and shouldered my way through.

There were a couple of plywood tables set up under the seagrape tree and under one was a pile of folded cardboard boxes. I pulled a few out, cockroaches scurried. When one flew up to the underside of the table I jumped and felt a silly fool.

The boxes were damp but they would have to do. I carried them back and Dock and I unfolded them while Jacob settled with the woman. We dumped the entire contents of each cooler into a box. The tails were frozen solid, curled up tightly and crusted with ice. When we had everything we each reached down, got our hands under a heavy box, put our backs into it and lifted.

"What kind of fool box this is?" Roberts asked.

"The only kind."

I could feel the bottom of my box go soggy from the melting ice and hoped we could make it. We staggered down the ramp muttering "Excuse me, excuse me" the whole way. Most people didn't hear and I had to nudge them. That got nasty stares. I thought, my God, how far away this is from a fine day spearing on the boat. I wanted to get out of there. My fingers were starting to break through the soggy cardboard and so I tried to spread my hands and forearms under as much of the underside as possible for support.

The crowd was drunk and pressing in. Jacob was tight-lipped and gray-faced. Suddenly he slipped, either on fish guts or conch slop, and a fell hard on his ass on the concrete.

"Shit!" he screeched, sliding towards me. I quickly sidestepped him and Jacob crashed into a group of girls. People laughed. The girls screamed and staggered and then their boyfriends were right in there.

"Boy, I ga kick yinna fuckin' ass!" they shouted.

Jacob got up quickly and pulled on the top of his box rather of lifting from underneath. The entire bottom fell through. The machine ice lumped out and the tails dropped. He slipped again and came down face first in the ice.

"The crawfish," he yelped.

The frozen curled tails tumbled, spilt and rolled down the ramp. Jacob grabbed at them, stuffing them in his lap. The boyfriends and the drunk crowd surged in. I could feel the press all around me. Hands reached in and grabbed up tails as they cartwheeled down the ramp and even snatched for those Jacob had fallen on. Tails were stuffed into shirts, others brazenly held high in triumph as their captors jumped around.

"Wait!" Jacob called, trying to pick himself up, kneeling. "Stop! That's mine! Wait!"

Dock and I forced our way to Jacob, still carrying our own boxes. I felt mine slip. People were pushing and elbowing, hoping for a second bonanza. Jacob was trapped on the ground, hunched over the frozen tails, fending off the hands that were reaching in all around.

Dock started shoving people hard. "Boy, get from round here! Hey!" He cursed them, his box between his legs. His head angled high in challenge. "I tell you carry your fuckin' Congo hip!"

We got some space. I squatted to gather the remaining tails into my box while Dock stood guard.

"Fuckin' hell!" Jacob spat, his face speckled with ice and grit, his hands a lattice work of brown scrapes and a little blood.

We made our way to the boat past hostile and mocking stares. My hands were cold from handling so many frozen bodies and it made holding the heavier box even harder. Just as I got to the gunwale of Jacob's openfisherman I slipped, spilt my box into our boat and the tails went avalanching across the deck. I was appalled but relieved they had fallen in our boat. Still, the crowd laughed at my mishap. Jumping up, I turned around to help Dock with his box. Jacob climbed in and kicked crawfish tails aside as he went to the controls. He got the engines running and put her in reverse. I fended us off the go fast boat while Dock hoisted the stern anchor.

The dark man with the gold chain was sprawling on the console seat of his cigarette boat, a woman in his arms. He was laughing at us, showing a fashionably gold-rimmed tooth and his tongue sticking out lazily. Enjoying the spectacle, he pointed his Guinness bottle at us and then doubled over in a great show.

"Shut the fuck up!" Jacob screamed, taking the anchor from Dock. The man's head snapped up.

"What you say, bitch?"

"I say shut the fuck up before I come there and mash your fuckin' watermelon head!"

"What!"

I felt cold. The last thing I wanted was a mob rushing the boat. Jacob might swing the anchor at a few on the bow but they'd take him down by the ankles. And how many could Clint shoot before he ran out of bullets? Then I caught myself. Christ! What the hell was I thinking? But Jacob didn't wait for a fight. He threw the engine throttles back and reversed into the harbor. The man in the go-fast boat stood akimbo, his face quivering, shouting challenges.

Fireworks streaked up into the purple dusk from the center of the party and the crowd cheered. The rockets rose on trails of sparks and pale gray smoke and exploded overhead with a raport that made us jump. I saw a bright streak and was blinded by the sting of smoke. There was an explosion and the boat was showered in crackling sparkles. We all ducked, throwing our arms over our heads shutting our eyes tight. When I looked again my vision was streaked with color.

"Jesus!" Roberts exhaled, recovering. "Rockets!"

We all looked at each other, alarmed. Jacob spun the wheel and headed the boat back in toward the ramp. I wondered why he didn't just get out of there.

"Hey," he called out, his hands cupped to his mouth.

But everyone was too busy drinking, dancing, and setting off fireworks to notice.

"Hey! I'm talkin' to you!"

The closest ones and the man on the cigarette boat turned and regarded us arrogantly, their eyebrows arched.

"Yeah! You! Why don't y'all watch out with those fireworks! Y'all hit us," Jacob said.

They turned away.

"Gad damn it I'm talkin' to you!" Jacob's voice shook, his teeth showing as he screamed up at them over the mindless music. "Watch what the hell you're doin'!"

"Boy fuck you!" they shouted.

The first bottle smashed on the deck. The brown glass splintered into fragments and spun about our bare feet. Then a hail of bottles and rocks barraged down. I could see our man on the go-fast boat pitching them. Mostly they were badly thrown and went down in the sea, but some hit the side of the boat and smashed across the bow. I ducked behind the gunwale and peered out at the jeering partygoers, who were pitching anything handy at us.

With a quick touch on the throttle, Jacob got us out of range. We looked back in disbelief. Jacob's face went cool as he lined the bow up to face the ramp. He kept the props trimmed up and then pressed the throttle all the way down. I didn't have time to ask what he heck he was doing. The twin two-fifties spun into action and the boat shot forward toward the ramp.

The faces that had cut us stared in horror at the boat

barreling down on them. At the last moment Jacob spun the wheel, the boat came about violently, the stern dropping deeply with its own momentum. The crawfish tails and broken glass slid everywhere. Jacob gunned it again and two tremendous sprays of seawater shot out from the props.

For a moment, the water obscured everything and seemed to hang impossibly in midair. Then it slapped down and people collapsed and slid, taking other's with them, the speakers tipped over and tumbled. The white water rushed in a torrent and overtook everything, kicking up against the scattered and sputtering partygoers, flooding back down the ramp into the sea. As the last water dribbled and pooled, people stood or lay splayed in still, hunched shock.

"ha-HAAA!" Jacob howled into the silence.

We sped off, barreling eastward with our running lights off. I felt dazed and weak. I was angered by the mean reception we'd received, and the others seemed to feel the same. But what had we done? Yet there was just a touch of devilish humor in what Jacob had committed that might make it all right.

In the deep channel, the boat sped over the flat sea on a plane as we arced toward the creek and home, with the frozen tails slowly defrosting all about us in the humidity. Taking advantage of the smooth water, I collected the tails, sorted them from the broken glass, and packed them in the coolers.

Unexpectedly, the colorful little fishing boat loomed large at anchor off the sandbar that narrowed the channel. Jacob wrenched the wheal to keep from ramming the wooden boat. We came within feet of it, our wake rocking it violently.

"Damn stupid place to moor a boat," Jacob spat. "Makes me angry the way these people just don't care."

It was the third time I'd almost slammed into something of Caleb's. I wondered what his problem was.

Glancing over at Jacob I noticed the smallest hint of a smile on his face and wondered at that expression.

Jacob never slowed until we were just short of the mouth of the creek. We entered at a gentle pace. He took out his cell phone and dialed Arial, told her we were coming in.

"She's up at the Cabana," he said, looking distracted, and I figured he was trying to sort out what he might tell her. He rubbed his face as if trying to adjust his mind. "She says the power's off."

The creek was empty and still. The peace of it was numbing after the noise of the market and roar of the engines. The moon shone down and the overgrown bush hung out over the bulkhead. *Orion*'s white hull came ghosting out of the dark.

Two sandy-haired boys sat night fishing on the dock of another creek property, their bare legs dangling, a hurricane lamp at their side. As we idled past they both raised their heads to hail us.

"Catch anythin'?" I called out.

"Jacks," one said.

The other boy eyed our coolers and our gear.

"Y'all been jookin'?" he called.

"Yup," Clint replied, opening a cooler for them to see our purchased crawfish and the two boys looked after us with awe and longing and I felt a terrible fraud.

"You the man," Jacob muttered back to Clint.

At our mooring, Jacob put the port engine into reverse and spun the bow neatly around to face the creek mouth. The tide was coming up and he maneuvered the boat into its spot behind the stern deck of *Orion* with the current helping to keep the bow straight.

Arial met us in her shorts and bikini top with the two Rottweilers panting at her side. She gave us the double thumbs-up when she saw the coolers.

"Sweetness," she laughed, "my big strong man home!"

Jacob shook his head.

"What? Y'all didn't get nothin' but little tails, hey?" she joked.

"Skunked."

"But didn't you spear today?"

"There's nothin' left on those reefs."

"Oh Jacob!" she sympathized. "What about the party?"

"I had to go purchase crawfish. We'll have plenty," he shrugged as she handed a torch down to him.

"What happened to your clothes, Jacob? You're a mess."

"Let's just not talk about it."

"And your palms are bleedin'."

"It's nothin'."

"I'm just askin'."

"Look! Hey! Why don't you clear these dogs from round here before they snap up the few crawfish we have!"

"Fine! I'll put 'em in the Jeep," she huffed, whistled for the dogs and strode back up toward the Cabana with them at heal. Jacob was looking at the sky and then at me.

"What? I know what I'm doin'."

We set about cleaning the boat but my heart was not in it. I hosed the deck down, tilted the engines up and washed the salt off the props. Removing the fuel filter, I set to work on it with the pressure hose. As I worked I could feel the day's sunburn on my back and arms.

Dock mopped the deck. The suds ran back to the stern where they were flushed out. Jacob laid the spears out on the concrete quay and washed them, the stainless steel gleaming in the bulkhead light. Clint stood about unemployed.

"Wash that boat down good now, University Boy," he laughed.

I wanted to hit him. I wanted him down so fast so I could put the licks on him. Sometimes it was hard to forget that I was the hired hand and that Clint was a guest. I swallowed my anger and got on with the business at hand.

"Clint! What's your fuckin' problem!" Jacob demanded.

"What I look like? Your boat bitch?"

"Come on, Clint," Dock said. "Roll up those sleeves and get mucky, m' boy."

"Sorry," Clint said. Then he dragged an empty cooler over and started pilling it up with crawfish.

"What you doin'?" Jacob asked.

"Takin' my share of the loot," Clint shrugged, grabbing handfuls of ice from another cooler and spreading it out on the crawfish.

"What you talkin' about?" Dock asked, whipping sweat.

"I figure these are my share and I takin' 'em."

"No man! That's not the deal. All these crawfish are for my party," Jacob said, fixing Clint with a smile that said he must be joking.

"That was for your traps. That rule doesn't apply when we're jookin'. I don't remember anythin' about me jookin' for you."

"First of all, we didn't do no jooking and second you didn't touch that water, much less carry a spear!"

"Now I was the one drivin' the boat!"

"We bought those crawfish!"

"Which was my idea!"

"No, no, no my boy, the whole idea of the trip was to stock up on crawfish for my party I tell you!"

"Man, that ain't right!"

"You signed up! Now get cleanin'!"

"Sorry," he said.

"What you mean?"

"I must be off," he said flatly.

"Off? We're not finished as yet! We got crawfish tails to clean!"

"You guys go ahead. I've got to split."

The three of us looked at him but we didn't say a thing. I couldn't believe it. You don't go out in a man's boat and then not do the work required. Jacob's lips were puckered and the vain in his forehead was standing proud.

"I have a client first thing," Clint said lamely.

"That's right, and you don't want to stink of fish. But your ass too late. You was born stink," Dock said and laughed awkwardly.

But Clint wasn't laughing. He was looking at his cooler laden with the crawfish Jacob wouldn't let him keep.

"You guys got it under control. I'd just be in the way," he shrugged and shouldered his tote bag and gear. "See ya." Leaving the full cooler behind, he turned and walked off to where his car was parked behind the cabana.

"Ass," Jacob spat.

Clint's car tires ripped down the gravel drive.

I kept silent and handed the crawfish up to Jacob one by one while Dock lined up the coolers. We worked quickly and quietly, hosing off the remaining grime and glass, packing tails neatly in the coolers in layers with ice between. Jacob was moving fast, sweat beading at the tip of his nose as he bent over each open cooler.

I looked up at *Orion*. It didn't seem to matter how many times I buffed it her prow was still dull. There was no bringing it back.

XX

Bare-chested and in shorts the three of us, wet and dripping, came up from the creek toward the Cabana, lugging the coolers and unused spears. Drumming rose up from the direction of the fish ramp. We trudged along in the slipping sand, listening to the beat. Dock stumbled and dropped his end of a cooler.

"Fuck!" he screeched, grabbing his naked foot.

"You gettin' bitten by snakes again?" Jacob sneered.

"Somthin' stab m'foot! Look!"

It was almost impossible to see. Only a faint blue marked the sandy beach and black marked the sea. I switched on Arial's torch and cast the light along the sand. We saw little conch shells littered all about. They were very small, juveniles. It's illegal to take conch when they're that small.

"Jesus, Jacob," Dock whistled, rubbing his foot. "Someone's using your property for a dump."

"Typical." Jacob ground his teeth. "They take the young ones. They don't worry about reproduction. They don't check. That ain't me boss. I met it like that," Jacob spat. "No wonder there's nothin' left out there on the reef. And on my beach! My land!"

His face flared. He grabbed a shell and hurled it at the bright fishing boat bobbing just out there in the dark. I heard the thud of the shell hitting.

"Bitch! Take blow!" Jacob shouted.

"Hey!" came a voice from off down the shoreline. "What yinna doin'?"

"Who that?" We span toward the voice, guards up. I

focused the torch beam. All it illuminated in its week circle of light was bush.

"Who that say who that?" the call came back.

"Show yourself!" Jacob demanded.

"I comin'! Don't worry! I comin'!" A man stepped out from the bush into the torchlight. He carried a hammer and chisel for bashing conchs out of their shells. A long main of white hair blew about his shoulders. It was Caleb. I felt instantly embarrassed. He had seen Jacob throw the conch shell at his boat and was angry. But much of it looked to be show. "Now, I comin' and I ain't scared," he said. "I don't play you see."

We set the coolers down to free our hands.

"Excuse me," Jacob said, putting on a good show of being understanding. "This is private property!"

"Who?"

"I own this land."

Caleb sucked his teeth and put on a drama.

"I'm not havin' illegal fishin' on my land," Jacob said.

I was shining the flashlight in Caleb's face and he was holding up a hand to shade his eyes. Surely he could not identify me.

"I fish in the sea," Caleb replied.

"These conch are juvenile. Don't you realize that if you clean 'em out then they will not…"

"Who you is? You ain't from here!"

"I'm from right here!"

"Ha! Well you don't look like it! You don't look like you from here! That's for true! Ha, ha!" The laughter was affected.

"What's that supposed to mean?" Jacob demanded.

"This land is my birthright! This my country!" Caleb declared, puffing out his chest and thrusting his chin upward.

"You're trespassin'!" Jacob spat back.

"No foreigner's goin' to tell me what's what!"

"Foreigner? Foreigner? Boy, get off my land! Carry yourself!"

"I ga cut your skinny hip!"

"Get off!"

"I ga beet one foreign bitch!" Caleb shouted, his teeth flashing white in the lamp's light and the hammer and chisel waving dangerously in his hands. "I ga beet you!"

"Get out now!" Jacob pointed.

Caleb hawked up and spat at us. Jacob stumbled back, involuntarily kicking up a foot load of sand that hit Caleb in the face. Caleb dogged, then charged, the chisel brandished ice-pick style, ready to stab. Dock picked up a conch shell and pitched it, striking Caleb in the shoulder. He lost his footing, spun comically in the air, and landed on his back. Instantly he hunted about with his fingers in the sand on all fours for the missing tools.

Dock had another shell ready but Caleb scooped up sand and let it fly. Jacob and I turned away. The grains stung my neck and naked chest, but Dock let out a cry and I knew that the sand must have gotten in his eyes.

When I cast the torch beam back, Caleb was gone.

"Come on!" Jacob picked up one of the spears and Hawaiian slings. I grabbed Dock, who was doubled over rubbing his eyes, and we fled up the limestone path toward the Cabana, leaving the coolers of crawfish. I was simultaneously steering Dock and casting the flashlight beam behind us, half expecting to hear Caleb pounding up the steps in pursuit.

Panting hard, we made it to Arial's Jeep. The Rottweilers were barking inside the cab and watching us keenly. Jacob swung the hatch up and the dogs sprang out. They reared on their hind legs and tried to lick us. They sniffed the ground. We stood, heaving, looking back toward the threat. Dock tried to wipe away the grit. We were winded from the run but soon anger took over. The dogs sensed it and they began to whine.

"Let's…let's get him," panted Jacob.

He bounded back down with the spear notched in the harpoon sling. The Rottweilers raced alongside. I pulled out a cleaning knife from its plastic scabbard and went after Jacob.

Caleb made a break from the bush and sprinted, his white mane streaming, making for the wall. The dogs tore flat out. The first gained quickly and was about to lunge. Caleb's eyes rolled back. He screamed in fear and struck out at the dog with a stick. The blow sent the dog cart-wheeling and yelping across the ground. The thickheaded bitch was soon back up in pursuit, but the blow had given Caleb time to make the wall and start scaling it.

Jacob crouched, pulled back the sling's rubber and let his spear fly. The metal shaft glinted in the torchlight. It hit the wall's hard stone and ricocheted, spinning back to earth.

The two dogs ran up to the wall and jumped just as Caleb reached the top. He was straddling it, heaving. The dogs jumped and barked savagely. They went for his dangling foot. Their paws kicked up the fine dirt and their bodies twisted and spun.

Caleb stared white-eyed at the dogs. He began to shout at Jacob. I couldn't hear what was said because of the barking. When I came up I shone my flashlight in Caleb's face. He recoiled, swung his leg over the wall and disappeared.

Arial rushed out the Cabana.
"Jacob? Jacob? What's happenin'?"
"Stay down by the door," he shouted.
"Why? What is it?"

"There's a man on the grounds. We're seein' him out. Stay put."

"But I was alone inside." As she said it we both considered the implications. Jacob looked grim all right.

"Let me deal with it."

"Did he come up here? It was only the screen door," she said.

"He was just down by the beach," I offered, hoping to calm her, to ease the fear. "He didn't come up beyond the beach."

"I just walked down to the beach."

"The dogs were with you, sweetheart," Jacob told her. He clapped his hands at the Rottweilers, encouraging them. The dogs' mouths were pulled back, the snout skin rippled, the yellow teeth ferocious and dripping with saliva. They ran about with their snouts to the ground and their stump tails wiggling. They followed the scent whining, snapping at each other. A rock came over the wall. I saw it mount its arch, spinning, then begin to drop, accelerating down.

"Rock!" I shouted and we both scrambled away.

It hit the dirt. Rolled. One of the dogs watched it, head cocked in confusion. Jacob and I crouched, picked up rocks and hurled them over the wall. We heard them cascade down the branches of the wooded lot next door.

"Y'all!" Caleb shouted. "Yinna ain't no fuckin' good! You hear? I say fuck you! Y'all ain't invincible. I ga kill yinna dogs. You ain't shit without them dog!"

"Come on!" Jacob growled, grabbing my arm, and we set off at a trot along the wall. He whistled and the dogs followed. A little further on, the stone wall ended and a chain-link fence began. Jacob hurled himself at the wire and yanked. It shook and wobbled. Another rock came down. On Jacob's third pull the fence broke off the post and he fell backwards in the dirt with the chain link on top of him. The dogs whimpered and scurried. He tossed the fencing aside, got to his feet.

"Let's go!"

He jumped, the dogs bounded after him, and I leaped through. The overgrown lot was dim and my flashlight illuminated tree trunks, thin saplings and hanging lengths of vine. The dogs stood erect, sniffing, and then they were off through the bush. Jacob pushed his way after them.

I was beginning to have doubts. Pure anger was no longer all I felt. I wondered what would happen if the dogs got Caleb. They would have him down fast enough. Those Rottweilers would get him down and they would maul him. There was no question about the intruder being one of us. He wasn't one of us. The dogs knew it all right and they would tear into him. What would we do then? Could we call the dogs off? How do you call off a dog that's gone crazy? Or do you just let it happen?

Jacob hunched low, hands forward, the fingers outstretched. The branching veins on his forehead pulsed and small red lines of blood snaked across his back where he'd been scraped by sharp sticks and vines. Sniffing and scratching, the dogs circled nearby in the undergrowth, their noses to the trail.

I wanted to tell him that we'd left Dock back there with sand in his eyes. That we'd left Arial. But the dogs plunged into the bush before I could say anything and Jacob jumped and pushed his way between the saplings.

"Wait!" I called, the flashlight beam shaking as I struggled to keep up. Emerging into a small clearing, I saw Jacob standing stock still. The Rottweilers were at his side, their noses testing the air.

Strange forms rose up, groping and reaching in the dark. Quickly I scanned the area by torch and saw that it was the ruins of the old home. The abandoned building gaped out of the bush, falling apart, the concrete floor lifted by roots. The rotten shutters hung loose from their hinges. My light showed up a rectangular, empty hole in the ground with a slopping floor. A swimming pool. The Royal Palms that had stood sentinel in regimented lines about the dry swimming pool had died and only the trunks stood rudely above the ramshackle bush.

"I wish we'd Clint's gun," I whispered, holding my knife ready.

"Shut up about Clint."

I focused on what we were doing, wondered where Caleb was hiding. He could be behind any of these walls, crouching, ready. He could be quite close. It made me think of that first night in the Cabana, of the intruder standing next to me with only a closet door between.

I got low, bending my knees, my arms held out, the blade point forward. Christ. I wanted to run away.

Jacob nodded indicating that I go left.

"Flush him out," he whispered as he moved right.

I swallowed and started to creep off, flashing the narrow torch beam from the building's bulk to the dense bush. I studied the building, wondered if he might be behind. When I looked at the bush I couldn't help but fear the empty weight of the abandoned building. What was I supposed to do if I found him?

I went still.

Something was out of place. Up ahead I saw a pile of things, red and blue, plastic in appearance. I licked my dry, slit lips, hefted the knife to see how it might cut and thrust.

The objects were a fishing tackle box and a cooler.

Caleb's gear. Flashing the torch about I combed the shadows for him, supposing that he might defend his property.

Dogs barked.

I looked up, thinking that the Rottweilers had caught Caleb's scent, only to see them galloping for me. Their hind legs flew out, tongues lolling, fangs bared.

I could never outrun them. I would be down, mauled. Standing firm was the only choice. But my legs twitched and wobbled. Telling myself that standing would sap the Rottweilers' confidence and confuse them. I knew I would have to be decisive and fast when they reached me. I got low behind the knife, told myself not to slash but to drive it home, to use the point and not the blade. First one, then the other dog.

A sharp whistle brought the dogs up short.

"Poonkies!" Jacob called and they looked back, their tongues lolling, confused.

"Hey, Gavin. Man. Those dogs caught your scent and they tore off."

"Jesus," I whispered, my knuckles white on my knife, my body still moving into a moment that had never come.

"Sorry."

"I thought my life would flash before me."

He came up and touched me on the shoulder and then the dogs were about my ankles, licking my trembling feet. Jacob stopped, his hands on hips, and peered at the assortment of fishing equipment.

"Look at this," he muttered. "Now we know where he's based. That son of a bitch. I'll soon show him." He peered through the dark coppice, grabbed the torch from my hand and cast it about.

The trail had gone cold and I could feel that we were alone.

"He's gone," Jacob confirmed, the return to his normal tone of voice disturbing me. "He got away." He turned about and looked at me. Then he shouted, "That God damn bastard got away!"

I didn't know what to say and I just stood there gawking at him. Drumming wafted over the coppice. I went cold. I thought, what if the whole time we were out there Caleb had circled back?

"Come on. Let's go," Jacob said, perhaps wondering the same thing. He whistled and the dogs were at our heals. We retraced our steps through the bush, leaving the abandoned homestead.

In the blackout, Arial sat on a chair in the front room of the little two-room Cabana, cleaning the sand out of Dock Roberts's eyes with a wet flannel by torchlight. I was pleased to see him look up at us when we walked in, relieved nothing had happened to them.

"Your wife's a good nurse," Roberts joked, with a hint of embarrassment. "You get him?"

"No," Jacob said, biting off the word. He threw himself into a big rattan chair and kicked his legs up on the ottoman. "The bastard got clean away."

"What did he want?" Arial asked, wiping Dock's face. It was dark in the room with only her torch and mine casting circular, blue-tinged light. The pool furniture looked strange in the false illumination.

"What did he want? God! I don't know. Maybe he thinks that as he moors his stink fishin' boat just offshore there, that he has natural rights to my land. As he sees it, he can come and go as he pleases, clean his illegal catch on my beach and leave his garbage all about. Perfectly natural, of course," Jacob said, crossing his bare feet on the ottoman.

"Why, it's simply outrageous of me to want to stop him, especially as all of this is his birthright."

"I was just askin'," she said, "I want to try and understand it. It could happen anytime. And often it's just me one here when you go off fishin' to the cays."

"Nothin's goin' to happen," he said, folding his arms over his head and leaning back.

"But Jacob…"

"Listen! Nothin's goin' to happen!" Then he shouted at her. "You understand me? Nothin's goin' to happen!"

"Nothin'?" She shouted back. "Nothin'? Well somethin' just did happen. It right now just happened. Not to someone else. To us. To me. You want your wife tied up?"

"Arial, I…" he lened forward.

"Oh, come on, Jacob," she complained and span around, her hair flying, as she returned to tending Dock's eyes. He sat silent and still and I felt suddenly very hot in that little room with no light or ventilation, since we'd locked up all the doors and windows.

"I'm sorry," Jacob said, "I didn't mean to get at you. God knows that's the last thing I want. It just all makes me so angry."

"I get angry too," she whispered, tenderly wiping away grit.

"I told you kids," Dock said, trying to be jovial, "get a gun. Just a little one. Or a big one. But get one. Don't let me have to tell you again."

Jacob looked at Dock like he didn't need to hear it.

"My father had a shotgun," I said in a low voice, relating a story from the days just before my father had to leave, "and when we were broken into he chased the man out of the house with it. The man ran off through the bush and my Pa fired a warnin' shot. The police got mad. They said not to fool about. They said aim low. Gun 'em down. I don't know how comfortable Pa was with that. With meanin' to kill a man."

Jacob ran a fingernail across the herringbone work of the rattan. Arial lit a couple of candles. The sulfur from the match's ignition was pungent but the golden light of the flames soon softened the room.

"You know," Dock sighed, "I remember the good old days when you could go abroad and leave your doors unlocked…"

"But its not like that anymore, is it?" Thesinger hissed.

"Jacob!" Arial said sharply.

Jacob's eyes circled to the ceiling and he rapped the knuckles of his hand on the arm of the chair.

"Oh hell, Dock. You know I don't mean a thing," he leaned forward, his elbows on his knees, and he ran both hands back through his sweaty, short hair. "I'm sorry, Tiger. Look. Let's move on. Let's get cleaned up, hey? Let's shower, put on fresh duds. We could go down to the Creek, to *Orion*. She has a generator onboard and we can have all the light and music we want. We could have a couple and fix somethin' to eat."

"I have steaks in the fridge," Arial looked at him.

"Yeah. Barbecued steak under the stars," Jacob said slowly, nodding his head. "Very civilized!"

XXI

Outside I heard the drums. The properties all around were dark because of the power cut and the trees and the water beyond were still and silent. The drumming pulsed between the palms and stroked over the flat water. It quaked from the fish market down the road. Even with the power outage the party there was still in full swing. People were forging their own noise. It was an itchy, wearisome beat.

Nerves pinched as I walked alone from the Cabana to my billet on *Orion* while the others showered shoreside. I felt eyes everywhere, watching me, sizing me up. And it made me mad that I couldn't just walk through a garden without a tingling feeling running up my neck. I remembered coming up as a boy in Pa's house covered in bars, on the windows, the doors, at the top of the flight of stairs to the bedrooms, after my father had gone. Bars everywhere. I hastened my step.

At the creek *Orion* rose singular, gleaming and improbable, her gangplank lay open as some portal to another time. Onboard, I locked the salon door fast, went below decks and powered up the generator. I latched the louvered door to my cabin and showered quickly. The hot jet of water poured over me, washing away salt and sand. I dressed in clean khakis, a polo shirt, pulled on chukka boots and climbed the spiral stairs up through the salon to the sundeck aft of the flybridge.

While I waited for the others to emerge from the Cabana, I kept watch for Caleb. He would be a damn fool to come back with us angry and the Rottweilers restive and roaming the garden. But then there's no accounting for people.

The security light illumination felt false, attended by a Florescent buzz that together took the depth out of the world and left only surfaces, as if this were all some fabulous mock up. Or perhaps it was my feelings. Beyond *Orion*, the white and black mosaic of the waves winked in the hush out in the harbor and the heads of the wild palms bowed, fanning me gently with their fronds. Above the open sundeck the stars were made blazon in a pale, blue cloud, visible so intensely tonight because our city had been laid dark.

Sitting there, waiting for Jacob, Arial and Dock, sensing the slight motion of the yacht as the current in the creek pulled against it, the drums pulsing, I thought that we could just take off in the yacht that very night. We could head out there, over the horizon, and never come back and never care. Not care that the creek was empty, that the bush would grow, the sandbar fill in and the Cabana fall apart. I could forget my papers. We could move out into new territory, be free and inhabit a world that was clean and open. There we could catch all the big game fish we could handle on a rod behind the openfisherman, there where the sandbanks rise pristine at low tide, the sand unmarked by the feet of humankind. We could breath in the peaty air of the open space and the ocean. We could look out and view no civilization save our own.

Except that the ocean out there isn't empty. It's full of people who steal your traps and boats that cruise by at night to check you out. Its full of young couples on sailboats who must shoot boarders dead to stay alive.

Except that my Pa had said that you must never give ground.

When they mounted the spiral stairs from the salon they smelled of soap. Dock climbed first. He was carrying a spear threaded through a Hawaiian sling.

"Roaches," I grinned sympathetically, patting his weapon. He gave me a wink as he took the last tread and then made a rumb line for the booze.

Arial came carefully, both hands on either stair rail. I wondered how she could ever have skin-dived all those shells with that leg. I must have been staring for she gave me a self-conscious smile and stroked her wet hair. She stumbled a bit on the last tread.

"Oops!" She fussed. "My shoes are too strappy."

Jacob was right behind. I watched him move, trying to read him, wondering was he still angry, still upset? He came up bouncing, all grins and cool exaggeration. It seemed to me that he was trying to play nonchalant. He had on a white, wicker Panama hat, for Christ's sake, with a perfect, raised groove along its crown. And he wore white leather Weejuns without sox. An unlit, thick Robusto cigar was clenched between his teeth.

At the landing he put his arm tightly about my shoulder, all bulla-bulla, and we walked locked together with his cigar pointing the way to the wet bar.

Dock was mixing mojitos, the loaded spear handy against the gunwale. I stood next to him and sliced limes into wedges while Jacob hung on to me and gazed at us both keenly.

The scent of the limes I cut was tart, the smell of rain out to sea was sweet and the soda water fizzed in the tall glasses. The drums beat on and my legs trembled slightly. A balmy breeze blew in off the ocean and ripple through my shirt, and I shuddered.

"Well, boys," Jacob grinned falsely, "wasn't that somethin'?"

"A tale worthy of the rounds," Dock agreed, mixing, still blinking and rubbing his red eyes from the sand.

"Man, I tell you, I'm just glad Arial is all right."

"Sure," I said, slicing limes.

"I'd hate a thing to happen to her."

"Hey," Dock patted him on the shoulder, "man, you don't need to tell me this, you know. You don't need to tell me."

Dock Roberts took out a butane lighter and fired it

under the tip of Jacob's cigar, charring the end evenly. Jacob drew in, the rubusto ignited and blue smoke curled. He puffed away from us, careful not to get smoke in Dock's eyes.

"I just suddenly had all these visions," Jacob admitted. "Of things happenin' to her."

"Don't sweat it. It's over. Look. Have a drink."

"Terrible things."

"I've made it extra strong for you, papa." Dock handed him the glass and gave me another wink. His frequent winks were large and meant to reassure.

"Remember Sammy's wife was raped last week and Hanna's maid the week before that?" Jacob frowned.

"Hey, Gav," Dock said, turning from the wet bar with two more drinks, "here's your own and one for Arial."

I took the cold glasses and walked to where Arial was leaning over the railing admiring the view. Paradise Island lay strangely dark were there should have been a fantastic sparkle of white and blue.

"Thinkin' of all of the shells out there?" I asked.

"Oh? I didn't see you comin' up. Is that drink for me? Thanks ever so much." She turned her back on the view and rested an arm on the top railing. I put a foot up on the bottom rung and leaned into it, holding my glass up for a silent toast.

"You boys did well this afternoon," she said, looking at the ice cubes in her glass. "You know, I was quite scared for a moment. What a horrid thing. It was such a lovely afternoon. Just me potterin' around doin' this and that. And to think the whole time that that man was here. It's terribly unsettlin', speakin' as a woman."

I nodded slowly and didn't mention that the man had been Caleb. I didn't see the point in upsetting her.

Our hands played nervously with our cocktails as we

gazed at the stars, and at Jacob and Dock busy now at the barbecue. They had the coals hot and the hickory smoke wafted across the deck mixing with the cigar aroma. The steaks sizzled on the grill, the fat spitting, the flame searing the flesh. The gorgeous fragrance of cooked meat made me tingle. I looked at my wristwatch, the hands lit up by lime green phosphorescence. It was late.

"When are you safe?" she asked. "One minute you're lookin' at the beautiful light fallin' on the trees in the garden and the blue of the sea and the next a guy comes runnin' out of the bush and bludgeons you and then you're being raped."

"Wow!"

"Sorry! That's what I was just thinkin'. I wasn't lookin' out there dreamin' about shells. I wasn't lookin' out there at all. But I should, shouldn't I? I should think about nice things, like shells. And it's a beautiful night and a wonderful view."

"Certainly is," I nodded, inhaling the salty air, still trying to achieve calm and balance.

"It's awful when you live right here and you look out there and you can't ever see it anymore. You can't see it because you're all twisted up and blinded. But I'd like to see it again, just the way it used to be," she said.

"Yes. Well. If you could just forget everythin'," I shrugged, hearing the drums and the dogs whining down on the dock, enjoying the smell of the cooking.

"I know what you mean," she sighed. "It's just nature though, isn't it? That's all it is, here, there, wherever, just nature." She bit her lip, turned and leaned over the railing and looked out to sea. I found that I liked her and that I liked listening to her talk. "Oh! Its beautiful though, isn't it?" her voice quivered.

I could see Caleb's little fishing boat out on the bloody sandbar, blocking the passage. It seemed an act of defiance, of aggression. Caleb's boat was a blot on the horizon. An ugly little thing. I thought about Jacob's wall mural in the Bahama Room, with its painting of this view empty of buildings and boats. How lovely that would be. Damn the sandbar, damn all the intruders and damn Jacob for giving in and selling off *Orion*.

"Sometimes," Arial continued, "some part of me desperately wants to leave here. To be free."

"When I was away on my travels," I said, "all I ever wanted was to come back here. I was enthralled. It held a mystery."

"Perhaps you need to be enchanted before you can be disenchanted," she smiled.

"Yes. I was so very enchanted."

"Grub's ready," Jacob called out from the grill just as I was about to suggest a long yacht trip on *Orion*. The meat was beautifully flamed, the fat at the edges charcoaled but pink at the center. It was served tender, red, with a spicy jerk sauce. My mouth was wet with saliva.

We ate in silence, perched at the ends of the deck chairs. I shook with anticipation, sawed into the flesh. Grease covering my lips. The fatty leftovers and bones Jacob took to the edge. He whistled for the dogs, then threw the remains onto the grass. I could hear the dogs snarling and snapping.

When we were finished Jacob set a canvas bag on his lap. He gazed at each of us in turn, the twinkle in his eye telling me he was up to something. Unbuckling the bag, he reached inside and pulled out an old square box, which he set on the deck. He unlatched the lid and swung it open to expose a turntable. I watched in amazement as he pulled a handle out of the box and slotted this into the side, pulled out an old record sleeve, slipped out the black disk and placed it on the turntable. He worked a small brush over the surface lovingly to clean off lint, cranked the handle, and the record started to spin. The needle touched the vinyl, crackled, hissed and bosa nova played.

We leaned back to listen. Jacob sat cross-legged, in his white linen trousers and open-neck Cuban shirt, his cigar smoke curling about him, the ash long. The white whicker Panama hat was perched forward. His Rolex glinted in the deck light and his white leather slip-on shoes hung off his toes.

But it was difficult to enjoy the music with the drumming coming from the market. You could just about force the intrusive noise from your mind, but then they started letting off fireworks again. They were not particularly spectacular fireworks. They just rose on a trail of thin, twisted smoke, screeching, and then smacked open in a shower of white sparks. Cheap. Nothing to watch and the evening was ruined.

"Oh hell!" Jacob spat, jumped from the deck chair and strode to the gunwale. Behind him his garden stretched up the ridge toward the little Cabana, the trees standing in black relief against the deep blue of the night sky with so many stars. Before him the creek opened up to the view of the small fishing boat and the water's of Montagu Bay that dazzled momentarily in the firework's glare.

"Damn drums!" Dock shuddered.

"Mix up another round," Jacob ordered as he strode back to his canvas bag. He pulled out wire, plugged an end into the record player uncoiled it along the floor and disappeared down the spiral stairs. When he came back up he cranked the record player, lifted the needle onto the vinyl disk and suddenly music was blasting out of the yacht's hidden speakers.

"Jacob!" Arial called, a finger immediately stuck in each

ear. Her look wiped the grin of her husband's face. "It's too loud!"

He yanked the needle off with a terrible scraping. I bolted upright at the horrific clawing.

Arial's face was stony as she got up, limped to the spiral stairs and disappeared below deck. Jacob watched her but didn't move. All I could hear after that were the drums.

I couldn't help but think, as I gazed around the company, that perhaps we were pretending. That the ceremony of the evening, the herb-marinated meat, our camaraderie around the coals as we roasted the joint, where somehow all a cover-up.

"Don't you think," I asked Jacob after a lag, "that maybe somethin' should be done? About this noise, I mean? Surely there's some law? You know, disturbing the peace? They can't just carry on like that, can they?"

He didn't answer right away and I felt suddenly stupid for having asked at all.

Finally he sighed. "I have to be careful about what I say, about speakin' out, about politics. It's not like back in my daddy's day. The more time goes by the more wary I become. There's too much at stake, and too much to fear in terms of reprisals. Victimization. Now, at election time, I just shut up my mouth and send in the check."

This wasn't what I'd expected from a son of Charlie Thesinger. Maybe he sensed that because he snorted loudly, leant forward, and we all leant forward with him to conspire.

"You know," he said to Dock and I, "I stand out on my piazza at night and I listen to that blasted music. Day and bloody night. I stand motionless, transfixed, and listen. It's an act of aggression. What else could it be played so loud? It's territorial. I have grown up with the sound. Internalized the threat. Considered the promised violence, the great human wave that will come for me. Maybe Gavin's right, maybe something should be done."

He paused for a moment and I tingled. His eyes lost their twinkle and became hard, cold, such that the mood changed, lost its humor, however ill-mannered that humor might have been. Jacob wasn't faking anymore. I saw him come into focus and the Panama hat, the stub of the rubusto cigar, were now solid things, invested with the weight of personal history. Dock was nodding slowly, the glass of his turtle-shell lenses catching the barbecue light. I stopped looking at them and looked instead at my hands and found that my hands were trembling.

XXII

I was practicing knotting an actual bow tie. My Sweeting's Boat Basin cap was on my head backwards, keeping my hair out of my face while I got down to the business of it. The black satin tongues of the tie crossed over in my hands about my neck. A book illustrating how a gentleman should dress lay open on the cot and I leaned into my billet's little pear glass while I glanced back to the page.

A clip-on lay in the drawer, but I didn't want to use it. I preferred to tie the real item. Working the awkward bat-wing strip of cloth under my chin was difficult. I had to practice tying the bow on my thigh before I got it right. The book's chapter on bow ties was awkwardly placed and the weight of the binding kept turning the page, hiding the stage-by-stage drawings I relied on.

I arranged the awkward knot under my spread collar, my thumb got caught in the bulbous silk and when I managed something it was tied at a diagonal to my face. I tugged it into some recognizable shape, my forehead beaded with sweat.

Then I pulled on my Bermudas and fastened opal cufflinks and studs in my white dress shirt. My black dinner jacket had piqued lapels. I threw it over my shoulder and decided to return on deck, find a drink, and survey the preparations for the following evening's grand party.

It was sultry topside, out of the air-conditioning. Humid and unbreathable, the kind of island heat that sits on you and doesn't move. The late sun sat radiating through a thin haze, biting into me, burning. Storms ringed the east.

Tomorrow night, I thought, it will be full moon and the mutton snapper will run. The fishermen will go out to make a haul. They will line up at the edge of the bar by the deep water and hand line with fifty-pound test. I would miss going out.

The patois of the Haitian laborers carried across the vacant creek. On shore, they were putting up a marquee and strings of colored lights from one palm to the next, creating a sense of carnival. The Haitians, dressed in matching beige jump suits, went quiet when they saw me. I heard the clink of boxed glassware and leaned over the gunwale to look up toward the Cabana to see it all. It was very grand and I hoped it would go off well.

I sauntered down the gangplank and up to the Cabana bar and decided to get oiled for the evening. I'd learned to make the perfect martini; chilled gin with a dash of vermouth over the top to give it nose, extra dry, a lemon peal rubbed around the rim of the glass, the drink served neat.

I was just feeling pleased with myself when I noticed Clint Knowles coming across the lawn, wearing his usual

Cuban open collar shirt and large, black shades.

"Well, hullo," he said, "if it isn't University Boy."

"Hullo, Clint. Still sore?"

"Sore? Me? No." But the way he said it was exaggerated and I could tell he was sore. I knew he wanted what he called "his crawfish". He was half-cut and breathing rum fumes on me.

"Aren't you gonna say anythin'?" he asked.

"I guess I don't feel like talkin'."

"I don't want to put you to any trouble."

I shrugged like I didn't give a damn. And to tell the truth I didn't, now that Clint was no longer on Jacob's "One-Of-Us" list. I didn't have anything particularly against him, I just figured he should leave well enough alone.

He cut me with his eye and he was sweating from the booze.

"Boy," he said, "those are some fancy threads."

"It's a real bow tie."

"No kiddin'? A real one? Say, that's real fancy."

He was a bloody insect all right. I smirked, imagining his antenna and swiveling eyes.

"What do you want here, Clint?"

"Well jeez. Host of the season award to Gavin Blake. Man, I just came for my crawfish. Where they at?"

"What crawfish?"

"The one's I busted my back end boatin' and campin' for!"

"Now Clint, you know these are Jacob's own. You know that was the deal. All the crawfish are for the party."

"Just tell me where the crawfish are at, Blake."

"You're drunk."

The way I saw it he had guessed Jacob wouldn't be around at the Cabana and so he had come over to take what he could carry. Well, he hadn't figured on me. I felt an obligation to protect things and I smirked, thinking of the first evening when I'd met Clint Knowles and his sneer, that he wouldn't live down this way if you paid him.

"Who's the cockroach now, Clint?"

"What?" He was most taken back.

"I said who's the snake in the grass, boy?"

"Where's the crawfish at, Blake?"

I was about to tell him to go to blazes when I noticed his tote bag slung over one shoulder. It was the bag he kept his handgun in. The realization made me cold and I held my tongue. He was looking at me with purpose despite the booze, and I wondered what it would take for a man in that kind of mood to just shoot me. I studied the canvas bag for the outline of a weapon. Clint never even said a word about it. He just stood there with his feet set apart and his chin thrust up.

"I said where's the crawfish at, Blake?"

"Oh, hell Clint…"

"I mean to get what's mine! I came for my things!"

"Jacob won't be happy."

"I'm not happy!"

I took off my cap and wiped the sweat from my brow as a ploy to hide my face. I didn't want him to guess what I was thinking. I had about a second to make up my mind. Could I rush him, knock him down before he could get to his gun? Was it worth getting shot over a handful of crawfish?

I pointed with my cap toward the place where the coolers full of crawfish tails were being stored. Clint followed my direction. His head wobbled and he smirked.

"Enjoy the party, Blake," he sneered and turned, a swinging gate in his step. When he got to the cooler he lifted the lid of the first, and studied the contents. Then grabbed a handle and dragged the cooler full of crawfish toward his Jeep.

"Tell me, Blake," he called back. "Why d'ya think you can ever be one of us? How's it you think you belong in your fancy pant suit there when all you got is a foreign education and a boat basin hat?"

XXIII

I drove my truck through the purple evening toward *Bangalay*. The view flashed by, visible in the corridors between the old colonial properties. The sea out there was emerald below a featured sky that lay low and gun-metal to the horizon line, with slanted iron rain to the east and the heads of the last heavy clouds burning as the bonfires of a distant war in the deepening dusk.

I drove with urgency, wanting to get to the Thesingers' homestead and tell Jacob about Clint's theft. I wondered what the hell Jacob would think of it and hoped he wouldn't blame me.

After checking the drive for anyone who might be lurking in the shadows to ambush me, I pulled in. I pressed the buzzer and stared straight at the camera so they'd know it was me and waited for the security gate to swing in.

Pulling on my dinner jacket and touching my tie gently, self-consciously, hoping that it had not come undone, I waited at the door. I looked forward to the following evening when I could dress up for real.

Jacob opened up. He wore khaki linen shorts and an open neck short-sleeve shirt. It was dark blue with a white palm frond pattern. His nose crinkled. I got the sense that something was wrong. The mood was tense and uptight.

"Nice tux," he said, looking me up and down. I knew immediately I was a dope and wished I'd changed. "Come in. We're in the Bahama Room. Go straight down."

"What's up?" I asked.

"Just go down," he said with finality.

As I entered the Bahama Room the icy air moved across my hot face and I could hear the soft whir of the air-conditioner. Barely perceptible static came over the speakers.

Roberts was slouched in a leather club chair, his arms folded across his chest, lips jutting. A glass of Campari stood untouched on the side table, the ice thinned to slivers. His glasses were on the table, and he was staring into some middle ground. He didn't hail me.

Jacob's swaggering nonchalance was that either of a man fully in control of things or one tossing his cares to the wind. I couldn't tell which. He threw himself down into one of the club chairs and sharply scissored his legs, the top leg bouncing, the sole of his white slip-on slapping his hard-skinned heel.

"So. Gavin. Pull up a pew," he said, indicating that I sit. I did so in front of the great mural, took out the handkerchief that dressed my breast pocket, dabbed the sweat off my face and waited for whatever was about to happen.

"You know," he continued, "we were just talkin' about you."

"Really?"

"Yes. Really. Do you perhaps have anythin' you want to tell me?" his eyebrows went up and his angular face lengthened. He glanced at Arial, who perched on the edge of her seat, her rigid back to me. Her nose in profile was slightly elevated. She did not greet me either.

"Well, actually, yes," I said, leaning forward and

putting my elbows onto my knees, ready to tell him about the situation down at the Cabana. I was checked by Jacob's exaggerated "I see" expression made first for my benefit and then for Arial's. I could see her mascara blurred in tear tracks down her cheeks.

"Oh, do go on," Jacob gestured theatrically and I found myself swallowing.

Dock's expression came into focus, his glasses back on, the glass magnifying the eyes that watched me. His hands were together, his fingertips touched his lips.

"Eh, I just…came to tell you that…that Clint showed at the Cabana," I said nervously.

"Clint?" Jacob screwed his face up.

"Yeah. Clinton Knowles. He came down by me at the Cabana. Said he was lookin' for "his crawfish"…"

"You didn't give him any?"

"I told him they were all for the party."

"Good."

I realized he was getting the wrong idea and played with one of my laces while I tried to figure out how to tell him.

"He was…insistent," I said.

"Oh hell!"

"Just one cooler."

"You ass!"

"What could I do?"

"Boy, what do I pay you for? Hey?" He sprang out of his chair, leaning forward with his arms wide. "It's your job to look after things for me. We made that clear from day one. Day one! And you ask me what could you do? Stop him! That's what you could do!"

"But…how?"

"For God's sake! You tell him to get lost! And if he

carries on then you put an end to it. You understand me? You deal with him! Physically! You deal with it!"

"But he had a gun."

"A gun?"

"You remember…on the island…that night…when he shot up the snake. Remember?"

"You mean to tell me Clint raided my garden and took my property wieldin' a gun?"

"Well, not exactly…"

"How exactly?"

"I never actually saw the gun, not really, he just had his tote bag with him, you know, the one he carries his gun in."

"You got held up with a tote bag?"

I swallowed.

"Jesus Christ! Those were my crawfish, man! My crawfish! And you let that boy Clint saunter in and walk out of my place with 'em?"

I didn't have anything further to say. I just looked at my hands palm up in my lap.

"Sorry boss."

"Sorry hell."

Arial sighed and I sucked on my lower lip and wondered what this was all about. A few crawfish couldn't be responsible for so much anger.

"Well, at least you tell me this," Jacob clipped, hitching up his shorts and swilling his whiskey until it slopped. "You get me, man? At least you tell me this!"

"Oh Jacob," Arial pleaded. "Please. It doesn't matter."

"No Arial, you're wrong. It does matter. I pay him. He's my boy and he's supposed to tell me things. He's supposed to keep me informed. Isn't that right, Gavin? Hey?"

"Sure," I managed.

"Then why didn't you tell me about drivin' my wife

down to that filthy fish market?"

I was at a loss.

"You took her down there. That mornin' we were headin' out to the cays and you were late. That's where you were. Behind my back. Don't tell me you didn't!"

"What's wrong with that? It's just a fish market. She asked me to take her and I took her, so what's the big deal?"

"They attacked her is what!"

"Jacob! You're blowin' it out of proportion."

"Well what do you call it when a woman with a limp goes down there and a full grown man curses her and runs her out? I call it assault!"

"Jacob!" she screeched and covered her face with her hands.

I was suddenly worried that I'd made a horrid mistake. I'd never told Arial that the fisherman she had gone to get shells from was the same Caleb who we'd chased off the property that evening. I hoped Caleb hadn't done some damn awful thing and felt it would all be my fault if he had. I should have told her. Bloody stupid! But then Caleb had never seen her.

"Wait," I said, trying to stay calm. "Back up here. What happened?"

"She got attacked is what!" Jacob insisted.

"I went down by that way lookin' for that fisherman, Caleb, the one who was goin' to dive up shells for me," she said, defiant.

"And he attacked you?" I asked.

"I go down there first light to catch him right when he pulls up to the dock. And he tells me he has plenty shells and I better have brought his money. I told him I was happy to pay, of course. So he hefts this net bag up onto the wooden cleanin' table, up ends it and sends all of these shells spillin'."

She looked around at the three of us. Dock rubbed a hand nervously over his mouth and chin. Jacob stared into his drink letting her tell the story so she went right on.

"Some were lovely shells. Shells I've never seen in my life except in photographs and in the marine park."

"That sounds good," I shrugged.

"They were illegal Gavin. Protected."

"What? Shells?"

"They're endangered species he fished out. And he must have gone down to the park, where else? There were so many. And there was no chance they were dead or anythin' like that. There were simply too many. He must have taken 'em alive and then cleaned 'em. I am so angry. How could he do such a thing?"

"But you asked him to," I said evenly.

"I didn't! I most certainly didn't. I wanted dead, collectable shells. Not live endangered ones. But that's not the end of it."

"What happened?"

"Well, he wanted to be paid! Can you believe it?"

"Well, that sounds reasonable. Honest toil and all that."

"Gavin. I'm not goin' to pay for illegal goods. And I told him so. I told him you must be jokin', I'm not payin' you for this illegal stuff. He told me not to try that. He said we'd an agreement and he wouldn't barter, the price was agreed. I told him I was fine with that, but the goods where not the agreed goods. Shells is shells, he says. I got mad, I told him he had done a terrible thing and that he should feel ashamed, that he had no right to take 'em."

She was now facing me and leaning with her elbows on her knees and her hands gesturing and I thought that this whole country was full of people claiming their personal rights and wrongs. Clint, Caleb, Jacob and me and now Arial.

"So, he starts throwin' his arms up in the air like he's preachin' some sermon, sayin' that no one can take the sea from him, that God has provided all that is in the sea, and that its man's bounty to take as he will. He says that he will take any shell or any fish from any reef anyplace, anytime, and let any man try to stop him. And then he said that God had ways of dealin' with sinners like me, that I would be cast out, struck down. He said the Lord is comin' and justice will be visited upon me." She shook her head. "I was speechless. Here was this man breakin' the law and he's makin' out like I've done some wrong. He kept demandin' that I pay him what I owe him and naturally I refused. So he says, go carry your fuckin' skink ass bitch self. I felt like I was in a foreign place, it was so alien and strange. I didn't know what to do," Arial cried.

"That's outrageous!" I said.

"Damn right it is!" Jacob slapped his leg. "We can't let him get away with it!"

"What're you goin' to do?" She looked up.

"Teach him a lesson's what!"

"Oh no! Please don't!"

"I can handle it. I'll march down there now!"

"He's only a fisherman on the beach. What's the big deal?" she sobbed.

"What's the big deal? What's the big deal? I'm sick and tired of this, is what! I'm a man, for cryin' out loud! A man! And this is my home! How dare they come in here! All the time!" He banged his fist on the chair arm. "You try and make somethin' nice and they trample on it, they just want to plunder you, rape your wife, and when you try to stop 'em you're the bad guy. That's what I'm sick to death of! I'm sick

GARTH BUCKNER

to death of always bein' typecast as the bad guy!"

"Oh Jacob," Arial choked, "why can't we just leave?"

"Don't say it, Arial! Don't." He raised a finger sharply.

"But you know I want to," she pleaded.

"No! This is our country."

"We could put *Bangalay* up for sale," she said.

"Never! It was my grandfather's house. He built it. My father was born here in the birthin' room."

"Oh Jacob, it's just a house."

"It's our heritage, Arial," he said, and now it was his turn to plead.

"We could sell it and live on *Orion*. We could leave this awful, terrible place and just head out there, out to sea, and never, never come back," she sobbed.

His chest was heaving and he tried to regain his composure. But his voice cracked as he spoke. "Now... Arial...you know...that's just romantic nonsense."

She was teary-eyed, her breath uneven, her mouth drooling with saliva. I was embarrassed.

Jacob gripped the table and tried to speak softly. "You know we have too much invested here. Too much of ourselves. Too much at stake financially. Sweetheart, we would risk losing everythin'. Everythin'!"

"So we stay and are forced to play their game?"

"Not just their game, but the game behind their game."

"We become corrupted?"

Jacob looked at her with such terrible longing. I felt my throat go tight. I knew Arial was right, and not just about Jacob. It was the same for me. It was the same for all of us, I supposed.

When she continued her voice was very small and halting. "We...stay here...and we try...to keep things...just the way they were. But…we are not the way we were…are we? We have become such horrible people…with such horrid ideas. I don't think I like what I am." Then she fled the room.

Jacob slapped his palms on his thighs and went after her. The door slammed. I could hear his voice receding down the corridor as he called her name.

I exhaled, looked over at Dock who nodded knowingly, as if we all knew the reasons for this scene and it had come as no surprise. Personally I was stumped.

Dock shook his head, got up with exaggerated effort, the gold medallion glinting, and labored over to the bar with his glass full of warm Campari.

"Gavin, you want a cool drink? I need a cool drink," he said, then his eyes widened in alarm at the clamor of shouting coming through the house.

"Cats and Dogs," he said. "What's your poison?"

"Whiskey?"

He discarded his untouched drink, stood the glass up on the bar and placed a clean tumbler next to it. The ubiquitous ice bucket stood full beside him and he dropped a handful of cubes into each glass, pulled the stopper from the bottle and splashed in the Scotch. It shone gold in the light as it settled about the popping ice. I thought it might be a good idea to shift the subject onto Clint.

"Clint?" Dock sauntered over and handed me my glass, then relaxed back in his club chair with his own red concoction. "Damn! That's one son of a hog for true. He has it comin'. Think we should take him out?"

"Sure," I joked, happy for the off color humor. "Pay the Jamaicans a couple dollars and they'll chap him up."

"They'll plant a few bags of cocaine on the body to implicate him in somethin'. That always shames the family."

"Hot damn," I toasted, raising my glass in mock salute.

"Seriously though. That bitch needs a reminder."

I went tight, feeling like an accessory to some future gambit. "You don't really mean it though, hey, Dock?"

"Shit bulla! You kill me."

"I just…" and then I shook my head. "Dock. You've been friends with Jacob a long time. Why's he so upset?"

"Why? Man, I thought you knew."

"Must'a missed it."

"Well, because of Arial's accident."

"Accident?"

He sighed and smoothed out his shirt. "Okay. Jacob's upset because of an accident she had, years ago. An accident, or, as he always insists on callin' it, an "incident". An incident with a fisherman."

"Not Caleb?"

"Well now, I wouldn't know who this Caleb is."

"Is that how she got her limp? Because of this incident?"

"She was run over by a fishin' boat while snorkelin'. You know how she's so mad about shells. Well she was down in the cays with Jacob and me, divin' 'em up, when she got hit. Jacob was on deck and saw it all. Saw her wave at 'em as the boat came at her. I guess they didn't check, they went right over her. She tried to dive, which saved her. The blow knocked her unconscious and, well, the prop mangled her leg. Jacob thought she was dead. The boat stopped and its crew looked back to see. They saw her floatin' face down at the surface. One of 'em pointed, that's how we know. Then they sped off. Unbelievable. Totally unbelievable."

"You mean they didn't offer any assistance?"

"They were gone. They weren't checkin'. Jacob, to his credit, he kept a clear head. He dove right in, swam to Arial and turned her over so she wouldn't drown. There was all this blood in the water from her leg. I was below deck fixin' another, you know," he held his glass of Campari up and made the ice tinkle. "First I heard of the accident was his screamin'. Needless to say I came up topside wonderin' what on God's earth was happenin'. I wasn't prepared to see her bleedin' and on death's door. Shit!" He paused and made the ice tinkle again.

"I mean, I'd all my canvas unfurled. It was a sunny day. I was piss drunk, hey! I had to do the best I could for her when we got her onboard. I had to make do. Luckily Jacob raised a seaplane on the VHF. It was doin' a safari with some tourists a few cays down. That boy flew right over and airlifted her to the hospital in Miami." He leaned back in his chair and crossed his feet on the ottoman. His brow was perspiring and he patted his close-shaven dome with a cocktail napkin.

"My God," I muttered.

"She was a lucky girl, our Arial. And unlucky. Speakin' as her doctor, and maybe I shouldn't say, but her injuries make it harder for her to swim, but not impossible. I think she's just afraid, poor thing. She was such a good diver. A little fish. Always comin' up with the most extraordinary shells. I don't know how she found 'em, but she did. Now she doesn't dive."

I exhaled, puffing my cheeks. We were silent for a moment and I took a swallow of whiskey. I saw the mural with the blockade-runner stealing through the night, and the mate up at the bow with his lantern, peering ahead into the dark.

"I think," Dock continued thoughtfully in his baritone, "that it was an accident. Well, started as an accident. What turned it into an "incident" for Jacob was them not helpin'. He says they had no decency. They didn't care. That's the truth. They just didn't want to bother. Knowing Jacob the way I do, I'd say that's the unforgivable part. He could excuse the accident, but not the leavin' the scene. Maybe he's been carryin' that around. Of course, he couldn't go after 'em the way he would have liked because he had to stay and keep Arial alive. So I suppose he never got any satisfaction."

XXIV

We don't have the energy to feed all our hungers. We choose one and try to make it perfect. One thing to polish. One thing to shine. A single path to keep to over the turmoil of years. That we have just this one choice is intimidating. Some never decide. Thesinger had chosen his path. He knew who he was and I envied that. But once you begin to feed that lonely burn, it becomes law.

Later on that evening, he and I sat silently in the Bahama Room. Dock had said goodnight. Arial never returned. Beyond the open French doors the palms swayed in black relief against the blue background of night. Clustered lights illuminated the view across the harbor. The lights of the hotels, the waterfront homes, the dock lights and navigation lights, all a multitude of color and luminosity, even so late it was quite a spectacle. To the east, where the harbor widened to the open sea, the moon, one night short of full, sat fat and salmon hued above the india ink waters.

I tried to be part of it. I was kicking back, a drink at hand, my bat wing bow tie pulled out so that the tongues hung loose. But the view did not move me as it once had. My neck was tight, my bowels in a knot. Jacob sat brooding. The only sounds were of the chime of ice cubs on cut crystal and the hum of ceiling fans.

I wanted to tell Jacob how sorry I was about Arial. How awful it was for someone to run her over and not even help. But I didn't say anything for fear of apearinging self-serving.

"You know," he said at last, his voice surprisingly cracking. "I've never gone out fishin' and come back skunked." He looked at me, unconsciously scratched a scab on his elbow from his fall at the fish market.

Abruptly everything went dark, the table lamps in the Bahama Room went out, and the gleaming windows of the hotels and the bulkhead lights across the harbor went out. Jacob disappeared. The view out the French doors collapsed into a void. The hum of the fans lowered in pitch as the blades slowed and came to a halt. Our world dissolved, every sight and sound manmade came to stop. For a moment I was lost, frozen in my seat, the leather my only contact.

"Is it too much to ask for to have electric power?" Jacob said, seemingly to himself

I could make out his outline. He was sitting bolt upright in his chair. I felt his tension. He was ready to leap—but at what? Only the vanishing of things. He was already too late. The things were gone.

"Fuckin' hell," he hissed and I heard him stand and stride out the open doors, down the piazza steps.

The view had changed. The red glow of the moon splintered across the wave caps. At the end of the garden, out in the water upon the bar, I could just make out the little fishing boat in the moonlight. The calls of nature had taken over, the soft call of insects and the surfing rustle of the palms.

Then the generator ignited and the lights came back on. Jacob came back, and behind him I could see that the hotel generators were kicking in.

"Come on," he said to me.
"What's up?"
"We're goin' for a ride."

His Continental cruised down The Eastern Road as we headed west through the dark. The engine whistled and the hood of the car chewed up the center of the lane. The humid air riffled through the open window and pressed against my face. It felt good to drive at night on the empty road. It was our road and we knew every turn.

"Where we headed chief?" I asked.
"You'll see. It's a surprise."

I raised my eyebrows and gazed out beyond the endless walls at the raven gardens that rushed past and the hardened homes reduced to outlines, at the trees without order that hung down low over the road and I wondered at our destination.

Jacob steered the big car off the road and onto the broken limestone area next to the fish market. He parked behind a large seagrape tree whose bulk secreted us from the road.

The marketplace's wooden shacks stood empty and the few boats pulled up above the tide line lay still. Everything was quiet except for the rustle of rats gnawing through garbage.

Jacob got out and I followed. No one was playing drums that night. It was even beautiful back lit by the moon. Walking toward the market I trod on the litter of burnt firecrackers and crunched broken beer bottles. The memory of the other night was vivid--Jacob falling, the crawfish spilling and the crowd pressing in not to help but to steal. I remembered the frustration of being without recourse. Remembrances flooded back of the shanties and the filth of my travels. Shaking, I knew that I had not got anywhere, I was not home. Was I still out there in the lost world? I searched for Caleb's stall, but I was unable to distinguish it from the others. I shivered. Why had we come?

I heard the trunk open and turned to see Jacob pull out a couple of gas tanks.

"Hey!" he said. "You want to help out with these?"

"We out of gas?"

"No man, we came here to take care of things."

"What things?"

He nodded toward the market. I looked at it and then back at him.

"Hey, very funny. You're always on at me about my university days so what about this? Some fraternity gag? Hazin'?"

"I'm goin' to take care of this once and for all," he winked, leveraged a can in each hand and lumbered toward the wooden shacks with a comic and almost lunatic swagger.

"Come on," he whispered back to me. We'd started whispering, and he waved that I should follow.

I stood there, watching him go. As he approached the stalls, a small group of mongrel dogs, their ribcages severe, broke skittishly from under cutting tables and spirited out into the dark. Jacob jumped perceptibly, then turned back to me smiling sheepishly.

"Hey, Gavin!"

"I can't," I whispered back.

"What? Why?"

My stomach twisted. I leaned to one side, my pulse thumping in my head as I realized the enormity of what he intended.

"I can't do it. I mean, that's people's things, their livin', you can't just burn it!"

"Oh come now. The whole market's illegal." He waved his hand at it, meaning everything. "Don't you see? They're criminals! Crooks! They have no right to be here!"

"So, get an injunction, or somethin'."

"An injunction? What planet do you live on? It's all payoffs and corruption, man. They don't give a shit! We have to do this ourselves. We have to do this my way. Want your home to be overridden? You asked me the other night what could be done. Well, it's up to us."

"Hold on there now…"

"Hey! This is the right thing to do." Jacob walked back toward me. "I mean, never mind the fact these people have no business license, never mind the fact that they never pay a cent in tax, this market is a health hazard, all those fish guts and conch slop sittin' out in the hot sun at low tide and then gettin' carried down to the bathin' beach when the tide comes up. What kind of bacteria do you think's in there? People get sick, Gavin. People die. Look, there's no runnin' water, there's no toilet. Where do you think these guys go to the toilet? What do your university ideas have to say about that? It's disgustin'. It's a public health hazard and a blot on the environment and it needs to be cleaned up!"

He had worked himself up into a right mood. My heart was wrung with sympathy and pity for him. He was passionate, juggling self-preservation and self-delusion with high intention, the two becoming blurred in flight. I would rescue him. I'd rescue us both.

"Is this because of Arial? The incident?"

"And what about Arial?" he snapped, breaking off and striding back toward me, a finger pointed. "Hey? Did you stop to think about her? You know, I bet the fishermen who hurt her, the ones who ran her down, I bet they're from right here!"

"Don't do it," my whispering was strained.

His action loomed large. Abominable, surly? My moral compass sort equilibrium and I wondered why we were whispering. There was no one around to hear us. I suppose its just one of those conspiratorial things. When you conspire you whisper. Except I wanted no part in it. I stood up straight and told him aloud, "Don't do it."

"Hey, I thought you were one of us?" He turned and started sloshing the gas onto one of the wood shacks. I could smell the lovely scent of it. Some of the petrol ran down the ramp where Jacob had fallen and it glistened in a vivid paisley rainbow in the sea. If he threw a match the sea would catch a fire. "Aren't you with us, Gavin?"

"Don't do it, Jacob," I warned.

"Who the hell said you could call me Jacob?"

I stared in disbelief as he worked his way down the line of shacks, dousing them all. At the very end of the first line he was barely visible, all I could make out was the white of his shoes flashing in the moonlight as he strode. They were brilliant blurs, crossing and dancing, spinning, looping in the dark.

His preparations complete, he walked back up the ramp toward me, huffing slightly from the effort. Pulling out a matchbox he dragged a matchstick across the side, igniting it. I decided it was all a farce, a sham. He would never follow through. Then he turned and tossed the match. The flame ran fast and blue across the broken concrete and blazed up the sides of a stall. The old wood caught abruptly. Ribbons of fire swelled and gorged in a crimson blooming. I was made breathless by it. My cheeks roasted and my eyelids shut against the brilliant heat.

When I opened them Thesinger was swaying slightly,

a silhouette backlit by the fire. The flames were burning into the canvas roofs of the stalls and taking up twisting bits of cloth into the sky. Blood ballooned in my temples. I saw him go to douse more stalls, watched the ponderous immensity of his moves, the carrying out of a kind of ritual cleansing. He walked with a studied, mythic stride near the conflagration as if conducting some sacrament and I went to stop him. I reached out and grabbed the arm that held the can.

"The fuck are you doin'? Hey! Hey, Blake! We need to get this done before someone comes."

Looking him in the eye I gritted my teeth and leaned my weight backward to stop him advancing on the next line of shacks. His lips went tight and I saw the square fist come at me. The punch landed on my jaw, a knuckle catching the cartilage of my nose. I went reeling onto the concrete and lay there stunned, until focus collapsed back to heavily salted breath and righted sight. Then came the sweeping rush of confusion. This is silly. A mere lapse on Thesinger's part. But anguish shook me. Through spots I saw him burn the last shacks. Beyond him was a vision of fire. I was fuzzy, distant, and, oddly, I thought it was all very pretty. Even the sea was gorgeously alight, the water curling with tongues of short purple flame.

"Oh, for God's sake, don't look that way. Get up and get in the car, will you," Thesinger complained.

I propped myself up, wiping blood from my lip, touching my nose to feel if anything was broken. I gaped at the fire and then at his car and back to him. He stood with the flames raging behind, the empty fuel cans under his arm. He reached out an open hand to me.

"We've got to stick together," he said.

"I'll walk," I said, ignoring his outstretched hand.

"Don't be an ass. Someone's goin' to come lookin' and if they find you in your bloody tux on the street they'll take care of you in the bush. You want bottle glass in the face? You want to beg for your life?"

"I wouldn't be in this if you hadn't burnt 'em," I said, still sitting on the ground looking up at him.

"You know what you are, Blake? When it comes down to the crunch, you're a pussy."

I stared up at him in disbelief.

"We have to fight for what's ours. And your laws, your university ideas, they don't exist. Got it? They do not exist!" I hated the way he talked about me. I hated to think he might be right.

"All there is is who's biggest, Blake. And you know what? I'm biggest. Now, mount up 'cos we're rollin'!"

I could hear voices, the coming yowlings and people running down the road. There wasn't time for talk. As much as I hated it, I got in the passenger seat and we were off up The Eastern Road.

XXV

I went to pay the bribe. I entered Immigration, with all the cash I'd earned from working on *Orion*, to "facilitate" matters. My heart pounded as I trod the faded linoleum tiles under the chipped panels of the suspended ceiling and florescent lights. I was desperately afraid that I was doing the wrong thing, that I was revealing myself and making a bad choice. Sitting in the waiting room with the Haitians, I didn't announce my presence. Finally an Immigration officer sauntered over, her features the very bow of arrogance.

"You does want to see someone?" She stood above me yet she raised her head so high that her eyes peered down from slits. Apparently I warranted the entire face.

"Yes."

She turned and walked off and I understood somehow that I'd been summoned. We went down a hall passed photocopied announcements for church groups and union meetings. We passed secretaries reading the tabloids or talking on the phone. The officer kicked open a door with the toe of her stiletto, pointed to a yellow plastic chair and walked off.

In the room a window-hung air conditioner hummed and a Formica desk was piled with manila folders tied neatly with string. A number of Chinese government magazines littered the side table next to an International Development Bank report on farm subsidies and quarterly publications of the ILO.

I was sweating between my legs. I wondered if the officer had locked me in. I breathed long and slow to calm myself. I told myself that they were not coming for me. Suddenly the door flew open and I jumped.

"This him?" a new lady shouted down the hall, pointing a long press-on nail at me. The nail was painted with stripes like on racing cars. She walked in sucking on a straw in a fast food wax cup. Her large body was wedged into a tight pantsuit. She lowered herself into her chair and it stretched to accommodate her girth.

"All right then. How you is?"

Say something about God, I thought.

"Thank God for life," I exclaimed.

"And praise Him for his mercy," she smiled. "You wanted to see me? I only got a few minutes for you."

"Thank you. Very kind indeed. Its about my citizenship application...you see, I was born here...my mother's family, er, were here for generations and I was hopin' to..."

"Your father was foreign?" She accused.

"Ah, yes, from Florida."

"An' they was married?"

"Of course."

"Child, if they was not married, if you was illegitimate, then you would have got your mommy's citizenship."

I was stunned at the strange parceling out of rights.

"But I is against that on account of my Church. They should make these boys marry these girls or castrate 'em. I'm not for playin'. You know what I mean? But all these politicians is men and you know how men does go. All they want is the coochy. You know what they thinkin' when they write law. But I know you different. You ain't married right? You got good hair."

"Thank you."

"Now I could get you straight. Don't you worry, sweetness. They call me "Mother" an' I goin' to look after you."

"How does the...process work?"

"You make one little donation to prove your citizenship. Only one couple dollar. You won't notice it."

"I helped out the air sea rescue association."

"Love, this charity is personal to me."

"Of course."

"You want to make your contribution now?"

I wondered if it were a trap. Was I being taped? Was this a sting operation? Swallowing took an effort. My glands were up.

My money was divided in halves, one in each pocket

and I pulled out the crisp, folded bill notes from one. Her eyes went sweet and she blushed. I had the feeling of asking a girl I did not know to dance, the same excitement and uncertainty. The fear of rejection.

But I had to do this. After Jacob had burnt the market down I felt terribly exposed. I knew the double standard. Jacob had said one night: It is important in life not only to have good standards but also sound double standards. No place follows this advice more soberly than this island. If caught, Jacob would be cautioned strongly by a senior police officer, he would donate to a charity of his choice and the matter would be hushed up. An illegal like me would be deported. Then there was the fact that *Orion* was to be sold. I needed security. I needed my papers. I placed the fold of hundreds into her hand.

"Oh, that's very kind. You're a Christian."

"That's, ah, well, just the start."

"A down payment?"

"With the balance on completion."

"I got your file right here, Mr. Blake. Now you hold on. I got to see a man. Child, I goin' to Miami this weekend and you can pay me the other half direct. Wait out here. Mother comin' back."

She led me out into the hall and asked the secretary to make sure she looked after me right, then marched off. Suddenly I was a person worthy of politeness and attention. The secretary's eyes shone. She giggled. I felt the sickness that grips you when you are afraid the police will come at any moment. It was all so overt. My hands, sweating in my pockets, gripped the other half of the money. But I pretended, played along, as though there was an inner mechanism of righteousness to these strange workings. And there was a logic. Breaking the law seemed the only way to become legal.

For when the world is lawless you must become your own law. Thesinger excelled at this.

The civil servant returned smiling superciliously.

"The Deputy Permanent Secretary says there is no hold up with your application and he sees no problem with it. I am informed that the Minister will be approvin' certain applicants today and DPS assured me that he will place your file on the top of the pile. If you come back before the close of business today I should have your naturalization papers ready for you and we can finalize matters. Thank you so much Mr. Blake and have a blessed day."

XXVI

The evening of the grand party arrived. The Cabana garden was adorned with strings of colored lights hung between the trunks of the palm tress. The oily dance of tikki lamps in the balmy breeze set an enchanting mood as they flickered amongst the coconut grove with the amber of landscape lights shining up into the fronds. The lights traced lines across the still, jet water of the empty creek where *Orion* stood white, silent and impressive.

My anxiety of the last few days was waning and, aided by the night's ambiance, a sense of relief was washing through me. After all, I wasn't responsible for Jacob's actions, and I wondered why I should even stay.

I fingered the crisp new passport in my pocket and kept taking it out and opening it to the photo page. I ran my thumb over the black-and-white photograph of myself. My chest tingled as I rubbed the crisp, unmarked pages. Bringing the open inner spine up to my bruised nose I sniffed the document's official glue and ink

I nursed my swollen, tender nose and remembered Thesinger's white shoes waltzing through the flames. A hint of wood smoke still lingered on my jacket and I thought that maybe I should throw the jacket off. I should just get back into my old shorts and boat shoes, sling my backpack over my shoulder and walk out. But there was no point in missing the party now. I'd worked hard helping get this thing together and, a citizen at last, the event was sort of a coming out. Besides, I was broke again. All my money had gone on "dash" at Immigration. I needed the work.

Thesinger had left written instructions for me that morning. He wanted me to see to things and have everything ready for his arrival. I was to man the gate and make sure only those on the guest list were admitted. Apparently, sip-sip about the party had spread along the island's grapevine and he was afraid everyone would try to crash.

The list was folded in my tux pocket and I carried a drink as I walked passed tables littered with cone-shaped party hats and kazoos decorated with silver glitter and lit by candles cradled in halved coconut husks. Barmaids stood in white starched shirts behind their stations with the great ice filled coolers brimming with Champagne set before them. The caterers were poised to set out the spread of baked crawfish tail and roast wild hog.

I went down the gravel path to the entrance off The Eastern Road where the gates stood open and several hired security guards loitered in the orange streetlight. I nodded to them. They grinned back as I took up my post against the wall next to the varnished driftwood sign with "*Creek Cabana*" branded into its face. I gazed about and watched for the first guests as I savored my cocktail. I felt an expectation I hid with studied nonchalance.

"Boss," one of the guards called to me, "you could fix us up with some drinks, hey? It open bar straight through, right boss?"

I was taken back. "Y'all workin' security," I said.

"That's right, we right here. But it hot. I like it with tonic just like you got it there boss man," he grinned.

"Now, y'all ain't bein' paid just to be here you understand. Y'all bein' paid to work."

"If you could call this pay."

"That's the job, hey," I said, incredulous.

"You drinkin'," he said, looking hurt.

"That's different, I'm a guest."

"I thought you was workin' for Mr. Thesinger."

"It's different," I said. "Now, I've got this guest list here. Mr. Thesinger wanted me to give it to you so you can check all the guests as they come in. Only let in those on the list, okay?"

"All right then."

I handed him the folded list and that seemed to excuse me having a cocktail. Now I looked like any other partygoer waiting for friends. Leaning back, I sipped my drink and watched the night. They didn't speak to me again.

The guests came late, arriving the moment after worry had begun, when confidence in what had been laid on turned to anxiety. It wasn't my party but somehow I felt responsible. The emptiness of the place bothered me. I began to worry if the ice would melt, if the food would spoil. Of course that was all nonsense. I knew these people, they would come late and they would stay late. And when the first ones did pull in, perhaps confident that they were making a fashionable entrance, I felt embarrassed for them because all I had for a

welcome was an empty yard. I told one of the security guards
to run quick and tell the band to strike up and make sure the
barmaids were ready.

The guests came in big Jeeps, classic Caddies and Jags
with walnut paneling, and parked all over the Cabana lawn
and right out onto the street where they lined both sides
of The Eastern Road reducing traffic there to a single-lane
crawl.

They met out there on The Road, hailed each other
with plenty of back slapping and cheek kissing, and then
advanced up the drive in groups. The guards withdrew to
the sides, grinned widely, and nodded deferentially. They
never once even pulled out the guest list and I realized that
I'd made a mistake. They would never ask these people who
they were.

I wanted to rush forward and take matters into my
own hands, but it was too awkward. What would I do? Corral
those already walking up the gravel path and turn them back
to the gate to check their names? So awfully sorry, but do you
mind? Would I show everyone that I was otherwise than in full
control? I felt just a little sick and let it happen.

I told myself to relax. It would be a great party. The
weather was perfect, the sky a clear, vaulted dome lit by a
scattering of stars. There was just a hint of cool in the air so
that the ladies wore their shawls over their shoulders and the
men were comfortable in their dinner jackets. Some of the
men came in red velvet smoking jackets, and the women
wore pearls and extravagant nothings. Their mixed Trans-
Atlantic accents and The Eastern Road drawl carried on the
breeze between calypso beats.

I received them at the gate and ushered the parties
up the gravel path to the piazza for cocktails. Their faces
invariably lit up. All the older ladies greeted me with a kiss on

each cheek and "Hullo Dear" and "Don't you look smashin'". They were elegant in gowns with their hair pulled back and some were already drunk.

The bluebloods wore green and red pants with Sea Island cotton shirts and hand-rolled handkerchiefs angled with aplomb in the breast pocket of their jackets. They strode in with the gait of the leopard, a few in buckskin shoes. The older men shook my hand too firmly and winked and laughed at some inside joke that had never once been articulated, but in which they all forever shared. Their penetrating eyes regarded me and made me self-conscious. They stared out from bushy eyebrows and salt-of-the-earth faces. "Boy!" they said, shook my hand, laughed and swept past.

The young women were sparingly radiant, their gowns slit up their legs and cut shallow about their breasts. They all called me "sweetness" as we kissed. The young men hailed me as "papa" and "boss" and I passed on the old, silent joke by squeezing their hands too hard and twinkling my eyes. They all chortled and raised their eyebrows. They knew that joke.

When the crucial onrush of Thesinger's guests was done I vacated my post and made my way through the Cabana to the party. I didn't even think about the list now, it was too late for that. Guests packed onto the piazza. You could only move by letting your shoulder do a little negotiating. The waiters bearing hors d'oeuvres didn't penetrate much beyond the perimeter and the bar was packed with men backslapping and putting in multiple drink orders.

I got a Mojito and mingled. There were the pranksters with their spinning bow-ties and the clubmen with Royal crests on their blazers, there were the men trying to juggle having both their wife and their sweetheart unexpectedly at the same do. The old political insiders clustered in knots, whispering to each other and staring out at certain individuals, nodding carefully. I wondered if this was how it had been back in the heyday when Charlie Thesinger ruled the boys in the back rooms and when J. T. had made his fortune running booze to the banks off the Carolinas.

The sweat rolled, cold drinks were emptied and the talk began to clamor. Blue cigar haze hung in the still air and the ladies smoked cigarettes, ashing carelessly, crushing the lipstick-reddened filters underfoot. The music was quick and catchy, tripping. The band, in matching calypso shirts, were all burning eyes and moving hands. They're faces shone. People spread out on the grass and up on the bulkhead above the Creek dancing meringue in couples and stomping.

I spotted Jacob Thesinger across the patio in his signature white DJ and Weejuns. I determined not to tell him about my citizenship and wondered how seeing him would come off, and if we were still friends.

"Hey tiger." I said in a flat tone, sauntering over.

"What you say, killer?" Thesinger took my offered hand and we squeezed each other's knuckles. His speech was equally noncommittal.

"Just tryin' to get the bossman off my back," I joked.

"Well," he mocked. "You've come to the wrong address." And he turned cold for a second before smiling his winning smile. "Still," he said, "you won't have to worry too much longer. When I sell *Orion* you'll be free of the trouble."

He was lording it over me, but I no longer cared. I had my new passport in my breast pocket. Then he changed tactics disarmingly and put his hand on my shoulder. Without a word he ushered me over to the bar and ordered us dry gin martinis.

He told the girl not to shake them because it 'bruises the gin', he told her to stir it up. I could see the girl's eyes go wide. Thesinger had to tell her twice, but sure enough she took up the mixture in the shaker and gave it a good toss because that was what she knew. She slopped it out into the glasses and some ran down the side of the shaker and soaked into the tablecloth.

Thesinger sipped, moved with a jerk at the taste and spat it out. It was too sweet, the vermouth too strong. I felt he must be so tired of it all. He didn't bother to hide his disdain but simply dumped his glass onto the grass. I figured he had paid good money and he could do what he liked.

"A fool and his money soon parteth," he joked.

He took over behind the bar, set up two clean glasses and began to work his magic. The girl didn't bother to watch and learn. She stared off as if we might not be there at all. His cocktails were excellent and cold. We clinked glasses and tossed them back.

"Listen, Gavin," he said to me, "about last night."

"I'm sorry chief…" I began to explain.

"Okay, all right," he cut me off, perhaps assuming what my answer would have been. "Forget it hey. Have a drink." He made us refills, handed me mine and then winked. "You know," he confided. "There's a part of me who wants it to be always night, always the full moon over the languid bay, always time to dress up, have a martini and dance the meringue." He raised his glass for a toast, nodded the full glass first toward me and then his guests. "To us," he said and surveyed the success of his evening.

I studied the crowd. I saw many faces, a few I knew, most I did not. I noticed some faces were missing.

"I didn't see Clint Knowles on the list," I said.

He sniggered.

I felt a chill, remembering Dock and I joking about having Clint dealt with.

"You know," he said, "when mosquito have party he

no invite fowl." We chuckled. I was relieved. All that had happened to Clint was that he was being snubbed.

"But then," Thesinger continued, "the most awful thing happened to old Clinton Knowles." My breath became jagged as he spoke, his eyes glittering. "It seems his bank found it necessary to call all the poor boy's notes. They've demanded immediate payment in full. Hoy bulla! I mean, millions! I guess he don't keep that kind of cash on hand. He'll have to liquidate holdin's, property, whatever. That bitch hates to sell anythin'. And with this market! Ha-HAAA!"

"Christ! What happened?"

"Well now, I wouldn't know about that, hey. But what a free-for-all! I mean; scram-ble! I've got my eye on a few properties." He gave me the insider's nod, then gestured at the party. "Anyway, things seem to be gettin' into swing. It's certainly shapin' up to be the grand event. The fireworks have all been laid out on *Orion*'s deck, ready to set off. We'll take her out after the dancin' and burn up the sky. I can't wait to see 'em set off. Can you handle *Orion*?"

My throat tightened. I forgot all about Clint. Could I handle her?

"Sure! No problems!"

"I've got a surprise for later," he said, animated, leaning in. "Don't tell a soul, but I've got a scrap group to do a junkanoo rush through after dinner before the fireworks. It's a little quid pro quo for me raisin' a couple dollars for 'em." He glanced around, pleased as punch, giving the upward nod and big grins to whoever's eye he caught.

"Well, I've got to do the rounds. Here," he said and stuffed a torpedo-shaped cigar tube into my tuxedo's breast pocket. "Have a smoke. Mingle," he patted me on the arm, smiled and went off through the crowd, backslapping and kissing.

I slid the large ring gauge cigar out of the aluminum

container and ran the length of its dark wrapper under my nose, inhaling the tobacco aroma. I bit the cap off and fired up and stood there, my legs slightly apart, pulling on the Cuban, sipping my martini, looking out to sea. The full moon was just coming up over the eastern horizon illuminating the view. I felt more at ease than at any moment since my return. There was no question about me being a Cracker now.

Arial made her entrance in a bronze sequined dress fashioned to emphasis her swimmer's form, lifting and pressing together her breasts. I was dazzled by the sequins that blazed in the tikki torch flames, as she limped slightly across the lawn. It was the first time I'd seen her since Dock had told me about the incident. Now that I knew her leg had been destroyed, she seemed so much braver to me, and perhaps Jacob was that much more understandable. Making her way through the crowd, she joined Jacob on the bulkhead. He held his arms high and we all looked up at him and hushed.

"My friends! Welcome. You know, this party has been a tradition at this house since my father Charlie first held it back in the day. It seems on the inaugural night, matters got somewhat out of hand and there was a raid. Now the police captain was a new chap, out from England, and the judge had just been posted here from Burma. They didn't know the ropes and the captain hauled Charlie before the judge. The judge glowered at the accused in the dock and demanded an explanation. My father rose and said that it was impossible for him to mount a defense as he was drunk as a judge. The judge was indignant, "Sir," he said, "I think the expression you want is 'drunk as a lord'." To which old Charlie responded 'Yes, m'lord!'"

The guests laughed.

"Well," Jacob grinned, "the judge is gone and we're still here." The crowed responded with a chorus of "Hear, hear".

"Please," Jacob concluded, "enjoy dinner."

The food was served and we made our way to the buffet table. I could see our crawfish laid on, the tails displayed in the shell with the white flesh blossoming where their red backs had been cracked open, next to a bowl of steaming, melted butter. There was just enough. A line of us formed to one side of the serving table and we helped ourselves. The man ahead of me was eyeing up the catch.

"We speared those," I said to him. I don't know why I said it.

"Nice tails," he nodded, slapping his paper plate lightly against his thigh in what I took to be anticipation.

"We cleared out a whole reef."

"Man, leave some in the sea for the rest of us fellas," he grinned.

"Now you know we don't hold back."

"I see that."

"What's the sense in a man holdin' back?"

"That's right."

"You better get on out there before we skunk you for good."

"I'll just get yinna to jook it for me and then lay it out on a spread like this. I can live with this, you know."

The caterers had native hog skewered and roasting over the flames. The pork fragrance was pungent, skin crackled and crisped and I couldn't wait to savour that meat. There was chicken souse, corn, macaroni and cheese in deep dishes, peas n' rise, and for desert Guava Duff and Key Lime Pie. Bowls of goat pepper stood about for seasoning next to plump wedges of lime. My friend in line was giving the buffet table a good look over. He saw me noticing his culinary inspection.

"Very refined," he grinned.

"Very," I nodded.

The place cards at each setting were decorated with tiny shells that had been glued on. I found mine and sat with a full plate of pork and crawfish. I pulled the coned party hat on and reached for the wine. The guys at the table were talking shit and telling lies.

"Now is the perfect hour to go mutton fishin', man. The fishermen will be goin' down to their boats," one was saying.

"Boy, I wish that was me," said another.

As I ate they talked about the mutton snapper spawning and how if Thesinger had not thrown this awesome bash they would be out there right now. They said they don't mess. They said they would get they boat and one cooler and fill she with ice and beer soda and watch out because they comin' and they don't fool. They said they was worth they salt. They said no amount of cut ass could keep 'em back.

As I finished dinner I envied one of the boys pulling on his cigar. I patted down my tux pockets searching for another and I realized I'd left some in my truck. I rose to get one when people started calling out for bloody speeches. I sighed and sat back down to my empty plate.

Dock Roberts stood up on his chair and tapped his fork against his glass. He looked fine in a midnight blue tux with his newly shaved head shining in the tikki light. The ripple of "toast, toast" went through the crowd and everyone turned in their chairs expectantly.

"Pray silence for the Speaker," Dock called out.

People quieted down and for the first time I heard the wave-song of the palm fronds twine and turn as they swayed in the breeze.

"My friends," he began, "we come here tonight as the guests of a man who I am fortunate enough to call a friend. And as we dig into this feast that he has provided for us, I wish to recognize him. First of all, I don't know what's up with this white jacket, maybe he thinks he's in a Monte Carlo Casino or somethin', not that they'd let him in…" A ripple of laughter went through the crowd and I thought how very lucky Jacob was. "You know, that's the one place in the world where they just won't believe him when he smiles and says his background is French." That brought the house down with laughter, the outrage of it was exciting. I felt myself swell, checked my bow tie knot. Then I thought, boy, Pa, I came back against the odds but look at me now.

"Frankly," old Dock continued, "and yes this is a roast, frankly I have to say that this barefoot boy, well, he ain't no good at'll. He try to play the big man wearin' fancy clothes and t'ing, smokin' cigar and drinkin' wine, like he know the difference from grape soda. Now, I seen this boy in the water with a spear, all day in the water, jookin', never gettin' tired, and let me tell you that that is his true place, his true self, out there in the sea, in the wild. He was born of the wild palms, he is their son. And our brother. Ladies and Gentleman, if there are any present, please raise your glass to Mr. Jacob Thesinger."

The Champagne was popped, some bottles well with the wire unwound and the cork coming off in hand, others being shaken and the magnums sprayed over a table of guests. There was a great deal of screaming and heckling and then the glasses were filled and we rose to offer our toast. My glass streamed with golden bubbles, back lit by the landscape lighting, the surface smocked and I turned it bottom end up and drank the glass of brut down.

Another fella jumped up to speak, this one on the table, and the Champagne started to go round again. I decided I would use the break to slip out and get a cigar from my truck. I managed to make it to the Cabana before the merriment quieted down for the new speaker to launch forth.

A couple of people were already passed out on the pool furniture inside the Cabana and I could hear a girl giggling from the single bedroom, while the quiet, deep voice of a man encouraged her. As I made my way to the front entrance the louvered bathroom door wrenched open, giving me a start. A man slumped on the frame with his head dangling and the bib of his dress shirt wet. I walked out the screen door and back outside, where I collided with the hood of a black town car.

"Watch it man!" I was warned.

I looked up from the waxed hood and saw two guests at the open trunk.

"Hi," I said, "what's all this?"

"Pardon?" The woman looked me up and down.

"Well, why y'all parked right up against the door like that?" I gestured needlessly toward the front door.

"Oh, sweetness, this ain't nothin'. We just helpin' out."

"Helpin' out?" I was confused and peered over into the open trunk of their town car. It was stacked with cases of booze.

"What's all this?" I asked again, pointing.

"Man, these just a few things," the guy said.

"A few things?"

"It's part of the arrangement. With Mr. Thesinger," she said, stressing the name, using its authority, while the man walked around and climbed behind the wheel in the car.

"I'm not aware of any 'arrangement'. Whose booze is this?"

"Who're you?" the man at the wheel demanded, looking all superior at me, raising a hand on the question and holding it there.

"I work for Mr. Thesinger."

The driver snorted and looked away out the windshield,

shaking his head as if this were all just so typical and he was sick of it.

"Young man?" asked the lady, appealing to my rational sense, "don't you think it's right that we as guests should be allowed to help ourselves?"

"But this is not your property," I was amazed.

Her eyes fluttered

"But we were invited dear. It's all laid on for us."

"Look," I said, breaking it down with sarcastic simplicity, "when somethin' doesn't belong to you and you take it then that's called theft."

"How rude!" she snorted, climbing into the back of the town car, cutting me with her eye. The engine rumbled, the brights dazzled my eyes and the car reversed rapidly down the gravel track.

"Wait!" I bellowed.

The town car tore plumb out the open gate, bolting back onto The Eastern Road, gravel scattering on the tar. The driver didn't even check. He spun around on the road, came to a halt facing town and was off again in a screech of rubber.

"Security!" I shouted.

No one appeared by the gate and I hot-footed it down the gravel path, past the ranks of parked cars. When I got there the gate was unmanned. I ran out into the street, but the town car had vanished. Winded, I halted and scanned for security. There should have been several on duty.

"Security?" I called again.

I saw a shifting under one of the big tress that framed the entrance to the *Creek Cabana* and I could just make out the form of a man lying down. I marched back in through the gate and under the tree to see what it was about.

A single security guard was splayed across a beach chair. God knows how that chair found its way under the tree, but there it was, with this man just waking up from a nap and blinking up at me as if I was some strange apparition.

"Didn't you hear me call?"

"Who?" He propped himself up on an elbow

"I said, didn't you hear me call for Security?"

"I was over there," he said, pointing off someway behind him toward the property wall where the vacant house was.

"Over there?" I repeated stupidly, failing to understand.

"I was just over there checkin' on t'ings for you."

"You were right here asleep."

"No! No! No!" He waved a long finger at me, his dignity offended.

"But I saw you."

"That wasn't me."

"What?"

"That must have been one next one."

"Don't play with me, man. You understand. Talk sense."

"I was checkin' t'ings up in this tree. That's why I was lyin' low, so I could see up in the tree. I thought they might be comin' in through the trees. You understand me? Waitin' up there for the moment to strike!"

"What are you? Some kind of Joneser?"

"Man, don't be disrespectin' me like that!"

"What?"

"Give me my money!"

"A whole carload of liquor was just stolen right under your sleepin' nose and you think you're goin' to get paid tonight?" I spat venomously at him, the anger rippling through me.

He looked surprised and hurt, picked up his cap off the beach chair and walked out past me onto The Eastern Road. I watched him stagger slightly and realized with a sigh that he must be drunk. He made it about thirty paces down The Road and then he turned and insulted me at the top of his lungs.

I strode back up the path toward the Cabana to warn Jacob that his security guards were asleep, that I'd fired one and that his guests were stealing his liquor. Things had spread out, the speeches over people were moving, the order of neatly circled tables had dissipated. Couples were out among the tikki lamps Frenching. Two men were having a punch up between the palms, their dress shirts ripped. A handsome woman leaned out over the bulkhead edge, puking into the creek. It dripped from her pearls. The band, hands flying over the bongos, the saw whipping, played at fevered pitch, the dance square was packed, people on tables, one girl with her dress held up for the cool, showing a bit of panty as she moved. I caught a glimpse of a white jacket dancing meringue with a girl in a bronze sequined dress and I moved in their direction.

Before I reached them, a whistle blast cut through the night. The hubbub of the party died. I stopped in my tracks. The heartbeat of a bass drum struck up and the excited call went out from the other side of the Cabana.

"They comin'! They comin'!" people shouted from table to table. "They rushin'!"

The Junkanoo dancers came in a rush of color and shaking earth. They were all feathers and flashing sequin, bedecked in wonderful costumes of crate-paper strips, their faces hidden. The bass drums pounded down into the heart of me, their goatskins kept taut by the heat of little flames kept lit within the drum. The whistles called out the dancers and the horns blared the song and the cowbells rattled with urgency. The Junkanoo troop made its way into the center of the party.

Everyone jumped up to see the players. They wore their party masks of glitter and dyed feathers, blowing kazoos, lifting one foot, then the other in a jig, the women hoisting up their gowns, discarding shoes, showing leg. I pushed past people to get to the front of the throng to catch Jacob. People crowded in, shoulder to shoulder, with the Junkanoo players rushing between. The music took hold of everyone's bodies and they began to move. All of them broke away and banged their bones.

A circle formed with Jacob at its heart. He shook his legs, rolled his shoulders. I called out to him but he couldn't hear above the noise. He was prancing, jumping jaggedly from one foot to the next, bouncing twice and then spinning, arms out. The eyes of the players shone from behind their masks, mad and in a trance. They were coming on all color and sound, all spectacle. The air smelt sugary of rum and was sparked with electricity.

I called out to Thesinger. Oblivious to my hails, he kept dancing, the sweat rolling down his face, the back of his dress shirt wet and translucent. You could see his flesh where the material stuck. His white Weejuns were blurs as he jumped and bounded, tapped and stomped. He never heard me.

When my throat became horse I stepped away from the dance. At an abandoned bar I opened a cooler to see what was left. The ice had mostly melted. Only a few sodas floated in the water. I found some rum among the empties and managed to pour myself a cocktail. But the glass was sticky and the drink warm. Looking back at the dancers I thought that Jacob was lost in his own world, and now it was time I found mine. And I smiled, for I had come full circle back to the point where I'd started, alone at one of Thesinger's bars. But the social insecurity had gone from me, replaced by something more complicated and uncertain.

XXVII

Craving the cooler air off the sea, and a last look at the view, at *Orion*, I took the limestone path descending the ridge to the beachlet. leaving the light of the burning tikki lamps behind. The reverberation of Junckanoo drums and the merriment of the dancers receded as I sauntered through the shore-side trees and rocks that stood above the tide line.

The sea lay calm and the beach moved only with the creeping machinery of crabs, and the rush and stop of seaweed and silt in the halting current. The odd juvenile conch stuck up sharply through the sand, and I kicked them with the toe of my patent-leather shoe. Out to sea the full moon's pale luster reflected in a column across the surface toward the vague horizon and the little fishing dinghy nodded in the foreground.

It was a bloody shame the creek was going to seed. If only the channel mouth could be dredged, then the bulkhead would be lined with yachts again. I visualized the tall tuna towers and the arching grace of the long, wispy out riggers. Things were going wild, but that was no longer my affair.

I listened to the insect song, monotonous, speaking of a world untouched and hungry, accented by the 'chicka-chicka-chicka' of the diving night hawks and the soft mouthing of "*Cuda*" against the ocean with the rise and fall of the Junckanoo drums carrying out across the water to all points beyond.

I wished I'd remembered my cigar.

The unexpected scrape of shoes came behind me. My first thought was that Caleb would emerge from the shore side bush scrub by the abandoned house.

I ducked into the bush to hide, crouched on the sandy floor, camouflaged by the plants. To my relief, it was Jacob and Arial who stepped off the last limestone tread onto the beach. They came hand in hand, Jacob with his jacket slung over his shoulder and his white shoes bright in the moonlight. He was a sweaty mess of tangled hair, his shirt wet from his wild dancing and his chest heaving. Arial's dress glinted. They were both barefoot and they walked down to the surf line, but Arial stopped short and wouldn't let the sea touch her feet.

I watched them. It's not that I meant to spy. Actually, I felt foolish crouching in the bush. But I couldn't just stand up and walk out. What possible excuse could I have that wouldn't be farcical? I knew then that I'd allowed the drink to do the thinking when I'd become paranoid that Caleb was approaching. So I resigned myself to eavesdropping and I tried to make myself invisible.

They moved down the beach between the ever-shifting filigree of shadows, then reappeared at the point.

"Grand party," Jacob said, unconvincingly.

"It's not like what we thought it would be, is it?" she sighed.

"No, it's not. I keep bumpin' into gatecrashers and the staff are drunk. Wonder if dad ever had to put up with this foolishness?"

"Oh Jacob, imagine livin' back then," she said wistfully, looking up at him. "How grand it all must have been, like in that picture of your grandpa standing atop all those casks on Bay Street."

"Life was harder then," Jacob said.

"I know they didn't have all the conveniences we have, the things that make life easier. But that's not what I'm talkin' about. I'm talkin' about the way this place stopped being itself. How they wanted to reinvent everythin' and what a shabby job they've done of it. Everythin' seems to be slippin' away. All the crime, the threats, the pointlessness. But we remember how it was, don't we."

"Yes," he said. "We remember."

They had reached the gazebo. They had run out of land to walk out on. I suppose the ill-defined moment they had been walking toward had arrived. There are moments like this, the soft, intimate moments before our fate, the favorite music, the quality of the light, the being without care and the touch of one we love. These moments that, while we are still young, most of us wish impatiently to run from.

They didn't run. They touched quietly. I felt a knot in me tighten. She was so small and ready. He touched her waist, shifted the thin bronze material over her skin. I shivered. My throat dry. He leaned in to kiss her then on those lips and I closed my eyes out of respect.

"Don't," Arial whispered.

"I have to."

"We can't"

"Don't you want to?"

"Yes, oh yes. But someone might see."

"We could go down there. It's darker…" I opened my eyes and saw Jacob nod toward where I was hidden.

"We could go off somewhere. Leave this awful place and never, never come back," she said with such terrible longing.

Jacob's hands dropped from her waist.

"Silly me," she sighed. "I've gone and spoiled it."

"I'm not ready to go back just yet," he sighed.

"But we must. The guests."

"Oh, damn the guests."

"Jacob!"

"Sorry. I don't know. It's just that…well…it's not the dream I dreamt," he looked out at the view.

"You're my dreamer. My dream is to be with you," she said and stood on tiptoes to kiss his forehead. I was taken by the tenderness of it and by how vulnerable he seemed.

"I just wish you'd help me understand it all," she said.

"Don't you see?" he said quietly. "This place...Its... well, I suppose it's who I am...who I've always been. Where else would I go? Who else would I be? I can't ever leave, no matter what, not ever."

She looked toward his chest and leaned her head against him and he held her.

"It's important to have dreams," he said. "We used to have a dream. Remember those weekends together down in the cays? I used to watch you swim, divin' up all those shells. Your form in the water was a dream. I miss that."

"Oh, don't."

"You know your leg's not that bad, Arial."

"I can't."

"I think you should try."

She was silent.

"I want to see you like I used to. Do it for me. It's shallow just off the beach. I'll hold you."

He took her by the hand and started to lead her down the sand.

"I won't let go."

XXVIII

After they had gone I straightened up, touched my batwing bow, and walked off along the beach. Reflected moonlight danced festively across the open water as some allusion to chains of party lights and tinsel, and the water's surface was a strange reversed image of the cold core of the sky.

Something twinkled in the branches of a seagrape tree and bewitched me. A dress was draped over a limb, the sequins glinting in the moonlight. I smiled seeing it and despite everything I felt a sense of good will. I hoped they could do it, that she wouldn't be too afraid. I thought, please let her swim like she used to swim. Maybe I'm sentimental, but it seemed to me that the whole party up there was just nonsense next to what they were attempting.

Halfheartedly I made my way back up the limestone steps to the Cabana to keep watch over Jacob's party and earn my final paycheck.

The pulse of drums and the flutter of laughter were relentless. From the top step I gazed over the garden I saw tables over turned, girls dancing in their brassieres because of the heat that made their skin glow, a thick knot of dancers pressing their bodies in together and gyrating. Everyone held a bottle. There was an energy to it, an insistence, and I smiled at the irony of how much like the party at the boat ramp it all was.

A shrill scream split my ears. It didn't come from the party, but from behind. I thought it might have been a gull, but the sea birds go to roost at night. It might have been the shout of revelers getting busy in the bushes so I started off once more toward the party.

Clear and chilling, the scream stopped me again. I doubled back, taking the steps down two at a time. Leaping onto the beach, I staggered as the sand slowed my progress. My heart was pounding.

The beach was empty so I searched the sea. I thought about Arial. Perhaps it had not been so smart for Jacob to insist she go in the water. But there was no one out there thrashing for help.

A hollow wooden banging muffled another cry. A man's voice. My senses honed in on the direction of the call. The low moon cast its full light behind the fishing boat showing it up in silhouette and I saw it jerking spastically on its tether line. Then came a voice I recognized.

"Help! I...I...can't swim!"

Arial! Kicking off my shoes I thrashed through the low surf. Then remembered my new passport in my jacket pocket. Checking myself I dug the passport out and very carefully chucked it up on the dry sand before I waded on.

"I'm comin'!" I called out. I shouted it again and again to reassure her. I thought about her leg, how terrible it must be for her, how stupid Jacob was to talk her into a night swim.

My tuxedo jacked hampered my stroke. I couldn't hear too well in the water. I swam harder. After a minute I came up to the boat. Arial was treading water, frantic, trying to hold onto the gunwale. The boat rocked, dousing salt spray over me. I coughed it up, rubbing the sting from my eyes.

On *Cuda*'s small deck, two men wrestled. One had to be Jacob, but I couldn't tell them apart. Their bodies seemed to be the same size, the same height and build. They had their arms locked and with a twist both went down and out of sight below the gunwale.

Reaching out I grabbed the side, right below a varnished wood sign with *Cuda* burnt into it. Arial was slipping, her head at a desperate angle just above the water, breathing rapidly, the water lapping.

"Arial!" I called, and lunged. I got my arm around her waist and pulled her up and her bare breasts came out of the water onto my jacket. Confusion played across her face.

"Come on," I said sternly and that answered it and she

was business from then on. "Grab the side. Both hands. Do as I tell you. Now. I've got one arm under you, try to get your feet up on my arm, stand on my arm, that's it, now I'm going to launch you up and into the boat. Okay? And when I do you have to push with your good leg and pull hard with your arms. All right? And then I might have to push on your backside and your legs."

"I'm ready! I'm ready!"

"Right. And up!" I pushed with all my might and I felt my shoulder burn but she came up out of the water to her waist. She was mooning me and I put my hand on her ass and shoved so that she fell forward into the boat, her legs kicking in my face as she went over. I could see the raised welts of the scars from the propeller cut all down her leg. I spat water, pulled my jacket off and slung it up over the gunwale to Arial.

"Here!" I called to her.

I hurdled the low gunwale and landed on the deck boards, my body heavy with seawater.

A weight knocked me over and then the two men were on top of me, pinning me down. The boat was listing and the sea flooded in on top of me, filled my ears, sloshed up to my face and in my mouth. I was swallowing it and I strained my neck up not to drown, wondering what was happening.

"Hey! Hey! Can't breathe! Get off! Can't breathe."

They rolled off, but not because of my pleading. I sat in the pooled water surrounded by old conch shells and coughed. They were slogging it out terribly. Arial, crouched against the bow, trying to keep herself covered with my jacket. Between the stars that drifted across my vision I glimpsed Jacob, naked, fighting as some pugilist, his arms and hands wrapped about a man in a Speedo with a long, white ponytail.

It was Caleb and he reached around, got his hand over Jacob's face, stuck his fingers in both of Jacob's nostrils and pulled the nose right back. Jacob's head became an open mouth, all bared teeth below a giant hand. Blood started to drain over his upper lip. Jacob rammed his elbows back sharply into the man's gut. He was free. Caleb stumbled down among the bilge and came up with a cutlass. He smacked Jacob on the side of the head, not with the blade but with the flat side. Jacob went flying and landed on the gunwale, stunned, but not cut.

"Stop it!" Arial screamed. "Stop!" And then she was sobbing.

Jacob looked awful. Disoriented, he tried to get up but fell. I wondered what kind of fight was left in him. I thought he had had it.

"What's going on?" I blurted out.

Caleb turned on me with his cutlass.

"Boy, get off this boat!" he shouted.

I felt guilty. I thought about conceding, of just jumping out.

"Sorry!" I said.

"Kill you bitch!" Caleb shouted and I think my bladder just let go. I felt it warm all down my Bermuda shorts.

He was on me. I thought distantly that I must close the space between us so he couldn't get a good swing in. I lunged and hugged him tight.

"Kill you bitch!" He repeated, and I held on because I'd nothing else in mind to do. Then he bit my ear. It burnt and the blood was hot.

We both tripped backwards and I landed beneath him. The fall winded me and I couldn't breathe. His eyes bored into me. They were awful eyes. I was hypnotized. Hypnotized the way you see herd animals sitting there while the predator eats them alive. Just sitting, being eaten, alive. I could see the end there in the whites of Caleb's eyes while my open mouth failed to make any sound or draw any air.

I forced myself to move, fumbled in the water collecting in the hull to get a hold of something. I just had to get a hold of something. I found a conch shell and grappled at it with my fingers, but I only pushed it further away.

Raising the blade above his head, Caleb lined up to finish me. I wondered vaguely if it would hurt. Perhaps it would just be over.

Jacob tackled Caleb, one arm around his neck and the other grabbing onto the hand that held the blade. They tumbled over me, Caleb howling and dropping his blade. His face smacked into mine. His wet rope of white hair whipped me. I saw confusion in his eyes as Jacob took him down. Their hands and their kicks flayed and landed without practice while Caleb felt around for his lost blade and Jacob's hand searched for a conch shell.

I tried to stand up but I was dizzy and things spun before my eyes so I sat down again. I struggled and finally took a deep breath and felt the relief flow through my body.

Jacob was on top and wedged his forearm between Caleb's collarbone and chin and pressed down hard on his windpipe. Caleb's tongue came out fat and purple and the whites of his eyes went brown with blood pumping through them. His fingers closed around the cutlass handle and his eyes measured up the contact point on Jacob's skull.

"Wait!" I said, finding my voice. "Let's just wait! Can't we just wait?"

The cutlass moved. Jacob slipped his fingers into the mouth of the conch and gripped the inner coil. He raised the shell up to his shoulder, the three long spines of the queen conch pointing down. As Caleb prepared to swing Jacob pounded the spines into his face.

Caleb certainly looked surprised. The three neat dark

holes on his face started to gush blood. He screamed, his body convulsed and I knew it wasn't over. I wanted to talk to them, to calmly tell them to stop. I wanted to say, be reasonable, let's stop.

But he was enraged and Jacob hit him one more time, driving the hard points of the shell into his head. Jacob got right in on top of him and gave it to him hard, again and again.

When he was done Caleb lay inert in the bilge water and Jacob sat there on his knees, straddling Caleb, looking down.

I understood that Jacob had killed him.

I scrambled over to the gunwale and heaved up my crawfish dinner, tasting of garlic, butter and acid. The convulsions kept coming and I emptied myself into the sea.

Shivering and sweating, I looked at the bulbous moon over the sheer water, then I sought Jacob's and Arial's faces. They looked back, waxy and haunted. Jacob realized he was still holding the conch and he let go. It sank into the sea.

Jacob was holding his split nose between bloody hands. His face was dark where the flat of the blade had hit him. His hair matted with blood. His naked body was side on to me. Arial was sobbing and breathing jaggedly, with my jacket modestly pulled up about her.

"Gavin?" Jacob asked, still straddling Caleb, laboring for breath, his voice nasal.

"I was…walkin' the beach… heard a row… A scream."

"He… came up…out of nowhere. Scarred the livin' daylights out of me. I was…we were…"

"Sure."

"My God!"

"I swam out…when Arial started screamin'," I panted

and Jacob went over and hugged her tightly. She buried her head in his chest so she wouldn't have to look quite so much.

"Thanks! Really. I don't know what to say," he paused, frowning down at his hands and then at Caleb. It sounded strange hearing it like that out there. But what else could he do? He had to say it.

I didn't know what to say either. What was there to say? What does one say?

"Who the hell is he?" Jacob asked.

"His name's Caleb."

"You know him?"

"He's the fisherman."

"What fisherman?"

"You remember, from the beach?"

"The intruder?"

"Yeah."

"The fisherman who sold me the shells, " Arial whispered.

"Bastard. Had it comin'."

"I think it's his boat," I said.

"What?"

"This boat. I think it must be his."

A look came over Jacob's face. Something had clearly changed. He was seeing something very differently now. He took his hands from his nose, pressed the palms into his eye and rubbed deeply.

"Well shit," he said, "I didn't know that."

A peel of laughter came down from the ridge and everything up there seemed very gay.

"Oh, Jacob," Arial cried.

"We can't stay here," he said to her and then to me, "Gavin, we can't stay here."

"Do we have to swim?" Arial asked. "I don't know if I can."

Jacob leaned in to her tenderly and he said, "Buck up now, honey. It's no time to let it slip."

XXIX

Back on shore the blood throbbed in my ears. I reached down with a trembling hand and picked my passport off the beach. Sand spilled out from between the pages that had curled and softened in the humidity, and I found I was panting.

Jacob had wanted me to go with him on *Orion*. It had always been his intention to set the fireworks off at the end of the evening to finish his party in style. Now he had the idea of using them to cover the disposal of the body. But I had refused to go. After trying to stop him burning the fish market, I think that this refusal marked for him the final betrayal.

"Well, damn you Blake," he hissed. "So I guess you never really were one of us." Then he strode off with the gate of some uncaged beast toward *Orion* with Arial behind him. She turned and looked pleadingly back.

"We're put into these situations and it's just not our fault," she said, shrugging to me. "We're not responsible."

From where I stood I had a good view into *Orion*'s bridge and I saw them both come up the spiral stairs from the salon. The sight of the old ship's wheel with brass fittings seemed to confuse Thesinger. He grabbed it, as if it were the way to pilot the yacht, and perhaps it took him a moment to remember it was just a trophy and that it controlled nothing for he took his time letting go.

When at last he stood behind the real controls his face became bathed in their green light. He guided *Orion* away from the bulkhead with her thrusters and into the mainstream, compensating for the out-flowing current, then touched the throttles forward and the twin diesels slid effortlessly into gear. The sculptured hull glided passed me toward the mouth of the creek, the polished chrome work gleaming in the bulkhead lighting, out into Montagu Bay where the stars were thick and blazing and the full moon shone down upon the murky waters.

Arial was on the aft deck, making sure the fireworks were ready and as the stern cruised by she stood tall and waved to me before realizing what she was doing. I had worried when it had come time for her to swim back to the beach. But she had eased herself into the water and, despite her fear, she had managed a steady stroke, strong and natural in the water.

I'd watched her go. Looking at her had made me think of all the skin-diving she had done, all the shells she had collected and the time she had been run down and almost killed. I thought of Caleb. I saw the image of his big hands working the sharp blade of his machete into a red snapper down at the fish market. Now he was dead. These boats go through all kind of fool places where the bastards will chap you, I remembered Dock saying. You need to get ready because when they come they don't stop. None of these people ever stop, I thought, and they are all essentially the same. Especially Thesinger. His wealth aside he was no different from the lawless hoard he loathed and feared.

Orion moved fast. Thesinger took her out between the shore and the sandbank and soon had her along side Caleb's boat. I could just see him lean out over the gunwale into the small boat and pull the body on board. He disappeared again and a moment later the yacht reversed away from the little boat. Then *Orion* jolted into forward gear, accelerated, the bow lifting high out of the water and crashing down on top of the little wooden boat. Thesinger slid the gears into reverse and *Orion* stopped just short of the shallow sandbank that narrowed the Creek's mouth and began to inch backwards.

Cuda was destroyed.

I stared at the spot and saw a few splintered bits of wood and a slick rainbow of diesel in the moonlight. These dissipated quickly in the current that dragged them off into the vast sea. Empty water went on before me uninterrupted to the horizon.

A crowd of partygoers rushed passed me down onto the beach, knocking me in their haste. I was worried that they would see my damaged ear. But they didn't seem to care. They hollered and whooped. Champagne bottles were vigorously shaken and then the burst of wine sprayed into the air. Some of the men were play wrestling and they stumbled into the sea and collapsed into the water. The girls were shrieking and kicking and being held over the men's shoulders and hurled into the ocean. There was a great deal of laughter. Suddenly out of the bushes a number of naked people ran screaming and dove together into the surf. The crowd cheered. I watched the bathers, hoping they wouldn't swim to *Orion*.

Thesinger anchored the yacht in the deep passage. They were so far off shore now that the figures became small and indistinguishable on the deck. At this distance no one could possibly make out Thesinger wrapping Caleb's body in chains and then dumping him overboard.

A rocket hissed and spat on the deck, launched off its wood stick and sped upwards on a tail of sparkles and blue-gray smoke. The firework vanished into the night and then exploded, loud and powerful and delightful. The flash was brilliant and my eyes spun with spots.

Rapturous yelling erupted around me. The crowd jostled me and cheered for Jacob and their cheers reach a crescendo.

I gazed out to open water. It was changed. The little fishing boat was gone. Fireworks momentarily colored the black glass out there red and blue, the beauty was breathtaking, and it reminded me of the mural in the Bahama Room.

Things are what they used to be, I thought and the idea made me cold. I remembered my first night at *Bangalay*. I'd looked at the mural and at the wall-mounted lion head. Thesinger had caught me and smiled, raised his glass and toasted the trophy, "To us, brother". And he had surveyed everything he had preserved in that room, everything that he said was worthwhile, that he had kept safe from the horde that he said would trample it under its stampede and leave the world empty of the good things.

Thesinger had begun a dance to the music, the music he had kept alive, and his dance wasn't a display or a sex act or gratuitous, but a melding with the song. His dance was perfect. He had turned and he had danced and raised his glass to me and I'd raised my glass in turn. And I realize now that in his struggle to keep things the same he is the one who has been changed.

I looked at my passport. I pulled a strand of dry seaweed out from where it had been stuck in the binding when I'd thrown it on the beach, and I understood that now I could do whatever I wanted. I was free. At once free and so terribly weighted down and I knew I would never see Jacob Thesinger again.

"Isn't it wonderful," someone said.

The fireworks shot off high above, cracking open in the sky and booming out across the bay. They burst red and blue and white. They magically spun in the dark, circled, dipped, and cut back, leaving trails of luminescence. Each began a pinpoint in the great range of space that exploded out, arching and diving deeper and forever deeper.

GARTH BUCKNER

is the author of *The Origins of Solitude*
(Ravenna, 2005) and has published stories
in *Tin House*, *New York Tyrant*, *Avatar* and other magazines.
He lives in Nassau, Bahamas, with his wife and two sons.